The Cabana Murders

A Sergeant Cass Hasty Detective Story

By Joel Y. Dane

Originally published in 1937

The Cabana Murders

© 2016 Resurrected Press
www.ResurrectedPress.com

Published by Resurrected Press

This classic book was handcrafted by Resurrected Press. Resurrected Press is dedicated to bringing high quality classic books back to the readers who enjoy them. These are not scanned versions of the originals, but, rather, quality checked and edited books meant to be enjoyed!

Please visit ResurrectedPress.com to view our entire catalogue!

For updates on future releases, LIKE us on Facebook:
http://www.Facebook.com/ResurrectedPress

ISBN 13: 978-1-943403-35-6

Printed in the United States of America

Resurrected Press Books in
H. Ashbrook's
Spike Tracy Mystery Series

The Murder of Cicely Thane (1930)

The Murder of Stephen Kester (1931)

The Murder of Sigurd Sharon (1933)

A Most Immoral Murder (1935)

Murder Makes Murder (1937)

Murder Comes Back (1940)

Murder on Friday (1941)

RESURRECTED PRESS BOOKS FROM *THE
ETHEL THOMAS DETECTIVE STORY*
SERIES BY CORTLAND FITZSIMMON'S

The Whispering Window

The Moving Finger

Mystery at Hidden Harbor

The Evil Men Do

RESURRECTED PRESS CLASSIC MYSTERY CATALOGUE

Journeys into Mystery
Travel and Mystery in a More Elegant Time

The Edwardian Detectives
Literary Sleuths of the Edwardian Era

Gems of Mystery
Lost Jewels from a More Elegant Age

Anne Austin
One Drop of Blood
The Black Pigeon
Murder at Bridge
Murder Backstairs

E. C. Bentley
Trent's Last Case: The Woman in Black

Ernest Bramah
Max Carrados Resurrected:
The Detective Stories of Max Carrados

Agatha Christie
The Secret Adversary
The Mysterious Affair at Styles

Octavus Roy Cohen
Midnight

Freeman Wills Croft
The Ponson Case
The Pit Prop Syndicate

J. S. Fletcher
The Herapath Property
The Rayner-Slade Amalgamation
The Chestermarke Instinct
The Paradise Mystery
Dead Men's Money
The Middle of Things
Ravensdene Court
Scarhaven Keep
The Orange-Yellow Diamond
The Middle Temple Murder
The Tallyrand Maxim
The Borough Treasurer
In the Mayor's Parlour
The Saftey Pin

R. Austin Freeman
The Mystery of 31 New Inn from the Dr. Thorndyke Series
John Thorndyke's Cases from the Dr. Thorndyke Series
The Red Thumb Mark from The Dr. Thorndyke Series
The Eye of Osiris from The Dr. Thorndyke Series
A Silent Witness from the Dr. John Thorndyke Series
The Cat's Eye from the Dr. John Thorndyke Series
Helen Vardon's Confession: A Dr. John Thorndyke Story
As a Thief in the Night: A Dr. John Thorndyke Story
Mr. Pottermack's Oversight: A Dr. John Thorndyke Story
Dr. Thorndyke Intervenes: A Dr. John Thorndyke Story
The Singing Bone: The Adventures of Dr. Thorndyke
The Stoneware Monkey: A Dr. John Thorndyke Story
The Great Portrait Mystery, and Other Stories: A Collection of Dr. John Thorndyke and Other Stories
The Penrose Mystery: A Dr. John Thorndyke Story

Anybody but Anne
The Bride of a Moment
Faulkner's Folly
The Diamond Pin
The Gold Bag
The Mystery of the Sycamore
The Come Back

Raoul Whitfield
Death in a Bowl

And much more!
Visit ResurrectedPress.com
for our complete catalogue

Foreword

The Cabana Murders is a prime example of a style of mystery that flourished in the 1930's. The crimes are serious, but the tone of story is anything but serious. The subgenre is the literary counterpart to the "screwball" comedy films of the same era. The style is perhaps rooted in the most famous example, Dashiell Hammett's *The Thin Man,* but numerous other authors such as Craig Rice, Cortland Fitzsimmons, and Harriette Ashbrook were quick to jump on the stylistic bandwagon.

The hallmarks of the style are a crime, typically murder, that is played straight and a wise-cracking detective who attempts to solve it while cracking jokes and consuming large amounts of alcohol. Unlike the British mysteries of the "farceur" school where the crimes themselves are often comedic, the portrayal of the murders in the American mysteries is both serious and realistic, and the investigation, despite the comic banter, is pursued along the conventional lines of uncovering clues and looking for evidence. It is usually only in the interaction of the detective with the cast of secondary characters that the comic aspects of the story are fully realized. These secondary characters are usually played broadly and reference regional or occupation stereotypes.

In *The Cabana Murders* Sergeant Cass Harty and his partner Barney Stauffer are sent to the island of Sand Head off of Long Island to transport a minor criminal who goes by the name of Tootie McNiff.. When they arrive at Sand Head, they discover that McNiff has escaped and is at large on the island. With orders not to return until he is recaptured, the two detectives find themselves embroiled in the curious murder of a man and his son who are gruesomely shredded by a mysterious weapon while at a beach barbecue.

Cass Harty is a hard-boiled policeman with an interesting past. Having been at turns a war-hero, a college football player, a deckhand on an Great Lakes ore-carrier, and a stockbroker, he finally ends up as a New York City policeman when nothing else seems to satisfy him. He is tough and good with a gun, but also smart and reasonably well educated, though not too much so. He appreciates a good drink and a good-looking woman, but he never lets either of them get in the way of his job.

The mystery itself, is more complicated than most as it involves not only the who and why of the murders, but the how as well. The solutions to all of these questions are as clever as any, drawing on both historical and nautical lore.

Joel Y. Dane is not well known today, but *The Cabana Murders* is both very entertaining and well written. It is with pleasure that Resurrected Press presents this new edition of *The Cabana Murders*.

About the Cover

The Resurrected Press edition contains cover elements of the original first edition hardcover dustjacket.

About the Author

Joel Y. Dane was the pseudonym used by Joseph Francis Delany (1905-) for a series of four mystery novels featuring Sergeant Cass Harty. These include, *Murder Cum Laude*, *The Cabana Murders*, *Grasping at Straws*, and *The Christmas Tree Murders*. He also wrote articles and stories for magazines such as Esquire and Liberty under this name.

Greg Fowlkes
Editor-In-Chief
Resurrected Press
www.ResurrectedPress.com

TABLE OF CONTENTS

A Note On The Sergeant

CASS HARTY walked out of a classroom in April of '17 and became the third youngest soldier to serve in the A.E.F. With the infantry, and later with the field artillery, he acquired sundry wounds which inconvenienced him, and decorations which no one has ever seen him wear. With the American forces in post-Armistice Germany, he cultivated a taste for beer, played fullback on the divisional championship football team and, in an inspired moment, bankrupted a marathon crap game which had run for six days and nights in the Coblenz barracks. The money got away from him somehow, but his line bucking brought offers of athletic scholarships from three American colleges and he accepted the best of them.

Higher education was a dull business after the Argonne. Cass Harty quit at the end of his second year. His own restlessness and the post-war business doldrums combined to send him hoboing around the country for a year during which he found himself, at various times, a reporter on a Norfolk newspaper; drilling for oil in Oklahoma; acting as advance man for a second-rate circus through the Mid-west; deckhand on a Great Lakes ore-carrier; winning a ribald song contest at an American Legion convention in Kansas City with a masterly rendition of "The Good Man"; and, a good deal to his own amazement, functioning as stage manager for a painfully artistic Little Theatre group in Pasadena. He was working in a brokerage office in New York when a chance meeting with a wartime pal who was fast going ahead in Tammany first suggested police work to him. A session in a cramming school, some behind-the-scenes work by his friend, and an assignment to a Staten Island precinct followed rapidly.

The old restlessness was beginning to come back on him and he was thinking of resigning from the department when, in the middle of a well-publicized crime wave, he happened to walk into a filling station which was being held up. The gun fight which ensued brought him a reward on one of the stick-up men and promotion to a job as third-grade detective.

Other promotions came along at intervals and he had just been made a Sergeant when the sequence of murders on the uptown campus of Cardaff University shocked the city. His solution of these crimes brought him his first widespread public attention. Cass Harty lives alone on the top floor of a converted brownstone house in the East Thirties. Unmarried, but a long way from being a woman-hater, he has never expressed a preference as to blondes, red-heads, or brunettes—possibly, because, like the potential buyer of a car in a certain price class, he believes in trying "all three."

His battered old car and his collection of limericks are alike mildly famous, but less well known is his conviction that as a New York cop he is a member of the most effective law-enforcement body in the world. His detective methods are entirely his own and if he should ever be asked the chief reason for his success it would probably not occur to him that much of it is due to the point of view behind his remark: "I'm not one of those wonder boys who can tell you all there is to tell about everything he bumps up against—but I sure as Hell know where to go to find the guys who can!"

J.Y.D.

TUESDAY

THE REAR of the coffee-colored Rolls skittered across the washboard corrugations of the crossing. Atop a standard a bell clanged and the striped beam swung downward like a scimitar, cutting off pursuit. White teeth split the coffee tan of the driver's face as he grinned in triumph. He spun his wheel and curved out of sight beyond the tiny depot.

Fifty yards back Barney Stauffer's feet drove hard against the floorboards, applying imaginary brakes. He rasped, "Can't be done."

"You're telling me?" Sergeant Cass Harty's right shoe lifted from the accelerator and mashed down on the brake pedal, jamming it against its socket. Asbestos linings screeched their protest and tiny worms of rubber shredded free of the tires leaving a double trail on the surface of the sun-baked highway.

A dozen inches from their radiator shell the crossing bar swayed on its supporting rod, somber black and white striping indecorous in rhythmic dance.

"Anyway," Cass Harty murmured, "we made it close. Another quarter mile and we'd have passed him."

"If we didn't get killed going through the town. What makes you take chances like that?"

"I don't like drivers who crowd me off the road," the sergeant said. "And I like them even less when they make gestures after I spread a little language on them."

"Suppose he wasn't making gestures? He mighta been just waving at us."

"When a thumb comes that close to a schnozzle it's no wave," Harty chuckled. "Here's the train now."

Behind a slowing locomotive a string of dusty maroon

cars trailed leisurely into view. Dull gilt letters above their windows spelled out "Long Island."

"Maybe it wouldn't of hit us, but it's just as good you made that stop." Stauffer fumbled in his pockets for a match. "The inspector sent us out to get a prisoner, not to smash up no railway gates."

"Use this." Harty absently pointed at the lighter on the dashboard. He was studying each car as it slid past.

The electric coil glowed against the frayed end of the cigar until a cloud of smoke began to rise. "Y' know," Stauffer said comfortably, "it's hot in town. This made a nice ride."

"With a cell waiting for him at the end of it, McNiff won't think much of the ride back." Harty watched the lagging momentum of the train strangle in the air-brakes' grip. "I wonder if the honey in the little red hat is getting off here."

Barney sent up more smoke and grunted, "Who cares?"

"I do—very mildly." Harty half rose in his seat and stared through the club-car windows. "She's still there."

The girl sat at a small table whose top was untidy with the remains of a club sandwich, a novel, lying face down, an empty highball glass, some playing cards scattered in solitaire layout, and a chubby pocketbook whose catch was not fastened.

"She has food and drink and entertainment—not to mention plenty of the ol' what's-this," Harty told the bored Stauffer, "but she doesn't look satisfied."

"You're breaking my heart," Barney yawned his sympathy.

Dissatisfied isn't the word, Harty told himself as he continued to stare. Thoughtful is nearer the mark.

Elbow on table, rounded chin in hand, eyes contemplatively narrowed, the girl's mind was obviously faraway. At the slim end of a minor masterpiece in sunburn chiffon her right foot tapped slowly, gently, in careful ictus to the meter of her reflections. Completely unseeing, her gaze went directly through the detective.

Testing, he grimaced at her and got no reaction.

The small right foot continued to bob. From the ornament on the perky tomato-colored hat to the soles of her sports shoes, she was utterly oblivious to her surrounding.

Harty wondered if the word for her was not "calculating."

In white coat the Negro porter came sugarfoot down the aisle to stop beside her chair. He had to speak twice before he pierced the shell of her daydream.

Must've been going past her station, the detective guessed.

She startled erect, her hand hitting the pocketbook and sweeping it from the table. Erratic as a broken-pinioned mallard, it somersaulted twice in mid-air, spilling its contents. .

"You're missing things, Barney," Harty said. "You should have caught a load of what I just saw."

"Peeping Toms get a six-months stretch," Stauffer muttered. "Anyhow, I been married twenty years."

"Dirty-minded Barney, the boys called him," the sergeant said placidly. "And the boys were right." He tipped the black-banded brown hat back from his forehead. "But you got me wrong. The toots just scattered a whacking big roll of bills all over the car."

"Listen, Sarge; what these here debutantes do with their poppas' dough is nothing to me."

"That outfit she's wearing doesn't spell debutante," Harty said thoughtfully. "Not by a damned sight. It's more like . . ."

"So she's getting kept, then? I should argue?"

"Uh-*uh!* I still think you're wrong. Clothes aren't my specialty, but she bought that scenery south of Thirty-fourth Street or I don't know my New York."

"*Naafke,* or anything else—who cares? So, fortune-teller, what is she?"

Cass Harty did not answer. He leaned on the upper

frame of the windshield, eyes intent on the scene in the club car.

Driven by the gusts of a battery of electric fans, currency danced and spun along the aisle. Male passengers who had been hoping for a break ever since the train left Penn Station hopped gallantly after the fluttering bills. At peril to spotless flannels and peaty tweed jackets they dug beneath chairs and reached twisted greenbacks down from window fittings or coursed them along the car like rabbits. Faces reddened as blood pressures skied with the chase, and the watching sergeant checked an instinct for laughter with the sudden hunch that this, in its essence, might not be anything to laugh about.

The girl's action had given him the hunch.

After the first wild grab at her dispersing money, she did nothing. She stood dead still, erect and not very tall beside the wood and black leather of her chair, calmly content to let the men scramble. But her eyes were sharp and her lips moved slightly.

The detective would have risked a small bet that she was making mental note of each bill as it was retrieved.

The porter jabbed a brace of crumpled notes into her hand and hustled to the end of the car where he lifted two small bags down and said something to the conductor.

Telling him to wait, there's a passenger still to get off, Harty decided. With interest he watched the last few bills being hunted down.

Men straggled up in irregular procession and handed over their gleanings. She thanked each wordlessly with a mechanical, quick-perishing smile, her eyes uninterested in anything but the chase. The money disappeared into the pocketbook as fast as it was given to her.

Smart! Harty thought. She doesn't have to count it twice.

Last of the financial posse, a tall youth whose vague seediness made him seem out of place in the club car, edged into the ring of smirking masculinity and offered a wad of bills.

She took the green lump and made it vanish with a speed Thurston would have envied. Her mouth moved briefly—not in a smile.

Cass Harty could not get the words, but it was easy for him to imagine he had heard her lips click.

The boy's face reddened. He mumbled something, then reached into his vest pocket.

To show which side they were on, the men lynched him with their laughter.

The girl slapped his face and, with a swift protraction of the same gesture, whisked a single bill from his hand. Harty slumped down behind the wheel without waiting to watch her to the platform.

". . . in hell don't you answer me?" Stauffer was prodding him. "If I'm wrong, how do you figure her?"

"Figuring that babe," Harty said slowly, "is something, I am glad to say is no part of my job." He waited for the gates to go up, then toed his starter.

They bumped across the tracks and Stauffer brushed ashes from his decent blue suit and declared, "That's no answer."

"Best I can give." The sergeant nodded toward flat, trim-girdled hips flickering down the street between the two pieces of luggage. "There she goes. Add her up for yourself."

Grinding in second speed, the car passed her, and Barney stared back until she was lost behind a dejected movie theater and a row of small shops. "I dunno," he murmured. "I must be getting old."

Hands busy with the wheel while his eyes sought for the police station, Harty said indecisively, "And I don't know. You said debutante, but that's nonsense. She's dressed like a last-year's head-saleslady's idea of the debutante style of the year before that. The k.w idea's silly too. The babe isn't flash enough for a second-rate keptee, nor restrained enough for one in the important money. But she has important money—even if those bills were all ones. I guess this is it." He slowed the car. "Green light looks official."

The sole occupant of the little building was a weary, rubber-cheeked little man, well marked with liver spots. He took his feet down from the wastebasket on which they had been resting, popped a smut-magazine into his desk drawer, and turned the badge of office on his unbuttoned vest toward them before he asked, "Want anything?"

"Detectives Harty and Stauffer, from New York," the sergeant introduced. "We're here to pick up Tootie McNiff."

"Then y' come to the wrong place." The tin star caught the light as its wearer reached into the drawer to reclaim the delights of belles-lettres. "I hear tell they caught that *Mc*Niff feller yestiddy over on Sand Head. An' that's where they're a-keeping him."

No one had told Harty anything about Sand Head. He returned the papers on McNiff to his pocket and said, "Headquarters seemed to think he was here."

"Then they was wrong, young feller." A shift of the man's tobacco cud bulged his cheek to the bursting point as he leafed for his lost page. "They most gen'rally are. If y' want *Mc*Niff, y'll have to go get him. Them son of a bitches over there kep' him in their little one-hoss *dee*tention jail, 'stead o' bringing him here like they would with any other case. 'Fraid we'd try t' do 'em out'n their share of the *ree*ward, I reckon." His place found, he slumped lower in the chair. "Y' can ketch t' ferry if y' hustle."

"We'll hustle.". Harty had a date in town. "Where's the boat?"

"Cap'n Eben's dock. Foot of t' next street." A thumb as lean and brown as a nickel hot dog emphasized the directions.

Halfway to the foot of the next street open garage doors revealed bright chrome head lamps and a coffee-brown engine bonnet.

Cass Harty said, "Nice car," to a jumper-clad ancient who was resting his creaky bones against a gas pump.

"She is."

"High priced too."

"Ee-yep."

"For sale?"

"Couldn't tell ye."

"The owner could. Where is he?"

The ancient lowered his head to squint along the back of a knobby forefinger whose graphite-crusted nail was aimed at a widening streak of foam well out on the surface of the bay. "Mr Dunster's in that speedboat. He's going to the Head."

"So are we," Stauffer grumbled, "but not in no speedboat." He was looking with disfavor toward the foot of the street where kelp-fringed spiles upheld a width of sagging planking, and a canvas sign proclaimed: CAPTAIN EBENEZAR SOMERS. FERRY, FISHING PARTIES, EXCURSIONS.

Beside the ramshackle pier a broad, low-set sloop, from which the mast had been unstepped, rocked idly on the gentle tide. A stern, aggressive smell hung over the scene, a smell compounded equally of long-dead fish and sun-dried bait, sea wrack, the captain's gum boots, and the asthmatic gasoline kicker which provided motive power.

Cap'n Eben held the sergeant's bill up to the light before starting to make change. "It's thutty-five cents for a one-way to the Head," he declared, "or six bits for a round trip. Whut 'll it be?"

"It's not my money, so I don't care," Harty said. "But how come more than twice as much for a round trip?"

"Take it or leave it, I say." The captain frowned. "The extry five cents is for the reservation, like. Which do y' want?"

"Two round trips." Harty laughed. "It's worth it to learn."

Stauffer touched his elbow as he accepted the change.

"It looks like we got friends on board," he whispered.

Harty saw a familiar tomato-colored hat. "If she spills her money again," he said, "I suppose she'll want people to jump overboard after it. The hell with her!"

Aided by some whole-souled swearing, Cap'n Eben drew fire from his motor and the good ship Editha chugged away from the mainland. The two detectives sat near the stern smoking joylessly and in silence, dulled by the monotony of the sail and the fumes of the engine. Off to the west the sun was slacking down, managing to be high enough to give unpleasant heat, yet low enough to strike full in their eyes.

As they sailed endlessly on, Harty's growing hunger told him that it was getting late, but the ennui which settled on him made the task of taking his arm down from the coaming to consult his wrist watch seem not worth the trouble. He passed most of his time lamenting his broken dinner date in town. The culmination of a long and reasonably adroit campaign, the date, he was sure, would not have ended with the demitasse and brandy.

Once he roused from his sorrowings to watch a slim white sloop go ghosting across their bows in the light air and heard a fellow traveler say: "Randall Elrod's never satisfied. He has to own the bay as well as the Head," when Eben was obliged to yield the right of way. And again when Stauffer asked:

"How far is it across to the Head?"

"'Bout nine mile," the captain answered sourly. "An' asking how fur 'tis won't get ye there no quicker."

Part of the way Harty watched the girl.

She sat alone, up forward, and seemed to notice no one. Twice during the long trip she smoked a cigarette. She drew on it slowly and with an oddly unattractive mannerism of puffing the smoke out over a drawn-in upper lip, making it go straight upward and disappear immediately into her nostrils. The right foot no longer beat time to her thoughts but rested firmly on the smaller of her two bags.

Cass Harty felt her mood had changed from calculating to defensive and he wondered if the money had not been transferred to the bag. But as the dim outline of Sand Head began to rise out of the early evening haze ahead of them, he was admitting to himself that he still did not have her completely figured out.

Long and narrow and fairly high, the Head became clear at last. Its acres of dune stretched away to its twin termini, East Point and West Point, each a good six miles from the dock at the central settlement for which the captain was steering.

As the sergeant estimated the vasty empty spaces he recognized that it was not at all a bad spot for a lamister like Tootie McNiff to choose for a hide-out. Only the accident of some anonymous and unusually wide-awake summer resident noting the resemblance between the picture of a natty-suited and slick-haired wanted man in a month-old copy of the *Daily News* and the unshaven fisherman recluse in a cottage near East Point had kept the little crook from making a go of it. That one small break had meant the difference between Tootie's continued freedom and being summarily yanked back to a cell in the Tombs.

With the careless skill that two hundred years of sea-going forebears had bred in his salt-cracked hands Cap'n Eben brought the Editha alongside the dock and heaved up a line. People piled out and, when the last of them had gone, Harty approached the skipper.

"If there's no charge for the information," he said, "will you tell me where I'll find the local peace officer?"

"Y'mean Rev Crane?" Eben looked as if he might have to tot up the proper fee before replying further. "Why, that's him a-coming. On the slope there." He pointed at the long incline of the Head where the sergeant could see a tomato-colored hat trailing upward. "And it looks t' me like he's coming in a hurry."

Even though the information was free, it seemed to be correct.

Peace Officer Rev Crane hit the end of the dock in a flurry of pounding brogans, flying sand and high excitement. "Eben Somers," he bellowed, "don't get out'n t'at boat." The letter h, when occurring between a t and an a, was beyond Rev's ability. "Y' got t' take me over to the mainland."

"Not in no such hurry I don't, Rev." Eben started to climb out on the wharf. "I'm a-going to have my supper first. I'll take ye back t' Keyesport on my reg'lar night trip."

Rev pursed his lips and blew out a breath heavy with official dignity. "In t' name of the law, y'll take me now," he roared. "I got t' get help afore those New York cops get here. T'at city crook has broke out of jail."

2

Cass Harty's shoulders were almost wider than the sagging, loose-hinged door before him. He spat reflectively and said, "So this is the calaboose?"

"No, *sir!* Jail's around t'other side. Right here's my office." Rev's tone was halfway between apology for the shabbiness of his official sanctum and pride at having one at all. "Uh-watch out for t'at loose board as y' step in."

"I'll see the clink first," Harty suggested. "We've got to know how McNiff was sprung."

Rev led the way along the wall of sand-bitten boards, turned a corner, and stopped by some wrecked woodwork that had once been a door. "S'pose it's m' own fault," he admitted reluctantly, "but, y'see he's t' first prisoner we kept overnight since *I* been peace officer. And t'at's twenty-two years, come next November. We're law-abiding folk, gin'rilly, hereabouts."

Stauffer eyed him suspiciously. "What's all that got to do with Tootie breaking out?"

"Well." The Sand Head police force looked unhappy. "Maybe I should of cleaned t' cell up a mite 'fore I locked him in. We kinda got in t' habit of using it for a storeroom, like, these last couple years and . . ."

Harty peered into the semidarkness of McNiff's quondam jail, cataloging its contents. A stack of rusting tools over there. A broken water cooler in a corner. Some odd lengths of lumber. A single pontoon from a lifeguard catamaran. And, presumably for the comfort of any prisoner so idealistic as to refrain from escaping, a disreputable bed, its enamel chipped, its mattress and spring sagging almost to the floor. The double-bladed ax with which Tootie had smashed his way to freedom had, considerately enough, been left behind. It was leaning against the shattered door jamb.

Cass Harty said, "Well!" He looked at Stauffer.

The stocky little detective looked back at him.

They both looked at the sand which showed footprints, too many and too vague to be of help. The sergeant said, "Well!" again and led the way back to the door of Rev's office. There he paused and let his gaze wander along the great seaward slope of the Head beneath him. A pleasant enough place in the right circumstances, he thought, still regretting his lost evening in town. He supposed he would have to stay until morning to find McNiff.

Somewhat to his left the houses of the settlement clustered and, beyond them, strung out far to the east were the handsome homes and camps of the Cottage Line. Offshore, and far to his left, a smallish yacht rode at anchor, bright with white paint, her brass fittings refracting the rays of the dying sun.

Not as far down as the yacht and nearer to the beach, a large buoy rocked slowly in sea rhythm, its melancholy occasional bell proclaiming the existence of a shoal. East of its gaunt framework, but still closer inshore, a girl in a white swim suit and a boy in maroon trunks followed each other in recurrent sun-tanned archings from the springboard of a wide high float.

A dog loped in circles about two men who gathered driftwood from the beach and stacked it beside the open brickwork of a barbecue furnace. A tiny private dock, east of the furnace, and a large substantially built pier, which Rev identified as the home of the Sand Head Ocean Club, to its west, jutted out into the blue of the water bracketing the scene.

"Not much like Coney?" Stauffer said appreciatively.

Cass Harty shook his head. He was envying the owner of the yacht his graceful toy; the bell, its placid importance; the boy on the diving board, his slim brown-legged girl; and the people who would attend the barbecue, their prospective feed—the feed most of all, he decided, and turned to Crane. "Where's a good place to eat?"

"Up t' my Sea Spray House," Rev said proudly. "M' sister, Gen, looks after t' kitchen. Nothing fancy, but what we got's good, and there's always plenty of it. Uh . . . how'bout A Drink afore we have the vittles?"

The sergeant said it was all right with him and Rev dragged from his office closet a heavy, gurgling demijohn.

"It's old New England rum," he explained, tilting the wicker-covered jug in turn above a pair of filmed glasses. "Finest stuff in t' world for a thirsty man. Tonic for t' body and a elevation for t' spirit, like they say."

The two detectives raised their glasses, toasting "Luck!" and Crane bobbed his head at them in agreement. His loose camel lips circled the mouth of the jug, resting mountaineer-fashion upon his shoulder.

At Harty's "Swell stuff," Rev uncoupled the demijohn long enough to say, "Have 'nother Drink?" and drag his leathery palm across its neck before filling their glasses.

The sergeant had yet to learn that "A Drink" was definitely a proper noun. Just as a New Yorker understood a "martini" to mean gin and vermouth in proper proportions, so to the year-round residents of Sand Head "A Drink" meant an overpowering slug of old New England, unmixed with any weakening adulterant, and had, since whaling days, meant nothing else.

A third Drink was not offered. Rev returned the

demijohn to the closet and beckoned them toward the door, saying, "Let's eat!"

"We're with you," Harty approved. He scuffed along in the Sand Head man's wake, silently cursing the grit that filled his shoes.

"'What about McNiff?" Stauffer asked, trudging beside him. "The Inspector 'll be mad as hell!"

"That won't be a novelty," Harty grinned. "But the sun will be down in half an hour, and we can't cover the whole island by then. Tootie can wait till morning. I'm eating."

Ahead of them, Rev called, "How do, Miz Packe?"

The woman was a dozen yards off the path. She stopped whatever she had been doing with some metal rods and said reservedly, "Good evening, Rev." Beneath heavy eyebrows her face was thin and forthright as a blade.

"Who's the duchess?" Barney questioned when they were beyond her hearing. "And what was that stuff she was monkeying with?"

"Summer lady—name of Melissa Packe. T'at contraption y' seen was t' stand for her camera."

"Camera?" Harty thought the black oblong on the sand at her feet had seemed larger and heavier than anything the average amateur snapshot fiend would care to carry around.

"Camera's right! Folks say she's a expert. I hear tell she's figgered out a bran' new way t' take pictures in color. If it's so, she d'serves all it brings her, 'cause she's sure worked hard. Sometimes I see her taking pictures of t' same spot ev'ry day for a week, prett' near, just so's she be sure to get it exactly right."

Barney looked back at the declining sun. "Getting dark for picture taking, isn't it?"

"Guess not—for t' way she does it. I seen her last week working away in the middle of a thunderstorm." Rev thumped up the steps of a barnlike clapboard building. "Right in here, fellers."

A few guests were finishing their meals in the bare

dining room. In contradiction of Harty's fears for the quality of local cooking, they looked like people who had eaten well.

Rev seated the detectives and wigwagged a tall, long-jawed woman in white to the table, introducing her as his sister. "And these is t' New York police," he completed the identifications. "What's good eatin'?"

Gen Crane nodded at the city men with just enough dourness in her manner to imply they might at least have the decency to keep their cosmopolitan lawbreakers at home. Proving she had her brother's difficulty with h's, she answered, "Corn beef and t' lobster's most et up, but t' steamers are t' best they been all year."

The sergeant said promptly, "I'll have some steamed clams," and hoped it would help to thaw her distaste for city cops.

Gen looked pleased; and when he added, "That's what my friend wants too," she came near a smile. "I'll bring you some lobster, Revelation," she said, and disappeared through the kitchen door.

"She's a right sociable woman," Rev assured them, "even if she seems a mite stiff necked with strangers. She takes knowing! By t' way, I ever tell you how we got named?"

Harty said, "No," and found it hard to keep from adding, "Not in the forty-five minutes we've known you."

"Well, Gen was t' first-born and since m' father was a God-fearing man he thought it'd be no more 'n right t' call her Genesis. But when *I* come along t' old woman took a hand in things. She vowed there'd be no more children in t'at family, so she went clear to t' other end of t' Good Book and rounded it off nice an' proper by calling me Revelation."

"I get it." Stauffer was bored by the recital. "Say, what's the chances of Tootie getting off the island?"

"Ain't many—it's too fur t' swim, and if he stole a rowboat he'd hafta paddle with his hands. Folks on t' Head don't gen'rilly leave their oars lay around. Course he might steal one of them catboats in t' bay."

"I'll risk that." Harty thought that a city crook who had lived most of his life within a territory one block east and five blocks west of Broadway, with northern and southern boundaries at Fifty-ninth and Fourteenth streets, respectively, would not know much about handling sail. "Yes, Tootie's safe enough till morning."

3

Rev got to his feet with suspicious steadiness and asked, "Y' wanta have another?"

"Sure." Harty had stuck to beer since dinner and, more than he wanted another order of suds, he was curious to see how long Rev could go on absorbing those thundering drinks of old New England.

It seemed likely that the Sand Head officer could continue for quite a while, for his course to the kitchen was a dead straight line.

"I want sleep," Barney grumbled; "it's getting late."

"We'll knock off a couple more and then quit—O.K.?"

"I guess so." The little detective leaned sidewise toward the window and pointed out into the darkness. "But I'm seeing double now, or there's another boat out there."

Two unwinking lights, one red, one green, glowed like small jewels in the moonless dark, well to the east of the yacht's anchorage. Between their tiny brilliance the sergeant thought he could make out the lines of a slender vessel.

"Rev," he called to their returning host, "is that another yacht out there?"

Crane put the glass-laden tray down and squinted through the window. "Coast Guard destroyer, I reckon. She puts in here every week or two. Works out good for me—helps trade at m' gen'ral store." He tasted his Drink appreciatively and said, "Now, gettin' back to this McNiff, is he a bad actor?"

"Not especially." Harty saw no point in explaining that he had always considered the missing Tootie to be more ridiculous than menacing. "He's a very small smalltimer."

"Yeah? What's his line?"

"That'd be hard to classify." The sergeant could have said that anything agreeably flavored with dishonesty, and, at the same time, neither too laborious nor tinged with physical peril was Tootie's line. "He's passed phony money, helped swing a badger game now and then, and robbed hotel rooms. He's versatile but not very smart."

"Don't say! Which of them's he wanted for now?"

"None. He was under conviction on another job— aboard the train for Sing Sing, in fact—when he gave his guard the slip."

Rev liked his facts factual. "A killing, maybe?"

The picture of McNiff engaged in a murder made Barney choke on his beer.

Harty slapped his back and explained patiently to Rev, "Tootie wouldn't have the nerve to kill a bedbug. He drove a car for some fellows in a fur robbery. His defense in court was that one of the guys had told him he was the owner of the store and wanted help in moving stock. The jury didn't go for the yarn, but Tootie's always been able to put it across judges and parole officers and people like that—he's such a mild-looking little cuss—so the judge thought there might be something in it. He gave Tootie a year and a half—just as a compromise."

"He don't look tough, for a fact. I wouldn't of looked at him twice if I hadn't been tipped off. Course there'd been some talk going around 'bout a city feller up East Point way, and how he never mixed none, nor come down t' the village much. Folks down thisaway are prett' good at letting one 'nother alone and 'tain't likely he'd 'a' been bothered if it hadn't been for the paper. Someone up to Mr Dunster's house seen the picture in it an' talk went 'round as how it looked like t' feller up by t' Point. So I went up yestiddy, just 'bout suppertime, and . . ." He stopped for another twirl at the old New England.

"He didn't squawk about coming?" Barney asked.

Rev put down his empty glass. "No siree, t'at he didn't. I figgered at t' time it was peculiar."

From past experience with McNiff Harty knew it was not at all peculiar. The little gyp artist would willingly submit to arrest and then rely upon weeping or begging or smiling his way out of his troubles later on. There was a good chance that Tootie, early in his stay, had scouted the Head thoroughly and learned that there was nothing to fear from being locked up in the rickety jail.

"I says to him: 'You're McNiff, ain't you?'" Rev went on. "And he says: 'T'at's me, mister. So I says: 'I'm the law, better come along peaceable!' And he kem."

"That was just like . . ."

A roar cut off the rest of Barney's words.

The next day Cass Harty was to remember that his first thought association after the sound was of his World War days—and that was true. But now, as the first smashing blast of the explosion rattled the windows, he leaped to his feet, spilling his beer, as he shouted, "What the hell was that?"

Gen scuttled in from the kitchen. "Sounds a leetle mite like one 'a' them gas ovens in the cottages blowed up."

"No." Stauffer gripped the edge of the table, his round face drawing into lines. "That was no oven."

Outside in the night someone shouted. Feet of guests pounded on the stairs, raced through the tiny lobby and across the porch.

Cass Harty listened for a repetition of the report.

None came; but distant, frantic and thin, from the direction of the beach, screams began to rise.

The sergeant said, "Come on!" He crashed a chair from his path and burst out of the hotel, running laboriously in the deep sand. Along the Cottage Line babbles of horror served him as a guide. Stauffer panted behind him, and after Barney, Rev Crane shambled.

A glow from the barbecue furnace drew Harty like a lodestone. His feet thrashed the sand with what seemed like dreamlike slowness, and as his breath began to fail he regretted the gallons of beer he had drunk. All around him the night was peopled with racing men and women.

Suddenly he was on the edge of the slope, the furnace plain beneath him. He stopped, drew longer breaths and, as he took in what lay in front of the heavy brickwork, his thoughts of the war were justified.

Barney Stauffer slid to a stop beside him. The little detective was a brave man, but he groaned, "God! That's awful."

A woman who had just run up began to scream in hysteria. Her husband, following, told her to be quiet. But when he reached the brow of the dune and saw what she had seen, he leaned far forward and was instantly sick.

4

Stauffer muttered, "The man is dead." And, a moment later, "So is the kid."

Cass Harty kneeled, studying the horrible lacerations of the bodies. When he straightened up, he said, "I'm glad they are."

A little to the right of the fire, but well within the radius of its glow, the third dead thing lay. In his descent of the slope Harty had thought it a small child, but he saw now, with oily a slight lessening of pity and disgust, that it was a German shepherd puppy. Like the corpses of the man and boy directly in front of the fire, it had been frightfully riddled.

For the third time in as many minutes Cass Harty thought of the war. There you expected things like this. Here they were all wrong. You could not accept them here. . . .

In the front row of onlookers a slack-jawed man in green pajamas crowed at his wife: "Now aren't you glad we decided to come here instead of to Fire Island? Just wait 'll we tell the folks in Brooklyn about this—whatta thrill!" He found a stick and began to poke with it, speculatively.

"Get back from there, you moron," the sergeant roared. He booted the green buttocks enthusiastically when the man was slow in obeying.

"Damned if I know what to make of it, Sarge." Beads of sweat on Stauffer's upper lip sparkled in the firelight. "Do you?"

Harty said, "No," very thoughtfully.

"Musta laid it into 'em with a shotgun," Crane suggested. "T'at's all I know of would do it."

"Maybe . . ." The sergeant's eye measured the separation of the three mangled forms. "But I doubt it."

"Got t' be a shotgun." Rev's positiveness was mainly to convince himself. "Lookit t' way they been hit."

"That's just the point! They're ripped to hamburger — but notice how far apart they are. I'm no ballistics expert, but I don't believe there's a shotgun made that will throw a pattern wide enough to take in all this and throw it with killing force."

They watched him pace the distances his eyes had gauged.

"From a quick look," Harty went on, "I'd say the dog caught the outside of the pattern. He stopped more than enough to kill him, but the man and boy were right in the center of the charge."

"Got t' be a shotgun," Rev said once more. His whole lanky frame quivered like a jib in stays. "What else could do it?"

The many perforations in the black trunks and white swimshirt that covered the man's plump body made Harty doubt his own verdict. He raised the corpse slightly, looked at its back, then, with surprising gentleness, set it down. "He was facing the gun," he said. "I wonder if he knew what was coming?"

"They mighta said something to him." Barney was thinking of the turn-around-and-get-what's-coming-to-you prelude to gang killings.

The boy's body lay face down, its back looking as if it had been worked over with a steel-tipped knout. Bits of his green sweater had been driven into the torn flesh. When Harty turned the corpse on its side he saw that the front of the sweater had carried freshman numerals of some college. Three of the felt figures were still in place though no longer white. The fourth had been torn away by metal which had passed completely through his body.

"Look at that." Barney pointed to a toasting fork in the boy's hand. "He musta been tending the meat they was cooking."

"Yeah." Harty sniffed the heavy odor of roasting meat and wondered if he would ever find it appetizing again. Still puzzled by the extreme penetrativeness of the charge, he whispered to Stauffer, "I know of only one thing that'd throw iron with that velocity."

"What's that? A riot gun?"

"Possibly—if it happened to be close enough to any one target. But we've got *three* dead with that spread between them. That rules out the riot gun. I was thinking of shrapnel."

Stauffer forgot to keep his tone low. "Shrapnel?" he exploded. "You're crazy."

"It sounds crazy," the sergeant admitted. "What's more, it is crazy. Shrapnel is about the only thing that'd do this job—but I know it wasn't shrapnel."

Rev goggled at him. "How'd you figger t'at out?"

"With shrapnel you get two reports. One when the gun discharges the shell, the second when the shell bursts." The corners of his mouth drew in defeatedly.

"We heard only one."

"S'pose it was a bum?" Rev ventured. "It coulda been thrun down from the slope."

Cass Harty studied the terrain briefly before he answered. "That's out of the question. If it had been a bomb there'd be evidence of it in the sand."

"Don't see why. It'd be all blowed to bits."

"I didn't mean that kind of evidence. A bomb would have left a crater at the spot where it went off."

Crane was audience conscious and he hated to abandon his single idea. "A bum could 'a' been put in t' fire," he argued. "Maybe it had a heavy cover, or something, t'at would take the heat a long time to get through."

"Then the fire would have been scattered, wouldn't it?" Harty walked to the furnace and examined its facade carefully. "Besides, the shot must have come from out there, someplace, or these bricks wouldn't be scarred." He noted, but did not comment on the fact, that no slugs were observable in front of the brickwork, which was additional evidence of the extreme speed with which they had been projected.

Rev scratched his head and murmured to the crowd, "I guess t' feller knows his business."

"Or is reasonably adroit in giving that impression," a consciously mellow voice called from somewhere in the background.

"I was waiting for this." Harty grinned at Stauffer and deliberately pitched his tone to carry. "The kibitzers are beginning to hit their stride."

A man whose darkly handsome face seemed vaguely familiar stepped into the firelight. On the pocket of a Chinese silk beach robe a dishearteningly intricate monogram was composed of the letters, "LeM D." The shrewdest guesswork could place his age no more accurately than somewhere in the forties.

"We have been treated to a very edifying bit of sleuthing," he said, facing the sergeant with controlled belligerence, "and I suppose these methods are all very well in .their place. But I see no reason to let the bodies lie on the beach all night. Who the devil are you, anyway?"

"Pal," Harty smiled benignly, "do you know it was only by the split-est of split seconds that you beat me to that very question?"

The man settled his robe a shade more perfectly upon his wide shoulders. "I am LeMoyne Dunster," he said, as though it were a cantrap, compelling reverence. "You have probably heard of me."

Recognition of the shadowed sardonic face came to the detective. He said, "I've seen you drive a car."

"And you prob'ly heard of him too." Stauffer came forward until the buttons of his dark suit almost touched the rich orange silk. "He's Cass Harty!"

"To be sure." The courtesy of Dunster's bow was satiric. "I dare say the sergeant is stopping at the sanatorium of the estimable Dr Larsen up the beach. Their treatment of cases of chronic alcholism is renowned."

"Not a bad gag, Dunster—for the league it was sprung in." Harty laughed. "If I thought you knew I was down here I'd suspect you of setting it up in advance."

Diamonds winked at the fire from the lighter that Dunster held to an initialed cigarette. He puffed slowly before he said, "You haven't stated, yet, what you intend to do about the bodies."

Harty timed his own delay as aggravatingly. "*I'm* not going to do anything. This is Crane's job. I have no more power to act than you have."

"Perhaps not as much." Dunster laughed deep in his chest. The nod of his head was an order to Rev to get busy.

The Sand Head officer could not have looked more forlorn if they had told him to compose a pandect on the ancient Roman civil code. His jaw sagged helplessly as he asked, "Uh . . . ennybuddy know these two fellers?"

"They were my house guests," Dunster said. "Hubert Messinger of New York, and his son, Gil."

"Messinger?" Another man moved out of the crowd. "When did he come down here?"

"Oh—hello there, Tenny. They came by car this afternoon. I met them in Keyesport and ferried them across in my speedboat. Frightful thing to happen to him, isn't it?"

"It's ghastly." Tenny fiddled with an earpiece of his glasses. "Where is Kay? Is she safe?"

Dunster said he thought so. His manner implied that amorous concern was making the other raise imaginary perils.

"Does Elrod know about this?"

Ash was tapped from Dunster's cigarette. He watched it critically as it fell, then said, "Which Elrod?"

Harty's side glance sought information from Rev.

"There's two of 'em," Crane said. "Randall and Morgan—cousins. Folks say Morgan's touched. . ."

"I meant Randall Elrod, naturally." Tenny's voice was sharp.

"I can assure you he does." Dunster seemed amused at his ability to bait the other man. "They've all gone up to my house."

"Thanks," Tenny said shortly. He circled the fire, heading for the slope. "I'll see him there."

"Now, Mr Dunster—if y' don't mind—how long did y' know this Messinger?"

"Many years. We were old friends."

"Uh-huh! What was he doing here on t' beach?" Rev put the question as though the burning steaks had no existence.

Dunster's reply was equally humorless. "We had planned a beach party."

"Know ennybuddy'd want t' hurt him or his boy?"

"Not a soul in the world."

Cass Harty was infuriated by the too respectful questioning. Why, he raged silently, why didn't Rev ask how many others had been at the party? Who were they? Were they *all* at the house now?

For all the sergeant knew, some of the guests could be looking at him from the security of the crowd. The varying stages of undress made it impossible to tell which were swimmers and which lately roused sleepers.

Why, Harty continued to storm, were the merry-

makers sent to the house instead of remaining on the
beach as would be more natural in the circumstances?
Had they been sent at all, or had a mass shock driven
them from the scene of the tragedy? And, probably as
important as anything else, who had been in the water
and who had not?

There was a faint darkening, as of moisture,
spreading on the fabric of Dunster's robe. Perhaps it had
been pulled on over a wet bathing suit. Perhaps . . .

"I s'pose," Crane maundered on, "likely you had other
folks at t' party."

"That is true. There were several."

"Well." Rev resigned the battle utterly. "B' George, I
don't know what's right an' proper. What'd you think I
oughta do?" The question was aimed not at Harty but at
Dunster.

"Now, there's an odd thing. In all the summers I've
spent here I've never heard whether Sand Head boasts a
coroner."

"We don't. Need for one never kem up. But they got
one over on t' mainland."

"Then he would probably have jurisdiction here. I
suggest you get in touch with him and ask him to come
over—possibly in the morning." Heat from the furnace
was great enough to make Dunster loosen the sash of his
robe, disclosing a white silk swim shirt and black flannel
trunks. The trunks were supported by a wide mesh belt
whose silver buckle had doubtless cost as much as robe
and suit together.

Harty noted that the suit was undeniably wet. It
might not mean anything, but the shot had come from the
direction of the surf.

". . . and I'm sure the Keyesport authorities will take
charge as soon as they get here," Dunster went on. "In the
meantime I suggest that the bodies be moved to some less
public place."

Rev would have consented, but Stauffer's basso
protest stopped him like a traffic signal. "Nothing doing,"

the little detective said hoarsely. "Those stiffs don't get moved till some county authority's had a glom at them. There's gotta be a formal inquest."

To offend one of Sand Head's most important residents was beyond Crane's wildest thought, but neither did he dare risk further displeasing the city police. Letting McNiff escape had been bad enough. "What d'you think, Serge-unt?" he compromised.

"We need not debate the technical properties of the matter." LeMoyne Dunster beat Harty to whatever answer he might have made. "The medical authorities should be summoned from the mainland—and without delay. I am afraid I allowed the desire to see an old friend's remains treated reverently run away with my better judgment. In the meantime they can at least be shielded from vulgar curiosity." He turned and addressed no one in particular in the crowd. "I wonder if some of you would be good enough to run up to my home for a pair of blankets?"

A youngster detached himself from the ring of gapers and started up the face of the dune. Rev followed in his path, saying: "I'll go up to t' Sea Spray an' give Keyesport a ring."

"I've got a call to make myself." The sergeant, too, was in motion. "Barney, you sort of keep watch and see that nothing happens here. Got your gun?" The last three words were purely for effect.

"I got it," Barney muttered, "but I won't need it." He produced his blackjack and thwacked it lovingly across the palm of a sturdy hand. "Just let anybody"—His eyes wandered up and down the orange robe—"anybody at all, try anything wise, and I'll tumble him over like a fish."

5

Rev leaned on the desk in the Sea Spray lobby beside the wall telephone "Why don't y' get y'self A Drink while I'm talking?" he said. "The demijohn's in the kitchen."

If it's a stunt to get me out of the way, Harty thought,

I'll let it work. He said, "Thanks a lot—I can use one."

In the kitchen he located the wicker-covered jug and had one Drink, very slowly. He nursed it long enough to be sure Rev had completed his call, then poured two more and carried them back with him.

Rev was lighting a stubbed cigarette; the receiver was forked in its hook. "Got hold of 'em, b'George," Crane said between puffs. "T'coroner and chiefa pleece, both's coming as fast as a boat 'll bring 'em." He saw the glass in Harty's hand and murmured, "Don't know's I feel much like havin' A Drink right now."

"It's likely to be a tough night. You'll feel better with one of these behind your belt buckle." He gave Rev the glass and went to the phone.

"I want New York City, Spring 7-3100," he told the operator. "Reverse the charges . . . Yes, they'll take it . . . Sergeant Harty calling."

"Y' gointa bring the city cops out here?" Rev asked hopefully.

"I couldn't if I wanted to—we have our hands full with what happens inside city limits. I'm calling my boss to report on Tootie."

A voice on the wire said, "Police Headquarters."

"Put me through to Inspector MacIver's home, will you?"

Inspector John MacIver, unwilling to lose time in getting onto any police work that might crop up in the small hours, kept a direct line from Headquarters to the old-fashioned brownstone house in Greenwich Village where he lived in monastic plainness.

"The inspector is waiting here for you," the operator said. "I'll connect you with his office."

There was a buzz, the hollow clucking sound of a released hook, and a cold voice said, "MacIver."

"This is Harty. I'm still down here . . ."

"When you are precisely"—The miles of wire in between the two phones did not keep Harty from picturing frost-blue eyes lifting towards the hands of a desk clock—"precisely four hours and fifty minutes overdue already. I want that man here tonight. We've all heard stories about your fast driving, Sergeant; this is your chance to make good on them. I'll wait for you and your prisoner."

"Just a minute, Inspector—I'd have been back before this . . ."

"I'm not interested in excuses. We're going to sweat out of McNiff the names of the men who helped him escape from the train."

Harty lost his temper. "Tootie's not here!" he roared.

"Pick him up wherever he is and do it fast. You're not used to standing on technicalities. The papers you have are good anywhere in the state."

"But you don't get me," the sergeant bawled. "Tootie's gone! He broke jail sometime this morning. A good twelve hours before I got here. They didn't call Headquarters about it because they thought they'd have him again before Stauffer and I showed up. I can't be responsible for the way these salt-water constables do their work."

"I don't care about them. I'm holding you responsible for Tootie McNiff." The inspector was in just as much of a temper as his subordinate, but the eternal frigid intensity of his voice did not vary by a hair's breadth. "You had your orders when you left here," the iced-scalpel voice flowed tonelessly on. "Those instructions still stand. I order you not to return to New York until you have carried them out."

6

Out on the lead-black stillness of the bay's surface a graceful feather of white foam rose. To the accompaniment of popping cylinders its swift curving line filled in the gaps between the channel markers as it sped toward the two watchers on the Sand Head wharf.

"It's t' Keyesport boys," Rev said. "You got back just in time." He looked as if he wanted to ask the reason for

Harty's brief absence from the dock.

The sergeant volunteered nothing. A cagey poker player, he felt he could do himself some good by keeping that part of his hand covered up for a while. The attitude of the county officials would determine the right time to show it.

These boys, he decided, probably wouldn't be anything extra in the way of cops but if only there were enough of them it would be all right. Finding McNiff seemed likely to be a matter of skimming the Head with an efficient dragnet, rather than of hunting for clews or indulging in heavyweight reasoning.

The jet of spray died to a mere briny plash against the speedboat's brass cutwater as her motor was cut off, and she slid alongside the pier. A man leaped from her deck to the creaking timbers, an uncoiling line trailing behind him. He expertly snaked a hitch, a round turn and a second hitch about a tall spile, then turned on Rev, snickering, "Looks like y' got y'r hands full, don't it?"

"It sure do," Rev admitted glumly. To Harty, he said, "Meet Frosty Davis, Chiefa Pleece from Keyesport."

Harty recognized the chief and said they'd met already.

Davis seemed to recall the encounter with suspicion.

"Yeah, I seen this feller," he muttered, "but I don't know nothing 'bout him. He mixed up in it?"

"*Him?*" Rev crackled derisively. "He's Cass Harty. You know."

"Nope! Never hearda him. He tol' *me* he's a *defective* or something. Had another feller with him then."

"Still has." Rev introduced the two men who followed Davis onto the pier as "Doc Tuttle, t' county coroner and Bud Kemp, one-a Frosty's deppitys." In respectful tones he went on to explain the sergeant and the cause of his presence on the island.

Cass Harty thought it a poor opening, since mention of McNiff was so much salt in Davis' wounds. To ease the tension, he said cordially, "We're damned glad you men came. It looks like a big job's ahead of you."

Chief Davis looked up from untidy efforts to seal a brown-paper cigarette. Presumably, official business made him leave his cud at home. "No need to be too hasty about whose job it is," he snapped. "Doc's here becuz he's the on'y coroner around. Bud and me come along to protect him. We're here in what you call a inn-cognito."

Harty flicked his own cigarette from him in a comet-curving line that ended hissing in the water of the bay. He thought: So it's going to be like that, is it?

"Aw, now, Frosty," Rev pleaded. "There's no call for you t' get up on y'r high horse like t'at. We got work enough here for ev'rybuddy—and credit too."

"Y' don't say?" The homemade butt twitched in the corner of Frosty's mouth dribbling tobacco flakes upon his vest. "Well, so far's I know, I'm chief of police *over yonder* and my job don't go no further than the water's edge. Seems like I heard some talk yesterday about Sand Head having a peace officer who was able to take care of things hisself. But o' course that was differentlike: there was a *ree*ward to be got."

Doc Tuttle lifted his medical kit from the speedboat. You fellers' quarrels are nothing to me," he said briskly. "Where's them deaders?"

"On t' beach." Rev seemed relieved. "I'll show you."

Cass Harty fell into step beside Kemp, the silent deputy, and the five men trekked up the bay slope, across the ridge and down the ocean side to where Barney's stocky figure stood protectively between twin oblong tumuli of gray blankets. The little detective relinquished custody of the bodies with obvious satisfaction and, the instant the officials' attention left him, gave Harty a wink and a jerk of the head which meant more plainly than words: "Let's get the hell out from under this pile of grief!"

The sergeant was similarly minded. He flung Frosty and the coroner a bone in the shape of a remark about "catching up on some sleep now that the job is in good hands." The two city men started off toward the hotel.

"You got the inspector?" Stauffer wanted to know.

"Yeah." Harty recounted the brief conversation.

"Well, where does that leave me? Do I stick too?"

"I guess you do—he told me original orders stood."
arty chuckled at the manner of the telling. "What
happened after Rev and I blew? Did Lao-tsze make any
trouble?"

"Who? Oh, the guy in the Chinee robe! Naw. He
swelled around for a while shooting off his bazoo about
how it hurts to lose an old friend, and did I think you'd
move in on the case, and so on. I fin'lly told him to clear
out before he got a kick in the *kishkes*."

"I thought it was funny he wasn't there." Harty
checked his stride and faced the husky little man. "How
do you dope him?"

"He smells from herring. Why?"

"Well, he seems to keep getting in our hair. First on
the road. Then Rev says the tip on McNiff came from his
place. And after that he shows up beside a couple of dead
men and tries to tell everyone how to run the show. How
long had he been standing there before he opened his
yap? Couldn't he have just come on the scene?"

"You mean he might-a been off somewheres, hiding a
gun?"

"I'm damned if I know." Cass Harty was again in
motion. This time he headed away from the Sea Spray
House back in the direction from which they had come.
"But we're down here to get McNiff—and Dunster's place
figured in his first capture. Do you want to bet it won't
work that way again?"

7

"We're at the right place, I think." Sergeant Harty
paused in the shelter of a pair of trim cabanas that made
deep shadows below the main house. "That big shack next
door is Elrod's."

There was a sharp smell of fresh paint in the air.

"These things must be new," Barney said. He saw a shadow move across one of the lighted windows of Dunster's home and added, "They must still be up."

"But they've changed out of their bathing suits." Harty pointed to where a sagging loop of laden clothesline connected two poles. "Wait here."

Stauffer watched him slide from the protection of the cabana's wall and pass rapidly down the row of suits, squeezing each in turn. One of them was a man's two-piece affair of white shirt and black trunks.

"That was a screwy performance," the little detective said, when Harty returned.

"I haven't gone in for fetishism—even if that looked like it." The sergeant laughed. "I thought I could find out which of them had been in the water and which hadn't."

"You'll check on the suits and see which belongs to who?"

"Not now. All of them are wet."

"Then everyone was in?"

"I guess so." Another thought struck the sergeant and he added, "But maybe I'm trying to be too foxy. It's possible that whatever servant hung the suits up rinsed them out first."

From the other side of the house a slap of running feet on duckboards and a voice calling "Mr Dunster!" came to their ears.

Metal chains of a porch swing creaked from the released stress of someone rising. "Who is it?" LeMoyne Dunster's baritone carried far in the still air. "What do you want?"

"It's me." Harty recognized the treble of the youngster who had gone for the blankets. "Rev Crane says tell you they're having an inquest down to the Stevens cottage. He wants you to come."

"You'd think he'd of been there all along," Barney whispered as they slipped around the side of the cabana to peer through the night. "The mugg never acts the way you figure him."

It was too dark to see what was happening on the porch, but the clatter of Dunster's flat wooden beach clogs across its boards indicated he was making for the front steps.

"Kay," he said suddenly, "where did I leave my robe?"

"Now, really," a voice neither of the detectives knew responded, "I'm neither a wife nor a nursemaid, my dear Moy, and you men here seem to need both."

"Happily, I am not in the market for either." The big man was surprisingly petulant. "Never mind—I'll take Charley's blazer."

From a position quartering the house Harty watched the speaker cross a peninsula of light from a living-room window, shrugging into a jacket of green flannel. It was far too wide for him.

"You'd just as well go to bed, Kay," Dunster went on. "No way to tell how long these yokels will keep me. I'll answer for all of you if the need arises."

Harty thought: You wouldn't get away with that if I had charge of things. "Did you see what I saw when he was in the light?" he whispered to Stauffer. "He's still got his bathing suit on."

"But it was on the line."

"There's a white shirt and black trunks there—I thought they were his. How many outfits like that were being worn tonight?"

On the steps Dunster checked his progress. "Ah . . . run along, like a good fellow," he told the courier. "I've just remembered something. You can tell Crane I'll be there directly."

The boy scurried away and Dunster spoke again. "Kay . . . I was thinking that it might be ... ah „ . . wise, if you would . . ."

The girl's laugh interrupted the halting words. It was a laugh containing more mockery than amusement.

It irked Dunster and he snapped, "I did not realize I had said anything funny."

"You hadn't—yet. But I can read the future sometimes. I knew you were going to tell me to lock . . ."

"Yes, dash it—why not? There's no sense making fun of me. Charley may come to, and you know what he's like when he's tipsy."

If I know anything about gals, Cass Harty thought, that babe doesn't need to lock any doors. There's something in her voice that lets you know she could take care of herself in a barracks of the French Foreign Legion.

"I know what *everyone* is like," Kay said. "Old Mrs Franklin's only daughter always locks her door—at house parties."

The man in the flannel jacket said something short and sharp under his breath. He tightened the blazer's belt angrily and told her, "I wasn't worried about you. But I shouldn't care for any further unpleasantness this evening." Then he stamped down the steps and was gone.

There was a long silence; then a voice as hoarse as a barroom baritone's called suddenly from somewhere in the upper reaches of the house, "Kay! Oh, Kaaaaaay—where are you?"

The chains of the porch swing creaked again.

"Can you hear me, Kay?" the voice bellowed.

A white-shrouded outline was faintly visible against the darkness of the building's wall.

"P'sst," Barney hissed. "She's starting . . ."

Seemingly on tiptoe the whiteness moved slowly along the porch to another set of steps at the rear, becoming gradually identifiable as a girl in a white terry-cloth beach suit.

The detectives faded back into the shadow of the cabana again as she came down the steps and headed in their direction.

The boozy voice upstairs continued to bawl, "Kaaaay! Will you come here, Kay?"

There was a vaguely heard "No, you slob" from the spot at the door of the cabana where the girl jigged first on one foot then on the other as she twisted out of the heavy beach clothes.

Peering out from his concealment, Harty could not tell the color of the swim suit she wore beneath them, but even the darkness of the night did not leave him in doubt about its fit.

The clamoring in the house went on.

"Can't you shut up, Charley?" A new voice, heavy with broken slumber, suddenly demanded. "Let the rest of us get some sleep!"

"If you don't like it here, Elrod, you can go over to your own house and take Tenny with you." Charley's tone was drunkenly plaintive. "I want Kay!"

A third man called, "I do myself—but I'm not keeping everybody awake to tell them about it." And the first voice to answer Charley's howls said, "Forget it until tomorrow. She's probably gone off somewhere with Dunster."

Charley began to sob.

Kay made a taut little sound of annoyance. She picked the beach clothes off the sand and stepped inside the cabana.

In the intervals of Charley's grief the night was so still that the detectives heard the slap of a wet bathing suit on a tiled floor, the clunk of fumbled soap, and the quick stinging sizzle of a hasty shower. The water's flow died to a trickle, feet pat-patted briskly, and the lock of a closet door clicked.

Charley's moans changed into rage. "Damn your soul, Kay," he roared. "Why do you treat me this way? Do you want to start looking for another job when we get back to town?"

"No." The voice of the girl inside the cabana was calm and deliberate, but definitely intended for no other ears than her own. "No, Charley my boy, I don't. At least not just yet."

Yammering in the house rose and fell while the detectives held their post, their ears catching small intimate sounds of hurried dressing; a grunting tussle with a girdle, the snap of a garter, and swift rakings of a comb. Cass Harty wondered if even Krafft-Ebing had anything to cover their particular case. In the afternoon Stauffer had mentioned peeping Toms—but listening ones were something new.

In the middle of an especially loud whoop from the unseen Charley the cabana door popped open. The girl burst out and, looping a bow at the shoulder of her dress as she ran, scudded on flat-heeled shoes across the open sand toward the house.

"Will you do me this last one little favor, Kay?" Charley begged. "Y'don't have to come up here—don't even speak to me. But go an' look in my trunk an' see if I brought ol' Dunster his present, will you? Ol' Dunster's only friend I got inna whole world—it'd break my heart if I forgot t' bring his present. Take a look . . . You can do *that* much for me, can't you, Kay?"

Barbed wire in the girl's path could not have stopped her shorter than her employer's words. She stood still, thinking, for a moment. Then she turned to her left and began to run again.

She's probably all kinds of a bitch in her heart, the sergeant admitted to himself, but she's one of the few women I've seen who could run gracefully.

"Damned queer," Barney muttered. "What's this present about?"

"It hit her one awful wallop," Harty said. "From the way she acted, you'd think the whole idea was new to her."

"Yeah! Say, look what she's at now!"

Kay disappeared through a door at the back of the house and, an instant later, a row of small windows a foot above ground level flooded light onto the sand.

"Come on!" The city men abandoned their shelter and sprinted for the nearest of the lighted panes. The dust-clouded glass above them gave a fogged view of the cellar and the girl's crouching form.

Her back was to them and her hands flicked like small whips as she dug through the contents of an enormous wardrobe trunk.

"She's hot after it," Harty said. "Whatever it is."

In the shoe compartment she found what she sought. Her body hid it from the detectives' vision, but the sudden relaxation of her tensed attitude told of the success of her search.

Harty and Stauffer watched, hard eyed, while she worked over it for a moment. They saw her folding and refolding something, then she tucked it into her dress where it bulged the smooth swell of her bosom line hardly at all.

She stood erect and, with an effort, wrestled the heavy gaudily striped trunk shut. Some object was in her hand as she moved across the cellar, away from them, toward the small pot stove that served the hot-water system of the house. She took the lid lifter from its hook and opened the stove.

The thing in her hand was thrust in upon the dully glowing coals. It leaped instantly into flame.

"What was it?" Barney demanded.

"Nothing that makes sense to me. It was some sort of thin wood—almost like a picture frame. It was small, though, for that."

Kay was motionless, watching the dancing fingers of flame until they died. With the lifter she poked the embers carefully, dismembering them. Then she replaced the lid, blew cellar grime from her small palms, and came toward the stairs.

For the space of a single watchtick, before the light went off, both detectives had their first clear view of her face. There could be no mistake.

"Even without the dizzy red hat, I'd know her," Cass Harty said as he and Stauffer snaked away through the night. "It's the same little candy we saw on the train!"

WEDNESDAY
(MORNING)

CHIEF FROSTY DAVIS looked out to sea, then back at the bricks of the furnace—anywhere but at the sergeant. "I'm durned if I can see m' way clear to order my men over here," he said evasively. "It ain't that I'm unwilling, y'understand. I'd like to help but I just ain't got the authority. I'm sorry."

"I see." Cass Harty was fairly sure that he did see. "If you can't do it there's no sense arguing about it. But I thought that with a known criminal, like McNiff, loose on the community you might be willing to stretch the letter of the law a little to lend a hand."

"'Tain't my community," Frosty reminded him. "S'pose I was t' do what you ask and then some o' my boys got shot up. What'd that make me?"

The sergeant resisted an impulse to say "The same crusty old codger you are right now" but murmured instead, "That's not at all likely. McNiff never went in for any gunplay."

"What about last night? There's always a first time." Frosty wagged his head. "Looks like McNiff's your problem, like the murders is Rev's. I got no right to risk none of my men."

"Frosty's right," Doc Tuttle said briskly. "Sergeant, you ought to get Rev to help you—after he cleans up last night's business."

Chief Davis yaw-yawed high, vacant laughter. "Won't take him more 'n a year or two t' get that done, will it, Rev?"

"Now, Frosty, maybe you're a leetle mite forehanded there." The face of the Keyesport coroner was set in lines of mock seriousness. "If y'ask me, I'd say Rev's gointa have lots of free time t' work on the case. He won't be any too busy at the hotel or the general store this summer. No sir! A couple deaders on the beach and a dangerous crook making free of the whole Head ain't the sort of thing to bring no rush of visitors. Not if they care about their health."

"Hard lines, ain't it, Rev?" Frosty laughed like a malignant chanticleer. "Wouldn't s'prise me if a lot o' them folks that usu'lly comes here would stay at Keyesport instead. Y' can't blame 'em."

"In other words," Harty snapped, "you two are glad to grab any excuse to keep from helping here, just so's it will bring a couple of extra customers to your tourist traps across the bay."

"Don't take on so, Sergeant," Doc Tuttle snickered. "You know Frosty's got no business neglecting his own duties just to give you a hand. And my job ended with the verdict 'Death by gunshot wounds, inflicted by person or persons unknown.' *I* got no further responsibility in the matter. It's all up to Crane."

"Some-a these smart city fellers don't know's much as they make out," Davis said enthusiastically. "Come 'long, Doc, let's be getting back t' God's country."

It took quite an effort of will for the sergeant to keep from telling them precisely what they could do with God's country and its surrounding territory.

Rev watched them climb the slope, then said mournfully, "I need help—bad!"

So did the sergeant, but he did not say so. He was thinking that the stunt of playing one's cards close to the vest buttons often got results. Now he turned one face up. "When I left you on the dock that time, I went back to the hotel and called New York again. I asked one of our men to see what he could learn about the Messingers— whether there was any possible tie-up with McNiff, and so on."

"Y' can't tell." The card was plain to see, but Rev missed it. "Gawd a'mighty, they sure was tore up something awful. Undertaker's gointa have a time with them."

"Who's slated for the job—a local man?"

"Naw. Mr Dunster tellyphoned someone in N'York to come get 'em."

Dunster again! Still, it was reasonable enough: they were his friends. Harty was about to offer another suggestion but his better judgment howled at him: "Lay off; it's not your job! Crane's too dumb to see the trade you're willing to make, and his help wouldn't be worth a hell of a lot if he did see it!" But a smaller, sharper voice, far inside him, whispered: "You and Barney need help to search this place thoroughly. Suppose McNiff is tied up with this other business someway, and you don't go into it, and then the whole thing comes out. You'll win the Pulitzer Prize for Dope of the Decade, hands down!"

"Let's take a look at this layout." Harty paced off a short distance and drove a board into the sand to serve as marker. "The pup was about here?"

"Guess so." Rev would have agreed to anything.

"That fixes—roughly, of course—the extremity of the shot pattern somewhere out here. But the man and his boy got the full blast."

Crane moved close to the cold bricks, then flopped awkwardly down on the sand. "T' kid was layin' right 'bout here."

"You've got it within inches." Harty moved backward and slightly to his left. He knelt, scratching up sand about the spot until he came to some that was lumpy and darkish red in color. "The father was here," he said, standing erect to measure off approximate height on his own body.

"He wasn't tall's you are," Rev reminded. "But he was a durned sight heavier."

That fitted Harty's own recollection. He found a pair of long sticks and jabbed them erect in the sand. "Now . . ."

"I don't see how they'll mean much," Rev said

skeptically. "You won't learn nothing."

"Like the guy in the story," Harty chuckled, "I won't say I won't and I won't say I will, but it's the best opportunity I've had today." He motioned Rev to follow him down the beach to the damp and solid sand of the tidemark.

Crane got the idea. "Trying to line up the position of t' gun?"

"More or less—I don't guarantee it to work." Harty alternately looked forward at the upright sticks and back over his shoulder at the sea. "What complicates it is the way the shot scattered—makes it almost impossible to project a line." He turned to face the water and gestured at the anchored boats.

"You think it could-a come from . . .?"

"There's nothing to prove it didn't."

Out there the pleasant white yacht rode at anchor in barely perceptible rhythm with the lazy swing of the tide. The bronze letters of her name plate spelled out "Sad Angel." Still further out, to be sure of calm water, was the destroyer of the Coast Patrol, her slim gray outline standing up from the blue sharply and as quiet as a painting. Tompions ornamented with polished brass stars shone in the muzzles of her guns. Their breeches were hooded with heavy canvas. A lone sailor, moving indolently along her afterdeck, was the only sign of life on board. Slower only than his drowsy motion was the dull infrequent tolling of the bell buoy as it echoed on the somnolent tide, timing the hours of the ships' inertia like a grandfather's clock running down.

Rev's interest remained ashore. He pointed at a high formless bulge of sand which jutted from the backbone mass of the ridge well onto the beach. "Seems a feller could-a shot 'em from up there."

"Possibly." Harty saw that the angle was much sharper than the quartering shot required from either vessel. "The only catch is, if it was done from there, would enough of the central part of the charge have hit the

Messingers to produce the wounds we saw? It's hard to guess at that without knowing more about the gun."

Rev seemed pleased at having had an idea at last. "I'm going up top," he said. "I want-a look 'round."

Harty said, "I'll wait for you." He doubted that Rev would find anything of importance. Footprints would be a dime a dozen since the crowd that had assembled had come rushing in from every direction. The chance of picking up an empty shell case seemed even less likely, for no shotgun that the sergeant had ever heard of could conceivably have done the job. Something on the order of a one-pounder—a small cannon of some sort—appeared much more probable.

He lit a cigarette and let his gaze wander seaward.

That Coast Patrol destroyer—plenty of guns there, any one of which was capable of such ghastly work. But there had been no double sound of shrapnel, and it would have been next to impossible for any member of the crew to turn the trick unobserved by the night watch. The idea was crazy, preposterous, and yet . . .

Recollection of his own wartime experiences made the sergeant admit that even iron military discipline did not always prevent the occurrence of the unpredictable. He thought of a grim night in the south of France when two groups of military prisoners had fought a pitched battle with fists and clubs inside a penal stockade—a battle that raged in murderous silence from midnight till dawn. At reveille men were dead, but the MPs on guard had heard no sound. He remembered also, and more pleasurably, the astounding incident of the newly elevated corporal of field artillery, the Rheims girl named Claudette, and the amorous and venerable brigadier general who was famed throughout the division as an extremely sound sleeper. It was an incident which the good Francois Rabelais would have appreciated and which, no doubt, he would have been pleased to record, antithetically, to the story of his own Hans Carvel.

Yes, Cass Harty reminded himself, queer things

happened in spite of discipline.

Rev Crane came ambling back from the dune, his face so dejected as to make the sergeant's "Any luck?" superfluous.

"Not a durn thing up there but a busted post about so high." Rev's hand was some four feet above the beach. "Got any idees?"

The sergeant did not remind Rev that he had already laid down a card. Better to let it stay and trade on it when something important showed. He said, "Those ships sort of take my eye."

They took it a great deal more compellingly as the first sign of life on the yacht appeared.

A deck hand was busying himself up forward.

"Coastal boat's got t' guns for it, no mistake." Rev pondered. "Figger any of 'em was fired?"

"The officer of the day would know." Harty answered about the destroyer, but his eyes were on the yacht.

That deck hand was still busy. He was polishing something, polishing it to a very high sheen. When he stepped back to survey his work the morning sun was reflected from it dazzlingly.

The detective asked confirmation of his own idea of what it might be. "See what that sailor's working on?"

Rev's bushy eyebrows drew down, shading the glare from the water. "S'luting cannon, I reckon. Them toys take plenty of elbow grease t' keep 'em looking good."

"I thought that was it." Harty also thought the gun's barrel looked somewhat longer and heavier than a saluting cannon needed to be. "What do you make of its size?"

"Dunno." Crane peered seaward again. "Kinda big, maybe. I expect some folks 'll do anything for show. Say— you ain't sayin' they put a charge in t'at popgun, are you?"

"A storybook detective would be able to tell you whether they could or not because he'd know all about ballistics; but I'm only a New York cop and I wouldn't bet on it either way. But it won't hurt to think about it."

"B'George, t'at's an idee!"

"Maybe. Whose boat is she?"

"B'longs t' Elton Gresham, the steel man, but he don't get much good of her. His son Ronnie's aboard—worthless young scamp."

"Well, if the shot came from there, some of the party crowd should have seen the flash. And there ought to be an explanation why no one but the Messingers was in front of the fire. You ought to know who was there and where they went when they left the fire."

"I know t' people," Rev said solemnly. "Mr Dunster, of course; his house guest, Charley Wade; and his sec'etary, Wade's I mean, Miz Franklin; and t' picture-takin' lady, Miz Packe; and Randall Elrod, who lives next t' Dunster; and his business associate, Mr Tenny; and t' two Albright girls from up t' Cottage Line; and young Gresham; and a friend of his from New York. Mr Dunster give their names at t' inquest." He took a slip of paper from his pocket. "Here they are. I wrote 'em all down."

2

Kay's black hair was tousled by the morning breeze as she swung along the ridge. Her pace was swift for so warm a day, and she batted carelessly, from time to time, at the taller spears of beach grass with the rolled newspaper she carried in her right hand.

From a window of the Sea Spray dining room Cass Harty saw her. He put down his coffee cup, thinking, That's a girl I ought to talk to.

Across the table, Stauffer asked, "And what'd the destroyer's captain say?"

"None of their guns were fired," Harty said. "And the other try I made was even worse. The Albright sisters had left the party half an hour before the gun fired. They were shocked because Wade was so soused and they got young Gresham to take 'em home. Their family backs up their story, so I guess it's oke. They're so upset they're clearing out for home today."

Kay brandished the clubbed paper in casual hello at someone outside the sergeant's line of vision, but she did not stop to talk. Her present course would not bring her to the Sea Spray House.

Probably heading for the general store, Harty guessed. "I'll see you later, Barney," he said, shoving back his chair. "I want to get a close-up of our girl friend."

By going out through the kitchen of the Sea Spray and doubling around small buildings he beat Kay to the store. He was inside leaning on a counter and arguing monotonously with Rev over being charged a quarter for a thirteen-cent pack of cigarettes when she entered.

"Mornin' Miz Franklin." Rev gave over attempting to justify the boost in price long enough to add, "Be right with you."

Cass Harty caught her eye and held it while he told Rev, "Go ahead now. I'm in no hurry."

The automatic smile she had used in the club car thanked him. It lacked some of the tension of that earlier occasion, but its quick demise was still intended to let the smilee know that he was erased from her awareness just as rapidly.

Harty thought: Maybe I am—and maybe not.

He rested his back against the counter, spread-eagling elbows on the glass top of a showcase. Carefully he made his concern about the store's other customer seem secondary to his interest in a row of fishing rods that lay on brackets on the further wall.

Kay accepted her role of opponent in the duel of mutual obliviousness readily. She swiftly purchased a bright yellow bathing cap, two packages of cigarettes, and a copy of the *New Yorker*, all without apparent further notice of the sergeant.

Crane charged a quarter apiece for the smokes, a dollar for the cap, and a five-cent markup on the standard price of the magazine. He wrote each item down and began to add them loudly.

Crossing the store, Harty took down one of the fishing rods and began, with little flicks of the wrist, to test it for whippiness. The maneuver put him in a better spot to observe Rev making change from a ten-dollar bill.

The purse into which she slipped the money was pancake flat, definitely no sheath for the enormous roll she had carried the day before.

Cass Harty thought he would like to know what had become of that minor-league fortune.

Shutting the cash drawer, Rev asked, "T'at all?"

"All—for myself." She left the magazine stand and detoured around a pile of boxes to the wooden grille that set a corner of the store apart as the Sand Head post office. "My boss wanted to know when these would go out."

The cylinder of newspapers slid under the grille.

"Afternoon boat." Crane slapped the bundle onto the platform of a midget scale. "Eight cents."

Harty watched a dime pass beneath the wooden screen and two pennies return. He thought: Queer stunt!

Snug feet carried Kay from the postal window and paused while she inspected the books in the rental shelves beside the door. Nothing there interested her and, with her hand on the knob, she turned, allowing another of the meaningless smiles to nicker briefly at the sergeant. Then she was gone.

Cass Harty knew what had to be done and thought it would take a bit of doing. "It's a shame," he murmured, "the way they don't get enough newspapers in New York."

"Hah?" Rev looked up from a ledger. "What say?"

"Nothing. I was thinking out loud that the publishers ought to run off a few extra copies of their sheets. Then Wade wouldn't have to mail his papers back to town after he's read 'em; so's there'd be enough to go around."

". . . an' six's forty-three. Put down three an' carry t' four. Feller's got a right t' send papers in t' mails, hasn't he?"

"You hit that right on the button, Rev, he certainly has." Harty broke out his overpriced pack of butts and began to stow them in his case. "But I'd like to know where those papers are going. Let's see them, will you?"

"Four an' seven's elev ... I will *not!* What business it of yours, anyway?"

"Maybe I'm nosy." He put out a hand. "Give!"

"Nothing doing. Be a vi'lation of postal reg'lations if I did—lessen there was some good reason."

Harty was not keen on uncovering the idea that had forced itself upon him, but he would tell half of it to gain his point. "Does it strike you funny the way the Dunstar crowd figures in both cases?"

"Both?"

"Mine and yours. The tip on McNiff came from there and two of Dunster's guests were killed last night."

"You said McNiff wasn't no killer."

"And he isn't! But I can't stop asking myself if their hunch on him was completely the accident they claim it was. I want to know why two men were killed—and in such a damned queer way—so soon after the McNiff thing broke. And what makes Wade mail papers off—if he is the one who's sending them?"

The man behind the counter had no answer ready but he was smart enough to see that the questions spelled Harty's interest in the case and forecast possible aid for a sorely bedithered Header.

"B'George, there's something t' what y' say." He reached into the wire basket and held the parcel to the light. "They're addressed to a Mrs R. B. Franklin," he announced. "She lives at . . ."

"Let Hawkshaw see them." The sergeant put a long arm around the edge of the grille and grabbed the roll. "The sender is important too."

A neat secretarial script had furnished "Miss K. G. Franklin, c/o LeM. Dunster, Sand Head, L. I., as return address.

"I'm not surprised," Harty said. "It didn't make sense

for Wade to be mailing papers to town." He gambled that
Rev would not be acute enough to ask why it should be
any more reasonable for the girl to do so.

"Now, fat's a puzzler. Why'd she say her boss sent
'em?"

"I'm not the guy who can tell you why a woman does
anything." The sergeant faked a laugh. "It's enough to
know that she did it." He gave the roll to Rev while he
weighed two plans of action.

The first was out; Crane would never stand for
opening the papers immediately. The second would be
slower, but it stood more chance of winning Rev's
approval.

Damning the peace officer's ironclad sense of duty,
Harty attacked the problem roundabout. "The mail
service is pretty efficient, isn't it?"

"Y' betcha. Couldn't hardly be improved."

"But every so often you read about some letter getting
to its destination months—often years—after it was
posted."

"Y' got t' allow for accidents. Ain't nobody perfect."

"Of course not. But how do those accidents happen?"

"Lotsa ways. Mail gets misdirected. Or a letter 'll fall
down behind t' rack, or get stuck in t' woodwork, or
something."

"Um-*hum!* I was just thinking that if that roll had
fallen on the floor when you heaved it at the basket it
might have stayed there for a day or two before anyone
noticed it."

"Say," Rev demanded. "What you getting at?"

"I want to see you make that throw again!"

Crane reached for the bundle mechanically. His hand
circling it, he stopped and asked, "Just what is this?"

The time had come to rub Rev's nose against the card
that had been lying face up ever since their talk on the
beach. "A New York cop is investigating the Messingers
right now," Harty said. "You want to get that murderer,
don't you?"

"Course I do!"

"And I want McNiff. Try that toss again."

Rev picked up the parcel. "Durned if I see . . ."

"You will in a minute. Your conscience won't let you open those papers, will it?"

"I sh'd say *not!*"

"O.K.! But the murderer and McNiff each have some sort of tie-up with the Dunster place. The package is from there. Since you won't open it, the next best thing is to delay it. If there's anything fishy about it the delay will hurt. If it's perfectly harmless a few days one way or the other won't matter." Harty felt that if circumstances warranted he could break into the store and open the bundle himself. "*Try that throw!*"

"Weel, I don't know's I'm doing right." Rev drew his arm back with as much trepidation as if he were signing a nihilist manifesto. He let the roll fly and it plunked against the underside of the desk, rolling far back, out of sight. "Durn it," he said, "I missed t' basket. Have t' pick up t'at piece of mail—when I get time."

"We've made a deal," the sergeant told him. "You help me on McNiff—until you get the killer. I help you on the murders—until *I* have Tootie." If he had obtained the better of the bargain Harty would at least live up to his end in the meantime. By way of an initial payment he asked. "What became of the dog?"

"Dog? Oh, t' one t'at got killed. It was trun out on t' tide. Couldn't leave it lay where it was."

"No, you couldn't. But I wish you'd spoken to me before you chucked it in the water."

"I didn't do it," Crane said surprisingly. "Mr Dunster did. It was his dog."

Dunster again! Cass Harty sighed and returned to the showcase. "How much," he asked, pointing through the glass, "how much are you asking for one of these pocket-knives?"

Sergeant Cass Harty's eyes struggled to accustom themselves to the dim light as he picked his way through the collection of junk that littered the cellar of the Sand Head jail. Relics lay all about in junglelike profusion, ranging in worthlessness from an ancient grindstone with one broken leg through some assorted lengths of half-rotted cable to a splintered gaff for a small sloop.

To the detective the grindstone was a sheer gift of the gods. He had not hoped for anything to aid his task so greatly.

At the far end of the cellar a huge square of mainsail, black-green with mildew, shrouded the outline of a large tin bathtub of the vintage of the 1880s.

Sand and sea and the sunlit morning outside became improbably distant and unreal as Harty lifted the canvas away.

Large chunks of sawdust-flecked ice filled the interior of the tub, covering the bodies of Hubert Messinger and his son. Side by side, like tortured carp in a grisly garden pool, the shattered corpses lay half submerged in water from the melting ice.

His dozen years with the New York police had let Cass Harty look upon violent death in many forms. The handiwork of razor men in Harlem; splintering auto crashes on the West Side elevated highway; a thing dredged up from the mud of the East River bed, solid set to the waist in a block of concrete, a thing that had been a living man even after the cement had begun to harden; he had seen them all and looked at them coldly, entirely in the line of duty. But now, as he shucked off his coat and began to turn back his shirt sleeves, he asked himself if there had been any he liked less than these.

He lifted a lump of ice from the near end of the tub. It had rested on the boy's face and, as Harty turned it over, he saw that the pressure of its weight had made the underside conform to the shape of the dead features in hap-chance death mask.

Something about it touched a fuse to the rage inside him. Tiny prickles of fury danced along his spine kindling a blood vendetta urge for vengeance. His upper canines were tight upon his lower lip as, with almost womanly care, he replaced the ice block, fitting its hollows gently across the broad forehead and enveloping the once-bold nose now pinched in death. Then he took the newly purchased knife from his pocket and approached the grindstone.

The desire to square the outrages committed against society ordinarily played small part in the sergeant's police activities. Society could, in the long run, look out for itself, and usually did. Hunting down criminals was work, work to be done to the best of one's ability; and work to which, perhaps, an occasional piqure was given by the cleverness of one's opponents—but it was essentially a job, after all.

This dead boy changed all that.

With each downward lunge upon the handle of the grindstone, with every scrape of the increasingly keen blade, words were driven between the detective's locked teeth.

"I'll get him," he snarled. "I'll get whoever did this if it's the last arrest I ever make."

Back beside the tub again with the knife honed to razor sharpness, the hardest-boiled dick in New York knew he had a job to do and knew he could not do it on the boy. He put down his knife, gripped the corpse of Hubert Messinger beneath the armpits, and lifted its flaccid, unresisting bulk onto the cellar floor.

There was a black irregular hole in the center of the man's forehead.

"Can't have penetrated very far there," Harty said. He closed his mind against the thought of the boy in the tub. The man was no more than another case to him as he set his knife blade to work, probing delicately at the hole.

A moment's delving showed his guess had been correct. The steel of the knife ticked against metal lodged directly above the optic chiasm among the splinters of the smashed frontal bone.

Working desperately to avoid tearing the flesh of the forehead any further, he pried the missile loose and got it to the surface. It was large between his thumb and forefinger, and of a shape no bullet had any right to be. He carried it to the water tap set into the wall and, when he had washed it clean, he cursed aloud, no longer in rage but in blank astonishment.

The thing was the clipped-off head of a large iron nail.

Deciding to try the torso next, he gripped the knife again.

As he dug into the suety chest he thought that a doctor probably would not mind the task, and he recalled having once arrested and taken straight to a certain ward in Bellevue a staring-eyed man who would certainly have taken a particular kind of pleasure in it; but, he told himself, I'm neither of those birds. And glad of it too!

It was not necessary to guard against the knife accomplishing any further mutilation of the breast. Both it and the stomach had been so horribly raked that such a thing was impossible.

Cass Harty worked on, and twice as the knife slithered through the deep fascia it met obstructions that were not bone but iron. The gun had unquestionably had great penetrative power, whatever strange species of weapon it might be. In the myocardium he found a fourth chunk, also a nail. It was not clipped short, as the first three had been, but bent double on its own length, as if by pliers.

When the belly had given up a fifth, and the leathery rectus muscle of the torn thigh a sixth bit of metal, and his stomach was becoming almost used to his job, Cass Harty decided he had enough for his purpose. He replaced the body in the tub, restored the canvas, and went to hold the last scraps of iron beneath the tap.

As water ran cleanly over them his mind refused to imagine what type of gun had flung this load. "No matter what the gun turns out to be," he said, as he turned off the water and started up the stairs, "the load was obviously homemade. One thing's certain: An amateur — and a damned nasty one—is what I've got to look for!"

4

LeMoyne Dunster sat in the lounge at the far end of the Sand Head Ocean Club pier, the dishes before him emptied of a late breakfast. He looked up inquisitively as the sergeant entered from the west promenade.

Cass Harty's thumbs were hooked in the lower pockets of his vest, the right one touching six scraps of iron. He said, "They told me you'd be here."

Dunster tilted his coffee cup, making dark dregs run in a small circle. "They were right."

"'They said Randall Elrod would be with you."

"He is not."

"Gone for a sail?"

"No." Dunster pointed eastward through a wide window. "You can see him there."

"In that?" Harty looked at the dinghy bobbing at anchor well beyond the moorings of both yacht and destroyer. A man in an enormous, field hand's straw hat sat on its middle thwart holding a fishing pole. As Harty watched, he put down the rod and raised something that looked like a bottle, making the sergeant murmur, "I'd think he could do that more comfortably here."

"*He* likes it there. And quite often he catches some fish."

Harty lit a cigarette and puffed a ring toward the ceiling where Tritons and Nereids gamboled Priapically against a background of marine flora. "Quite a place, this."

"We think well of it." Dunster's tone was complacent. "There are trophy and committee rooms, a kitchen as modern as you'll find in any hotel in town, a central hall large enough to accommodate the entire membership at meetings and dances, and we have one of the best collections of whaling relics that can be found anywhere. You ought to see it."

"I'd like to." Harty fingered the iron in his vest pocket and tried to make his next question sound casual. "Done any building or altering lately?"

"No. The pier was conceived and built as a unit back in '29."

Some other place, then, Harty thought. He strolled to the east windows and looked out at a long strip of the Head. The Sad Angel. The destroyer. The float. Elrod's tiny dock and, on the ridge above, his house, larger than Dunster's and easily identifiable by the tall mast on its lawn, with halyards vivid arcs in the breeze under the tension of twoscore snapping flags. He said, "Nice view."

Dunster smiled. "You didn't come to tell me that."

"No—I was curious to know how your guests were weathering last night's affair."

"According to their various personalities—and intelligences." The smile shaded into something near a smirk. "How else?"

"Isn't anyone going up to town for the funeral?"

"I had been considering that, but"—an impression of selecting his excuse from a possible three or four accompanied Dunster's pause—"after all, I have certain obligations to my guests. However, I intend to accompany the remains on their journey."

Harty went back to the guests. "Where's Miss Franklin now?"

"Probably enduring the courtship of Adrian Tenny. They were going to go for a swim later on."

"And her boss?"

"On the divan, over there." Dunster laughed. "Poor chap, he's having a siege of the bloggles."

"'Bloggles'?" The sergeant crossed the room and leaned over the back of the divan that faced the western windows.

"One stage worse than the screaming-meemies. It sets

in when you've lost the power even to meem."

"I get it," Harty said, and thought: That's a pretty large portion of whimsy for your age and weight.

The object among the soft cushions could have been either a very recently matriculated corpse or a still-living being in an advanced state of coma. Supporting the later notion, a coffee table in front of the divan held several empty whisky tots and a tall tom-collins glass, its sides streaked with whitish foam, the residuum of a bromo.

"He looks as if he'd had a rough night."

"Like many people who have made money too fast to know what to do with it, Charley is addicted to rough nights," Dunster said. "Someone or another has claimed it is part of his charm."

There was scant evidence of charm about the man on the divan. Rumpled clothes swaddled his pudgily fat body like so much sacking. His face looked like a slab of veal in a cut-rate butcher shop and his skin was slippery with a weak sudation. Irregular breathing labored between the thick, sagging lips.

The day before *that* happens to me, Harty thought, I'll quit drinking.

"Have you heard anything on that convict yet?" Dunster introduced the topic which Harty had intended to approach indirectly. "The last I knew of it, he was still at large."

"We're on a par there." The sergeant settled into a chair. "I understand the tip on him came from your home."

"I shouldn't care to claim all the credit—but if there's a reward out for him I won't pass it up."

"Did the tip come from you?"

"Ah—vaguely, yes. That is, I told Rev Crane. I can't say who first remarked on the resemblance—it grew out of general talk and everyone seemed to be commenting on it at once. There was that picture in the paper. I thought it wise to bring it to Rev's notice."

Cass Harty tried to pin him down. "You can't

remember who first spoke of it?"

"Sorry—no. Perhaps I did myself. You know how anonymously a topic can get under way in a cocktail group. The . . ."

"Pardon, please." A man with a cropped mustache was suddenly in the west doorway.

"Come right in, Doctor." Dunster seemed not at all displeased by the interruption. "Doctor Larsen—Sergeant Harty, of New York. The doctor is director of a sanatorium down toward the western end of the Head. Perhaps you've heard of it."

Harty decided the doctor had been called to whip Wade into shape. He grinned and said, "Yeah, you mentioned it last night."

"Where is Mr Elrod?" Larsen inquired.

"Fishing. Will you wait?"

"I do not believe I have time." The doctor looked at a green-gold watch and nodded as though its hands confirmed his doubt. "I would appreciate it if you mention to him that I was here. I will also appreciate his calling at the sanatorium at his earliest convenience."

Dunster assured him the message would be given, and Larsen bowed from the hips in Prussian ober-leutnant fashion, thanked him, and was gone.

"Short and sweet," Harty remarked. "Why does he want to see Elrod?"

"I dare say it has something to do with his cousin. Morgan Elrod is a patient up there. A bit mental, you know—been that way off and on for a long time. Things of that sort often crop out in these old families—the first Elrod came to Jamestown in 1628—but they're always hard to bear."

"I didn't know the san was a nuthatch."

"It isn't, exactly. But the doctor believes in accepting any patient who is able to meet his rather stiff tariff. Alcoholics, narocotic victims and, rumor has it, some of the less mentionable social complaints. The place doesn't lack for customers."

"Especially the latter." Harty punned horribly, "Whose name is lesion, huh?"

On the divan there were sounds of stirring. Wade muttered drowsily, "Oooooh . . . what a headache!"

"This Morgan Elrod," Harty said. "Did he have anything against the Messingers?"

"Nothing. Besides, Morgan is not at all dangerous."

Over the back of the divan came a thick-tongued, "The hell you say!"

Cass Harty watched the bulky Wade try to sit up. "Feel bad?"

"Terrible!" The man blew out a long breath. His mouth worked experimentally before he managed to say, "Where can a guy put in an application to get his head cutoff?"

Harty said, "Sometimes a hair of the dog does wonders."

"Yeh—and sometimes it don't. I already had six . . . no, seven." He rocked back and forth, almost losing his balance at each extreme. "I'm as bad off as ever."

"You ought to keep on trying."

Dunster pressed the table buzzer for the steward and said, "We'll be glad to join you."

"Okey-dokey." Wade's head wabbled vaguely toward the service door. "Wherzat damned Filipino? Never around when y' want him!"

"The club has been getting along with a skeleton force until the season opens," Dunster apologized. "I'll see if I can find him."

"Pssst!" Wade looked mysterious as the door closed behind Dunster. "You're a cop? I wanna tell y' somethin'."

"Shoot."

"You tell *me* something. When y' walked out onna pier, which side did y' take?"

Having come from the settlement, Harty had taken the nearer of the two promenades. He said, "The right side."

The fat man made a drunken fumbling gesture,

familiarizing himself with the difference between right
and left. "It wuzzen the right side," he said flatly. "It ..." A
creak of the door cut him off.

"I didn't locate the steward," Dunster said, entering
with a tray. "But I found the tonic." He put his burden
down and poured with suspicious generosity for Wade
and the sergeant. His own portion barely colored the
seltzer. "By the way, Charley, this is . . ."

"Knew him right 'way." Wade cut off the introduction.
"Elrod said he was down here."

Harty was puzzled by Wade's remark upon
awakening. To follow it up, he said, "Doc Larsen was
looking for Elrod a while ago."

"Then Morgan's prob'ly been cutting up." Charley
snickered. "What a wild cuss he is! Why, one time in New
York . . ."

"Is this necessary?" Dunster cut in.

"Can't tell till I hear it," Harty said. "What's the lay?"

"Morgan Elrod had a little trouble in a night club,"
Dunster said suavely. "The usual tipsy
misunderstanding."

"Misunderstanding, my . . ." Wade waxed anatomical.
"He was stinking drunk an' he beat a guy's head in with a
bar stool. Damn near killed him. Morgan'd be in jail today
if Randall hadn't seen about half of Tammany to fix . . ."

"Competent medical authority decided Morgan needed
mild restraint." Dunster grabbed the conversation once
more. "That is why he is at Larsen's. He need stay there
only when his attacks occur and, fortunately, they do not
come often."

"Only when he wants to use 'em as an excuse for his
rotten temper," Wade sneered. "If I was working on last
night's business, I'd . . ."

"You're talking rot." Dunster silenced him again. "And
to the wrong person. The sergeant is concerned only with
McNiff."

"Even so. I don't have to be a hick cop to want to know
why everyone cleared away from that fireplace."

"I don't mind telling why *I* left. We'd brought a vacuum jug of cocktails to the beach with us. When it was empty I went up to my house to replenish it."

"You had nothing with you when I first saw you," Harty reminded him. "What became of the growler you were rushing?"

"I had not yet reached my home when I heard the shot. I dropped the jug and hurried back to the beach. Anyone would have done the same."

"O.K." Harty turned to Wade. "What took you away?"

"Well, y' know how it is." Charley's balled cheeks and shrewd eyes made him look like a benevolent hamster as he grinned with embarrassment. "Y' get a load of drinks aboard and you're talking to a pretty girl. It's a nice summer night and the ocean's right there. Maybe I wasn't feeling as old as I look."

"Which girl's absence does that spiel account for?"

"Huh? Oh, my sec'etary. We took a walk up the beach."

"Which direction?"

"This way—toward the club pier."

The dune from which Rev had thought the shot might have been fired lay the opposite way. "Did you notice anything? A light out at sea—like the flash of a gun?"

"We couldn't exactly see the water. We were . . . uh . . . sitting down at the time. Sounded like it was out that way, though."

"*I* didn't think so," Dunster contradicted sharply. "And I didn't see a flash."

"No?" It was a hint to go on talking.

"Emphatically, no! The surface of the water, out near the yacht, was dark."

"You were climbing that slope and looking out to sea at the same time?" Harty said thinly. He was thinking that he had asked nothing about the yacht. "Damn lucky you didn't break your neck."

"I'd paused for a minute—to catch my breath."

A man *could* get winded on that climb. "Nothing

scared you off? You had no warning it would be safer up at your house?"

"Of course not. The idea is ridiculous!"

Charley Wade was staring fixedly at the sergeant. Purpose of some vague kind was reflected in his bloodshot eyes.

"Look at it this way," Harty told Dunster. "It's an absolutely moonless night. A gun is fired. Gun makes a flash. Well?"

"I saw the lights of the destroyer and the yacht." The man's tone was stubborn. "I did not see a flash!"

Harty was puzzled by the second unsolicited mention of the yacht. He thought: Either you're lying, or you weren't looking!

"Due to the convolutions of the slope I could not see all of the beach nor all of the water," Dunster went on, "but I had an excellent view of it far out. There was no flash."

Wade was still staring. In apparent carelessness he opened and shut the fingers of his right hand on the back of the divan. Then, certain he had caught the detective's eye, he ceased to move four of the fingers. The index alone went out. It pointed straight at the door of the eastern promenade.

The hint clicked in Harty's brain. Suddenly he saw that what he had supposed was mere drunken argumentativeness really possessed meaning. When he said "It wuzzen the right side" Wade had been distinguishing not between "right" and "left", but between "right" and "wrong."

"If you say you didn't see it, I can't debate the point with you," the sergeant told Dunster, pretending a grudging abandonment of his stand. "You were there— I was not." He drained his glass and got up to go. "And, as you mentioned, McNiff is my job."

Wade's heavy face broke into a smile as the detective opened the door to the eastern promenade.

Comfortable deck chairs and small wicker tables were

strung at random along the pier's rail. Eyes alert, Harty strode past them, their innocous rank making him wonder if Wade had been kidding him.

Then, two thirds of the way to shore, he realized that the fat man had been desperately in earnest.

Mounted just inside the rail, its base secured to the planks by heavy rivets, a strange-looking instrument reared its black metal bulk.

Some three feet long, the heavy tubelike barrel was mounted on a swivel. There was a thick wooden stock that ended in a grip like that of an old-fashioned pistol. Inquisitively he touched the grip, and the gun swung easily beneath his hand until its muzzle pointed northeast-by-east, directly at the distant bricks of the furnace.

He swung the weird gun back and poked measuring fingers into its mouth. The bore was great enough to accommodate index and second digits with ease.

She'd figure an inch and a half to three quarters, he decided. Room enough for a hell of a load! But I need more than guesswork.

The plate gave him little help. Small and oblong, of lettered brass, it was attached to the gun mount for the information of the curious, none of whom, perhaps, had ever had the same reasons for their curiosity as the sergeant.

HARPOON GUN
Salvaged from the whaler
NETTIE LEE
Wrecked off Prince Regent Is.
June 21st, 1872.

5

Young Ronnie Gresham sat alone in the splendor of Cabin A on the yacht Sad Angel and gnawed diligently at a ragged thumbnail. Hair rumpled and forehead creased,

he perched on the edge of his chair and stared unseeingly
at the pattern of the rug, like a modern-dress version of
The Thinker tottering on the rim of a nervous breakdown.

Through the cabin window the breeze floated gently,
bringing a sound of chunking oarlocks and a deep,
pleasantly hoarse voice trolling an old navy song.

> *"Ev'ry good ship has a captain,*
> *Ev'ry captain has a crew,*
> *Ev'ry young girl likes a young man*
> *Who knows how ... "*

Ronnie raised his troubled head and murmured,
"Some of the crew coming back, I guess," then sagged into
thought once more.

> *"... to haul away the mains'l,*
> *And put his helm a-lee,*
> *Ev'ry nice girl's unhappy,*
> *When her true love's at sea."*

The renowned naval architect who had designed the
Sad Angel had provided for a connecting door between
cabins A and B. It was a sturdy door, fitted with a
stalwart lock, and built of an excellent wood, resonant
beneath the knuckles, yet not too thick to prevent the
passage of importunate whispers. And, since the night
that he and his two companions had come aboard, young
Ronnie had gone in for some intensive whispering
without bringing about any change in the position of the
bolts of the lock. The susurrant sessions had all been on
identical lines. Each started with an earnest and naively
hopeful "Laura! Open the door. There's something I want
to tell you," then ranged on through pleading, impatience
and exasperation to an "All *right!* If that's the way you're
going to act," and silence until it was time for the next
assault to begin.

The towered maiden managed to grade her answers

nicely. At each outset she was content to intimate her readiness to wait till morning to hear Ronnie's message; but when he arrived at the door-rattling, Oh-for-God's-sake-be-reasonable! stage she would murmur with chilling sincerity, "Now, you know I on'y came down here because I thought I could feel safe with you."

Ronnie had not thought so himself when he extended the invitation to visit the yacht, but the futility of his best efforts was beginning to convince him that she certainly could. Now, sunk in despair, he had made up his mind to cease storming the stronghold. If only he could think of a way to get her off the yacht and back to town again without a word about it getting into Winchell's Monday column he would feel he had gained at least a Mexican standoff.

Meanwhile, in Cabin B, Laura Ladd was doing some thinking of her own. She was tired of being cooped up and sick of having Ronnie whisper at her. She knew that something odd had happened while Ronnie and his friend were on shore last night and she worried about what it might be. And, worst of all, she wanted a cigarette.

It was tough to do without a butt when you wanted one so bad. But it certain'y did make a girl look a whole lot more refined if she laid offa the smokes—everybody knew that. Sometimes these fellas got funny ideas about a girl, just on account of she happened to be in show business. And the same everybodies who knew about smoking could tell you that they were the kind of ideas that led almost anywhere except down the path Laura had envisioned when she said, "Yes, she'd love to see Mr Gresham's yacht."

Laura had been following that path more or less resolutely since the day when she simultaneously abandoned the name Lena Ludisczlawa and a job in a Worcester textile mill; and it was a splendid path for a girl to follow, since she hoped it would lead straight to a justice of the peace and mingled envy and congratulations from the other girls in the floor show, and a picture, leggy, but in good taste, y' unnerstand, on the front pages of the tabloids, captioned, more than likely, "Runaway Bride of Millionaire's Scion." It was easy for Laura to think that she was already halfway there.

The on'y catch was, she hadda figger out a way to mix with Ronnie and his friend, sociablelike, y' unnerstand, while she still got the idea acrost to them that they had a perfeck lady to deal with.

Laura stood at her cabin window and peeped through a slit in the shutters at the calm blue water. She could see a fella in a rowboat, coming toward the yacht, and hear the words of the song he was singing.

> *"Ev'ry good ship has a gangplank,*
> *Ev'ry gangplank has a rail . . ."*

Miss Ladd heard the song through and thought it over until she figured out what was wrong with its rhyme scheme. When she finally got it straight she did not have to remind herself about being a perfeck lady. She slammed the window shut and murmured, "The nerve of that guy! He's certain'y pretty ror."

There was a second connecting door in Cabin B. It gave on C but, unlike the other portal, it had been neither shaken nor whispered through. Nor was there any chance that its knob would be so much as touched while Chester Thornton occupied Cabin C.

A large square-rigged high-pressure gentleman, Chester had, during forty-three years of concentrated Living, made it a point to know exactly what he was doing, and why, one hundred and five per cent of the time. He insisted on being called "Chet" by the people he had known three minutes, liked being referred to as "Good Ol' Chet" by a circle of friends and business subordinates, and never even suspected that to many he was simply "That heel, Thornton." He sold things, ballyhooed organizations, and promoted sales campaigns with a vast enthusiasm and a keen prescience for the mathematically correct instant for stepping from under. This latter was a stunt which Chet had learned on an October afternoon in 1929 while watching a ticker tape; and if he had torn any pages from his calendar since then, they had not been used for shaving paper.

Under no circumstances would Chet shake a door separating him from a lady. He might whisper through it, provided he had an ironclad guarantee of the outcome of the act, but even then the gesture would be merely a concession to the lady's taste for the romantic. Chet's own romantic yearnings—although he would not have called them that—were customarily taken care of in a succession of walk-up apartments in the West Seventies and on a strictly cash basis.

Like Ronnie and Laura, Good Ol' Chet, too, had engaged in a morning of deep thought. It was a brand of cold-blooded avaricious pondering which had been highly productive of results for him in the past and which, he had every confidence, would be equally profitable in the future.

As the sound of rowlocks drifted through his window Chet rubbed a soft hand across the front hair which not even the most expensive of barbers, and industriously rubbed-in tonics could keep from receding. He put three folded sheets of legal-looking paper into a pigskin bag which was equipped with an almost unpickable lock. His tongue made small sounds of regret against the roof of his mouth as he shut the bag.

Chet's rue was no less genuine for sounding slight. He had a feeling that an entire morning's reflection really should have provided so astute a person as himself with the answer he sought.

The folded sheets of paper were contract forms. They had been drawn up by a swarthy lawyer named Koumidijian—since Chet was fond of saying that it took a Greek to trim a Jew—and an Armenian to rook the pair of them. Mr Koumidijian had said that the contracts were practically bulletproof, and Chet's mental effort had been devoted to an attempt to choose which of the three he could most easily, and profitably, persuade Ronnie Gresham to attach his signature to—in nonfading ink.

Chet put the bag away and, in the mirror, checked the set of his five-dollar tie, the hairlessness of his newly scraped jowls, and the security of his buttons. He filled a cigarette case and opened a door that led onto the deck.

Last night complicated things, but he felt that Ronnie should be over the worst of his jitters by now. It might be possible to talk a little business over the preluncheon sidecars. If only that damned tar . . . that girl could be depended on to stay in her cabin until an agreement was signed!

A dinghy, amateurishly rowed, was coming up under the Sad Angel's starboard side. The oarsman's back was to the yacht as he sang,

> *"Ev'ry good ship has a mains'l,*
> *Ev'ry mains'l has a boom . . ."*

Good Ol' Chet recognized the rower. His freewheeling brain whirred through a filing case of tried and proven attitudes for every occasion and settled unerringly on one which called for a show of deep-chested male-to-male rowdiness, faintly tinctured with a bit of dignified condescension which any really discerning onlooker would immediately comprehend. In a rich baritone he started to round out the chantey, "Ev'ry young man likes a . . ."

Sergeant Cass Harty rested his oars and turned to wave a broad hand. "Hello, Sad Angel," he called. "I'm coming aboard."

"Come right ahead," Chet urged. Stepping to the gap in the rail, he asked solicitously, "Will you make it all right?"

"Hope so—I'll keep swinging." Harty hooked an oar under water, purposely catching a crab, because he liked to have possible opponents underestimate him. With great splashing he worked the dink in and made fast at the foot of the steps. "Boats aren't my game."

Thornton shouted "Look out!" as the sergeant climbed awkwardly from the dink, resting a foot on the gunwale and almost capsizing it in the process.

"Right—I nearly caught a bath."

"A damned close squeak." Chet frowned. "Can you swim?"

"I wouldn't know," Harty stooged again. "I've never tried." He reached the deck and began, "My name's . . ."

"Sergeant Harty doesn't have to introduce himself to any real New Yorker," Chet said. The ancestral Thornton home was a corn farm, thirty-seven miles outside of Charles City, Iowa; which did not stop him. "We all know you."

"Thanks. I'm giving Rev Crane a hand—unofficially, of course—and I'm on the prowl for information about last night. We thought you people might have noticed something from out here on the yacht."

"But we weren't here." Chet supplied what the detective already knew. "Ronnie and I were both at the party. Possibly Lau . . ." He stopped short and offered Harty a cigarette to cover the break. "Possibly some of the crew could help, but I doubt it."

"Possibly." The sergeant was more interested in sizing up Thornton at the moment. "Were you near the furnace when it happened?"

"I'm afraid not." Chet's semi-laugh implied that no such outrages took place when he was at hand to prevent them. "You see, I'd had a plunge in the surf; when I came out I sprinted down the beach, a quarter mile or so, to get warm."

"A lot of people would have stood in front of the fire."

"But *I* believe in keeping fit. I jogged beyond the club pier and back." He twirled a gold football on the end of his watch chain, in muscular ostentation. "Can't afford to go soft, you know. We old Blues pick up too much blubber if we do."

"See anyone on your way?" Harty recalled Wade's statement that he and Kay Franklin had walked in the same direction.

"Not a soul."

The girl and her boss could easily have been unseen by Chet, but Harty thought it was wonderful that so many people had managed to lose themselves at exactly the opportune moment. "Did you get any idea of the location of the gun?" he asked. "See the flash?"

"I hadn't turned back yet at the time I heard the report. I guess we both remember our elementary physics well enough to know that sound waves travel more slowly than light. It follows that the flash must have disappeared before I heard the report."

Very logical, the sergeant thought, and very damned pat! He strolled slowly toward the bow where the elongated barrel of the saluting cannon shone brassily.

"A person would have a good view from here. A gun flash could have been seen."

Chet smiled. "By anyone who was here to see it," he said amiably. "If you want to question the crew, I'll turn them out."

"Good idea."

Leaning over an open hatchway, Thornton bawled, "Everyone on deck. Tumble out!"

No one answered.

"Probably all asleep—they're lazier than Memphis coons," he said. "I'll have them topside in a jiffy." He grasped the rails on either side of the stairs and swung nimbly out of sight.

Cass Harty moved fast.

Two strides brought him to the gun and, bending, he sniffed at its muzzle. A grin of satisfaction stretched his mouth briefly.

As feet thumped on the stairway he moved from the gun to lean against the rail, drawing deeply on his cigarette. It was one way of getting the mingled smell of metal polish and burned powder out of his nostrils. Like

Balieff's wooden soldiers, a seaman, a cockney steward
and an engineer followed Chet Thornton onto the deck.

"Line up here!" The man's tone was that of an
R.O.T.C. captain. "This man is a police officer. He will ask
you some questions. Speaking for Mr Gresham, I instruct
you to answer them frankly. There is no reason to hold
anything back!"

Quite a speech! Harty thought, and felt it would have
been even more impressive if he could be sure they had
not received their real orders before coming on deck.

"Did one of you boys stand watch last night?" he
asked. They gave him a triple "No."

He spoke directly to the engineer. "Who did?"

"Nobody, sir." The man fiddled with the zipper
fastener of his dungarees. "Wasn't no watch stood, sir. We
all had shore leave."

Peculiar! And Thornton must have known about it.
"No watch, huh? Captain's orders?"

"No sir. Owner's."

"Cap'n ain't been aboard for a week, sir," the tall
seaman put in. "He's been visitin' his fam'ly. Be back
tomorrow."

"I see." No captain, and the crew sent ashore—a
perfect setup! "Mind digging Gresham out for me?" Harty
asked Thornton. "I'd like to talk to him before I leave."

"Sure thing." Chet went briskly down the deck.

"Now, then," the detective took a whirl at the
members of the crew. "Who polished bright-work on deck
this morning?"

"Me, sir," the seaman answered.

"You shined this peashooter?"

"O' course. Don't it look it?"

"It looks swell. How recently has it been fired?"

"I dunno—maybe the last couple days. Poppa's boy ...
uh ... I mean . . . Mr Ronald Gresham shoots it off now
and then, sir. Seems to get a kick outa playing with it."

Good clean fun—if it wasn't a way of setting up an
alibi, the detective thought. "How long were you men

ashore?"

"Us three come back in time for Webb to get breakfast. The rest of the boys are still over on the mainland."

"Then the yacht was empty last night?"

The seaman looked unhappily toward his mates for guidance. "Uh ... well ... not exactly empty, sir."

"What does that mean?"

"Y' see, sir, Mr Gresham, he had a ..."

"A job's a job," the engineer grunted. "Here's the boss now. Let him do his own explaining."

6

Billowy doeskin slacks flopped above rope-soled espadrilles as Ronnie Gresham came along the deck, his basque shirt heaving in time with his nervous breathing.

Sergeant Harty looked him over and did not have to look long to decide that Ronnie was not a person on whom he would care to depend in any imaginable crisis. He thought the millionaire's son looked yellow, in the way that certain prize fighters or football teams or polo mounts will look yellow and manage to go on looking that way even while things are running in their favor. And at the moment things were not running for Ronnie. He knew it, and it made him jumpy.

A good loud "Boo" would make him fall right out of those fancy pants, the sergeant decided. As they shook hands, it cost him more than a small effort of will to keep from giving that "Boo!"

Ronnie's palm was clammy damp. Talking very fast, like a rattled sixth former going through a conjugation of which he was not especially sure, he said, "I'm glad to see you. I've heard a lot about you. Suppose we send the men back to their quarters and we'll go aft where we can sit down and have a drink."

Harty heard him perfectly, but he asked, "What'd you say?"

"I'm glad to see . . ." Ronnie would have reeled off the entire speech again if Chet had not stopped him.

"That's a smart idea about being at ease while we talk. And the drink has merit too."

"O.K. with me," Harty said, and followed them to a circle of chairs at the stern.

Chet juggled glasses at a low table, apologizing, "We're out of everything but brandy."

In deference to his prolonged fast, Harty said, "Keep mine tender."

"I want a stiff one, Chet." Gresham slid a sockless foot in and out of its flat sandal and avoided meeting Harty's gaze as he asked, "What did you want to see me about?"

"You were at Dunster's beach party?"

"Yes, but I didn't notice anything wrong. I . . . uh ... I really can't tell you anything about what happened. I saw the Albright girls back to their cottage and stopped off at Dunster's after I left them. I had to phone my father about the yacht. I was still talking to him when I heard the gun. Up to the time I left the beach there'd been no trouble. So you see there's no use in questioning me."

"Hold on," Harty said, "I only asked if you went to the party. You've answered that."

"But I wanted you to understand I didn't see—" Ronnie broke off and bounded from his chair as Chet offered a drink to the sergeant. "Not that one, you chump," he shouted, and grabbed at the glass.

Harty's hand closed over his wrist. "Why not this one?"

Gresham's face went mulberry red. "Because I don't want you to get sore at me," he finally explained. "This is a trick glass that I keep, just for laughs. When you tilt it to drink, the booze spills down your shirt front."

"Ronnie loves a good joke," Thornton said expansively. "Why one night in El Morocco he got the whole place in an uproar by pretending to be drunk and complaining to Perona that the zebra stripes on the upholstery were coming off on his dinner clothes." He hacked out a forced laugh of tribute. "Ronnie's a great kidder."

"I can imagine." Cass Harty raised the glass until he saw the tiny hole just below the rim. He set it down on the table and moved toward a chair. "I hope this doesn't fold up when you sit on it."

"No," Ronnie assured him, "it's an honest-to-Jake chair. Then everything is all right?"

"About the glass? Yes."

Ronnie missed the limiting phrase. His face was happy as he leaned over and twiddled the knob of a radio beside him.

"You knew Messinger and his son well?"

"I'd seen the old gent twice before." Ronnie stopped beating time to the swing tune. "This was Gil's first visit here."

"Had Messinger ever had any trouble with any of the crowd that was at the shindy?"

"Not that I ever heard of."

Harty abandoned that line as unproductive and took a new tack. "When you went ashore last night, you went together?"

Chet said, "We did."

"I'm talking to Gresham! You came back together too?"

"Yes."

"Neither of you were back here in the interim?"

They both said, "No."

"None of the crew here when you returned?"

"No—oh no. They were under orders ... I mean, I gave them leave until this morning."

"So no watch was stood?"

"I didn't want them . . . that is . . . there wasn't need for a watch. The weather was mild and . . . and so on."

"Someone was aboard." Harty based his accusation on the interrupted words of the seaman. "Who was it?"

Ronnie's eyes rolled an appeal for help but Good Ol' Chet cannily managed to be too deep in enjoyment of his brandy and soda to catch his friend's SOS.

"We haven't all day," Harty snapped.

"W-w-well, it was a woman."

Thornton had debated whether it would be policy to offer aid. Now he came to bat nobly. "A Miss Ladd," he offered. "An old and very dear friend of the Gresham family."

"That's right," Ronnie mumbled. "Pal of my mother."

Chet's face showed he knew that for a blunder, but there was an underlying hint that he was glad it had been made. He said, "She has been a guest here for some time."

"Waltz her out," the sergeant ordered.

Thornton may have been pleased to have Harty know a woman was aboard, but he set about preventing him from seeing her. "Um, that may not be possible," he said smoothly. "As a matter of fact, Miss Ladd has not been in the best of health. She has been more or less confined to her cabin. You see, her purpose in coming here was to achieve a rest cure. It's important that she avoid any strain."

"I'm not going to wrestle with her. Bring her out!"

"Really, Chet's telling the truth. She shouldn't be disturbed. She's quite an elderly lady—an old friend of my aunt."

"A minute ago you said it was your mother," Harty pointed out. "Let's have a look at her."

"Certainly." Chet seemed to think he had found a slick out. "I feel sure Miss Ladd will be able to talk to you when she is feeling better—perhaps tomorrow."

The sergeant was growing fed up on the manners and methods of Mr Chet Thornton. "I'll see her now," he growled, getting to his feet. "What cabin is she in?"

"B," Chet said. "But I strongly advise against disturb . . ."

Harty did not wait to hear the rest of it.

Someone inside Cabin B moved suddenly at his knock. A voice said, "Now, Ronnie, you promised . . ."

That hotcha contralto doesn't make the yarn about an

invalid look good, Harty thought. Aping the steward's
cockney accent, he said, "Mr Gresham's compliments,
miss, and would you find it convenient to come aft?
There's a visitor from shore."

Miss Ladd took time to think it over. "This ain't . . .
isn't just a gag to get me outa here, is it, Webb?"

"Oh, certainly not, miss. I saw the guest come aboard
m'self."

"O.K. then. Tell 'em I'll be right along."

Harty said, "Very good, miss," and started aft.

Behind him, the voice continued, "An' be sure you tell
Ronnie if there's any monkey business he'll be sorry."

The sergeant thought: I can hardly wait. He told the
waiting duo, "She'll be out—and she doesn't sound like
anyone's grandma."

Ronnie was too flattened to speak, but Chet instantly
had his new attitude in hand. He chuckled as he rose to
fuss with a new batch of drinks. "No, she's not. Matter of
fact, she's quite young and damned attractive. You were
too quick for us there, Sergeant, and I guess we're both
big enough to admit it. No use denying we tried to deal
them out of the middle of the deck to you about Miss
Ladd. I'll ex . . ."

"Whistle the patter," Harty snapped. "Gresham can do
the explaining. It's his boat—I want his story."

Explaining shaped up as a large order for Ronnie. "It's
this way," he began haltingly. "Chet's told you the truth
about Laura not being so old. She's a . . . We're very good
friends. I mean, I like her very much. So it was only
natural . . ."

"What Ronnie is getting at," Chet offered, "is that he
is a sincere admirer of Miss Ladd's technique."

I'll give him a break, Harty thought, and not ask, "At
what?"

"Chet is telling it better than I could," Ronnie said.
"I'd seen her often and she's really darned good. She's . . ."

"... a potentially great artiste," Thornton cut in again.
"Voice, pen or brush? Get it told!"

"Well, if you've got to know, she dan . . ."

"Her specialty is eurythmics." Good Ol' Chet grabbed the conversational reins once more. "If she were given the right chance to develop, I think there would be no doubt about her genius. As Ronnie said, she aroused his interest some time ago. She's by way of being a protegee of his."

"Thornton," Cass Harty grunted, "I'll shut you up if I have to. I want Gresham's story—not your version of it. A while ago you asked me if I could swim—can you?"

"Swim?" Chet laughed. "Like an expert."

"Good! Then crash this conversation just once more and you'll get a chance to prove it." Harty's patience was exhausted as he nodded to the frightened Ronnie to continue.

"It's like Chet said. I wanted to help Laura get a break. I put a little money in a show that's opening in the fall and I was going to ask them to make a spot for her. Her dancing's really tops. If you'd ever seen her in the floor show at the ... I mean, she really can step."

"Tap, muscle or fan dancer?"

"Well, she did do one number with fans."

"What of it?" Chet asked. "Fan dancing is practically a recognized art form. She's a real artiste at heart, and . . ."

"Don't say I didn't warn you," Harty growled. He bounced from his chair and grabbed Thornton, swinging him high.

Chet's heavy form cleared the rail neatly. He made a fine splash.

The door of Cabin B popped open and a girl burst out onto the deck. She yelled, "What's the matter?"

"Not a thing." The sergeant was equally interested by her gorgeous Mittel-europa blondeness and her obviously high excitement. "Chet Thornton's in the water."

Laura fitted an assortment of curves and bulges to the line of the yacht's rail. With an air of nothing-that-happens-here-can-surprise-me, she said, "But he has his clothes on."

"It's a good thing he has," Harty grinned at her. "Rev

Crane is hell-on-wheels against nude bathing."

Mildly interested, she continued to pose at the rail while the wind did tricks with her dress.

Another couple of years and she'll have to diet like the deuce, Cass thought, but right now she's pretty close to remarkable.

"Ronnie," Laura turned to them at last, "that stuff don't sound sensible. Chet wouldn't go swimming all dressed up. What happened?"

"He threw him in."

"This guy?" She seemed to see Harty plainly for the first time. "What's-a trouble with him? Is he sous . . . intoxicated?"

"Not even started." Harty showed her the almost full glass. "This is only my second snort."

"Then how come you threw Chet down there?"

"He kept asking for it."

"Well, it sounds nutty to me," she said, sinking into a chair. "Ronnie, you got some awful queer friends."

"He's no friend of mine," Gresham snapped.

"He's . . ."

"... a chance passer-by," the sergeant filled in. "A little bit on the order of the inquiring reporter, or something."

"Oh yeah?" The unclouded blue eyes were mistrustful. "Then where's your camera?"

"I'll bring it next time. Say—tell me, Miss Ladd, how did you like the party last night?"

"There wasn't no . . . any party, fresh guy. Ronnie an' Chet hadda go on shore to see a fella. I stayed here."

"Alone?"

"Yeah, alone. The crew all went before the boys left. I don't fool with sailors, anyhow."

"What did you do?"

"Me? I hit the hay."

"Mind if I ask how you slept?"

"I slept awright. Ronnie"—she turned on her bleak-faced cavalier—"is this guy trying to rib me?"

"No," Gresham sighed. "You might as well answer

him."

"Did anything disturb you during the night?"

"On'y Ronnie . . . that is, someone knocked on my door around two o'clock. I made out I did'n hear them and they went away."

Gresham dragged himself erect and, muttering about wanting to help Chet come aboard, removed himself from the scene.

"But earlier than that—around eleven or twelve?"

"I heard some kinda noise, sometime—I don't know when. It woke me up for a minute or two but I went right back to sleep."

"You didn't get up to see what it was?"

"For why? It did'n sound like it was on the boat, and I was sleepy."

Dripping brine at every step, Thornton came up the crew's ladder on the port side. Without looking aft he squdged his way to his cabin. Ronnie tagged through the door after him.

"You didn't ask anyone what that noise was?"

"Not me. I mind my own business. It's a trick a lotta people oughta learn."

"I already have. And you'd be surprised at some of the things minding my business calls for." He took out his cigarette case and opened it to her. "Smoke?"

"Ixnay—I mean, no, thanks—I never indulge." Her eyes yearned on the double row of smooth-packed cylinders, contradicting her words.

"O.K.," Cass Harty said. "I think I get the sketch." He took her purse from the table, opened it, and dumped all but two of his butts inside. "You'll be going back to your cabin later."

She did not know whether to thank him, or toss the cigarettes over the side. Saying, "Honest, I don't know whatcha mean," was her idea of a compromise.

"Sure you do. When did you come here?"

"Sat'day night. We drove down after the show."

"What about your numbers while you're away?"

"I on'y had one specialty, lately. Rest of the time I was in the line. My specialty was kinda cute though—sorta combination of a grind an' a military tap. I worked it up myself and all the girls said it was a real novelty." Talking about herself seemed to put her more at ease. "I got up my costume for that little number too. Everything black paten' leather—shoes, pants, hat, an' a brazeer about this wide."

Judging by the breeze and the pose at the rail, Harty thought that anything about that wide had probably been overburdened.

"Yeah," she said thoughtfully, "it's a shame you didn't catch the show when I was on."

To draw her, he said, "I will, when you go back."

"I mighn't be going back there."

"Got a better offer in another show?"

"No, not exactly. But a girl don't get any younger. She can't stay in show biz forever. If she knows what it's all about, there's a time when she's gotta think about the future and look for a spot to settle down." She sighed and started to take a cigarette but remembered in time. "Maybe she can find some nice young fella—know what I mean?"

"I think so. Like—Ronnie Gresham?"

"Well." She looked him dead in the eye. "And why not?"

"Don't get me wrong. I wouldn't care if you put a halter on the entire Racquet Club. But, offhand, Ronnie doesn't strike me as the husband type. He'd look a lot more natural getting heaved out of a Harlem black-and-tan joint on his ear at six in the morning than he would heating the baby's formula at the same hour—know what *I* mean?"

"I know—so what?" The blue eyes were still steady on him. "Maybe Ronnie ain't what you might call steady, but at lease we wouldn't hafta worry about where the dough for the landlord was coming from."

"I guess that's true enough."

"Of course." Laura nodded her spectacularly blonde wooliness. "It's up to a girl to do the best she can for herself when she's getting married."

"Sure! But has he asked you yet?"

"No-o-o-o. But he's li'ble to—any day. Why not? I got the looks; I can learn the words and music, the way his crowd troupes 'em."

"Go right to it—and with my official blessing." Harty knocked off the last inch of his drink and raised himself from his chair. "Give my regards to the future Mr Ladd. I'm going back to shore."

"Wait a minute." She stopped him short of the gangway. "It just come to me—I saw you one time."

"Where?"

"On the stem one night, about a year back. They had you in a prowl car with Cordes and Broderick and some of the boys from the Broadway squad. Remember them fellas?"

"I ought to. We're in the same line of business." He saw her sudden scared look and decided she had imagined Gresham had hired him to chase her away. "But don't let that worry you."

"I won't," she sighed with relief. "And I thought you was getting pinched that time."

Amidships, Chet came from his cabin in dry clothing. Ronnie followed him over the raised threshold and, pretending not to see the look Chet gave the sergeant, followed his friend forward.

"You got Thornton's goat," Laura giggled. "I don't like that guy. He thinks he's King—" She mentioned a monarch who had his existence in the vernacular rather than in history.

Cass Harty took her return to naturalness as an indication that she felt she could be on the square with him. Acting on a sudden hunch he showed her Rev's list of guests. "Aside from your boy friend and Thornton, did you ever hear of any of these people?"

She studied the paper, then looked up, her blonde

curls nodding toward the bow. "On the level, copper, you won't tell *him?*"

Harty said, "On the level."

"I know one of these guys," she said slowly, her voice held below a whisper. "I ... uh ... a girl I usta know was a friend of his."

The men at the bow were too far away to make whispering necessary, but Harty stepped close to the girl and pitched his tone as low as hers. "Which one?"

Laura's lush mouth was hard as she handed the paper back to him. "It was that dirty bum, Charley Wade."

WEDNESDAY
(Afternoon)

IN THE TINY OFFICE behind the desk in the Sea Spray lobby Cass Harty carefully wrapped a brown-paper parcel while he listened to an account of Stauffer's morning.

". . . and the Franklin babe was down to the dock to say bye-bye to the Albrights," Barney concluded.

"She didn't even look like she wanted to go with them."

"That makes you owe me half a buck," the sergeant said. "*I* got on board the Sad Angel."

"Sue me!" Stauffer advised. "What's out there?"

"A captive blonde Venus—among other things. Only instead of acting like the one in the limerick she's behaving as proper as all get out. Even so, she's still a whole lot of girl for anybody's money. She wants to phenagle Gresham into holy wedlock and she knows Charley Wade and rates him pretty low."

"What about the gun they got?"

"There's powder smudge in its barrel, but they say Gresham's in the habit of shooting it off just to hear it pop. Maybe so, maybe not so—but from its size I kind of doubt it can throw a load all the way to shore."

"Hell! Then we're just where we started."

"No, it's not that bad." Harty told of the harpoon gun on the club pier. "There's no powder burn in it, but that doesn't prove it wasn't fired. It could have been cleaned out."

"Is the gun big enough for the job?"

"Just possibly. I talked to an old bird who knows a lot about whaling days and he gave me some dope. For instance: the harpoon that gun used to sling was about four feet long and weighed twelve pounds. The gun could throw it more than a hundred feet and with enough force to sink it in a whale."

"But that's no good to us. The pier's more than a hundred feet from the furnace—a hell of a lot more."

"Sure! But the load that killed them won't add up to anything like twelve pounds. Cut down the weight and you'll add to the range—that's simple arithmetic."

"I guess it is," Barney agreed. "What else did you do?"

"I collected these." Harty patted the parcel. "And I borrowed a boat from Bandall Elrod after I got back from the Sad Angel."

"After?"

"Yeah, I don't mean the dink I rowed out in. I put the arm on him for a real boat—the Jubilee; we saw her on our way across from Keyesport yesterday. Elrod says she's the nippiest thing in these waters; she'll work closer to the wind than a shyster lawyer and run like a bat out of hell."

Gen Crane came into the office as Barney asked, "What do you want with a boat?"

For her benefit Harty said, "Sea air's good for you." He waited until she had taken some supplies from a closet and left the office before he explained, "I'm going to cruise around the island and see what's to be seen."

"Haw!" Stauffer laughed shortly. "And McNiff 'll be standing right out on the beach waiting for you to spot him."

"I wasn't hoping for anything as easy as that. What I want is to get a good idea of the layout of the place. If I see any likely spots we'll hike down and look them over."

"Maybe you got something there," Barney admitted. "How did you size up this guy Elrod?"

"I think he's square enough. He's a heavy-set iron-jawed old rooster. Big business with a capital B. There's going to be an article about him in Fortune, either next month or the month after. He works hard and, from all accounts, plays just as hard—athletics and that funny brown stuff that comes in bottles."

"Another rum-dum like Wade?"

"Not a bit—he can really hold the stuff. He spent the morning in a rowboat, jiggling a fishing line and taking belts at a quart of rye, but when I talked to him at his house he was as sober as you are."

"Did you get any dope out of him about his loony cousin? They say he has one."

"They do—and if you'll listen, you'll hear them tell that yarn a couple of ways. Randall Elrod claims the guy's a Grade-A screwball. The other version has it that the whole thing's a gag to help him dodge the grief from a jam he was in up in town."

"So?"

"I wouldn't know which is right. Randall Elrod admitted to me that the doc from the san had told him Morgan had gone away from there. Randall didn't seem worried—said Morgan had done it before and that he'd be back." Harty finished knotting the string on the package, scribbled an address across its surface, and started for the door. "And so will I."

2

"First-class mail, Rev." The sergeant shoved his little package beneath the post-office grille. "Que mucho?"

Crane put it on the scale, watched the bar sink and come to rest. "You city folks don't give a durn 'bout money," he said, ripping off stamps. "What you got in it?"

"Remember the gag about the guy who wanted a job writing headlines? Nuts, screws and bolts!"

"Hardware, huh?" Rev recalled what Harty had said about mailing a newspaper. "Ain't they got enough o' *t'at* in the big town?"

"I suppose they have—but none of it's like this. Some of the iron in here was taken out of Messinger's body." The rest, though he did not say so, had come variously from the newly built Dunster cabana, from a mended thwart in Elrod's dinghy, from an unweathered plank on the club pier, and from a recently added side porch on Melissa Packe's cottage.

"Y' don't mean it!" Rev hurriedly put the package down after glancing at the address. "Who's this Roscoe Bennet it's goin' to? Seems like I heard o' him."

"You couldn't have missed—his name was all over the papers last winter in connection with that big kidnapping job up in Rhode Island. Bennet's one of the crack metallurgical engineers of the whole country, and the work his laboratory turned in on that case came very close to equaling the scientific sleuthing Stanley Keith did on the nails from the Lindbergh kidnapping ladder."

"Y' think he'll be able to help us out?"

"I'll be damned disappointed if he can't—and I'm a guy who doesn't build his hopes high—nor disappoint easily."

3

From the shore Jubilee was a lovely thing but, as Cass Harty stepped off the landing stage of the club pier and onto her deck, the closer view was disillusioning. Whoever had brought her around from her customary mooring in the bay had not troubled to make her shipshape. Her jib was insecurely fastened to its stay, sloppily damp footprints tracked her deck, a filthy sail made a huge crumpled heap on the portside of her centerboard trunk, while to starboard a sheet lay in a tangled snarl that would have disgraced the worst land-lubber.

To calm his annoyance at seeing a graceful boat so miserably mistreated the sergeant reminded himself of the old proverb about gift horses. More than likely Elrod felt that anything was good enough for a cop who would probably not know enough to be critical.

Harty attended to the jib first of all, snapping the hooks of its luff properly to the stay.

"Not bad, Sergeant, not bad at all." A voice came down

from the pier above the stage. "You did that like a real deepwaterman."

The detective knew the voice without looking up, but he looked anyway.

Dunster was at the pier rail, a dozen yards from the projecting muzzle of the harpoon gun. He smiled irritatingly.

"I do the best I can," Harty said mildly. "It's a couple of years since I've been under sail."

"Really? I'd recommend you get your memory working then." Dunster nicked cigar ash gently down.

"You've made a good start—I wonder if you know the rest of it."

"We'll find out." Going into the cockpit Harty cast off the mainsheet and raised the topping lift slightly until the boom waggled free of its crutch. He snapped the scissor arms of the latter together and stowed it beneath the seat on the starboard side before he went to work on the halyards. Gaff and mainsail rose easily; even though Elrod might be slovenly about his decks he had seen to it that the mast hoops were well greased. He untied his bow line and, with no boat on either side to hamper him, drifted backward until he was far enough from the stage to let his sails fill with wind. "Did I do all right?"

"So far so good." Dunster began to walk shoreward, still smiling that irritating smile. "So far ... so good."

"And the same to you," Harty called. "Watch your step—you might trip over that harpoon gun."

The way the fly stood out stiffly from the truck in the freshening breeze decided the sergeant's direction for him. He would run before the wind first, setting his course for the eastern tip of the island, so as to get the feel of how Jubilee handled before he should be compelled to start tacking along the bay side of the Head.

Off his port bow he could see the strung-out houses of the Cottage Line, dominated by the imposing homes of Dunster and Elrod. The mast in front of the latter was bright with snapping colors, white beside a blue fork, blue with white center square, and white with red x markings flying above the rest. Striped orange-and-green duck beach chairs were careless on the lawn, a man in tan lounging pajamas napping in one of them. Through the binoculars he had borrowed from Rev, Harty could make out the bald head and strong features of the owner of the house.

Directly ahead of Jubilee's bowsprit lay the Sad Angel and, coming from shore, the arms of swimmers in progress toward the float thrashed the sea to green foam.

Some of the Dunster crowd, Harty guessed. He changed his course slightly to pass nearer to the wide high platform.

From the springboards slim brown legs swung beneath the extremity of a brief white suit. The yellow cap snug upon black curls identified Kay Franklin. She waved at the sergeant and called something indistinguishable.

He rounded Jubilee into the wind, letting her drift up toward the sun-baked square of boards. As she lost way, he said, "I couldn't make that out."

"I said you were so obliging in the store that I wondered if you'd be again."

"Why not?—with me it's practically a tribal custom."

Kay looked toward the approaching swimmers. "I'd like a sail—and a talk."

"And I could go for company." But not, he thought, while I've got this job of scouting to do.

"Very handsome of you." Before he could object, she rose and plopped neatly into the water with a small splash. The precise calculation of the dive marked her an expert swimmer, for the yellow cap broke surface a yard beyond Jubilee's seaward side.

"You made it." Harty moved the glasses to the floor of the cockpit to avoid advertising the purpose of his sail.

"I always do." She puffed out a spray of brine and trod water easily, extending one wet arm. "The lady wants a hand up."

Leaning outboard, he grasped the firm sun-tanned paw briefly. "Can we make it tomorrow? I'm only beginning to get the hang of managing this baby, and"— he alibied, his gaze shifting to the stiffened fly at the masthead—"the breeze is getting stronger."

Kay refused to let go. "Can't it be today? I'm so damned bored." Her free hand came out of the water and its index finger bobbed in the direction of the float. "Today?—*extra* please."

The sergeant watched Charley Wade drag his pudgy body up the ladder to flop exhausted on the cocoa matting. He lay there, puffing and gasping, while water ran from his limp hair over his forehead and cheeks.

"Fed up on the boss?" Harty asked. "That's not cagey."

"But it's true. And Tenny's even worse." She still clung to his hand, trying to make small intermittent pressures seem meaningful. "With Charley, fun's fun— and forget it; but Adrian's intentions are honorable almost to the point of a fixation."

"I don't get around enough to know, but I imagine a great many girls would consider that something of a break."

"Would they?" Kay kicked twice, making the ghost-like outline of her white suit shiver in the water. "When I do get married it will not be to a human adding machine. Adrian can go back out West to manage Elrod's interests there without a bride if he's depending on me. Just look at him!"

With awkward scramblings, the marital-minded Tenny was getting laboriously onto the float. He stood up, spreading his legs self-consciously wide and inflating a patchily haired chest. Ribs stuck out from the thin torso that was beginning to redden under the sun, and loose-cut flannel trunks sagged from his narrow waist.

"He's nobody's dream man," Harty admitted. "But didn't I see you swimming with him yesterday?"

"That was Gil Messinger." Black eyes held momentary regret. "He was just a kid—but lots of fun. Terrible, wasn't it?"

"Know Gil long?" the detective probed for a possible jealousy motive actuating Tenny.

"I only met him yesterday."

That was out then. It took more than a half-hour swim to turn a respectable businessman into a double murderer.

Charley Wade sat up on his broad buttocks and grumbled, "Where did Kay go? She was here when we started out."

"I don't know." Tenny squinted nearsightedly around, then called, "Kay! Where are you?"

"He can't see me." She giggled delightedly. "He can't see the end of his nose without his glasses and he's too vain to admit it."

"She might be under the float like that other time," Wade suggested. "Why don't you dive down and see?"

"Why don't you, if you're so anxious," Tenny snapped. "I'm going to sun-bathe."

"They're worse than a pair of old ladies," Kay said. "I scared them silly this way, last fall. I swam under the float and came up between the tanks and hung onto a crossbar for about ten minutes. There was no danger— the float's so high there's almost room under there for a bridge game—but neither of them had the nerve to come and look for me. They were talking about getting a lifeguard when I finally came out." She patted his arm imperiously. "Help me up."

Cass Harty looked down at Kay's smooth shoulders awash in brine and then across at the two men. "Did either of you boys lose a mermaid?" he called.

"Hah?" Wade recognized him for the first time. "No mermaid, Sarge. What's missing has it on one a dozen ways."

"That's a big write-up." Harty put his tiller over and let the mainsail fill with wind. Jubilee swung away from between Kay and the men, letting them see her yellow cap. "Will this do?"

"Meanie!" Kay said, treading water. "I wanted a sail!"

"Tomorrow, sure." Harty grinned. "Be seeing you."

"Will you, now?" Kay began to stroke leisurely toward the float. "How can you be sure I'll want to—tomorrow?"

4

Sunlight like counterfeit gold pieces danced on the wave crests ahead as Jubilee boomed down wind toward East Point. Harty's hands were casually busy with sheet and tiller, holding the little sloop to her course; his brain, like a prospector's sieve, tilted an assortment of odd items back and forth in an effort to select one truly meaningful fact.

It ought to be simple, he bullied himself. *You've already found two guns.*

But only one of them is likely to be worth anything, the answer came back. *Just try to work out a schedule that would allow anyone to leave the party and get out to the yacht in time to fire that gun.*

Gresham . . .?

. . . was phoning! You checked it yourself.

It's a damned queer setup on that boat of his. Sure, but that doesn't lessen the time needed to get out there; nor increase the range of that silly-looking saluting cannon.

You can't trust Thornton, he warned. *He's got the manner of a college-educated Rotarian and a heart full of larceny.*

Granted! But he had no grudge against the Messingers.

Well, take Laura Ladd . . .

For a short week end it'd be a pleasure—after that she'd begin to pall.

Quit gagging! She said she hated Wade.

Wade wasn't shot. He's still living—if you can call it that. Outside of the fact that Wade's a wealthy old rum hound he doesn't seem to matter much, one way or the other. Or does he?

Well, one inner self took a new lead, *there's still that gun on the club pier. Dunster acts funny and he keeps hanging around there.*

Why the hell shouldn't he—he's a member with full rights, the other argued. *You can't accuse a guy of murder just because he acts like a grand duke in the last stages of egomania. You've got to . . .*

The detective broke off his split-personality debate as a figure, moving high on the slope, caught his eye. Looks more like a woman than a man, he thought, as he grabbed the glasses from the floor of the cockpit and began to twiddle the adjusting cog. It's a cinch it's not McNiff.

In the powerful lenses the distant figure swam from obscurity to overmagnified vagueness before he got the right focus. It was a woman, all right, a woman he knew.

Melissa Packe was bent in concentration above the tripod she was setting up. As one bar failed to hold, Harty thought he could read the movement of her lips to make a mild "Damn!"

While you're asking yourself questions, smart guy, his conflict started up again, *what about that old gal? What's her game? If she's really taking color pictures, why come here to do it? There's damned little color in a mound of sand!*

I'll ask plenty—once I can convince myself why a dignified and respected woman should commit murder. There's no cause.

She's dignified as an Episcopal bishop—I'll give you that. But what else do you know about her? How do you know she can take pictures at all? Ever hear of her before yesterday?

The answer to that last was a solid "No!"

Feeling slightly down, the sergeant took Jubilee around East Point, dropped his centerboard, and began the sail along the bay side of the Head. It pleased him mildly to discover the perfection with which the little sloop worked to windward. She footed neatly along in the steadily freshening blow, heeled well over, her deck dipping underwater to within inches of the coaming.

The shore he passed was empty of life.

Jubilee ate up the sea miles in a series of tacks while the sun beat warmly on the detective, the salt air stung crisply in his nostrils, and exhilaration at the boat's aliveness beneath his hand prickled his nerves; but a nagging awareness of the loose ends of the case forbade contentment.

What about that girl? the awareness prodded.

You mean the girl in the yellow bathing cap? The one with the sunburned legs, and the black eyes, and the shoulders that looked so slick in the water—that girl? Quick on the uptake, aren't you? She's the one—the girl that handed you the come-on. Maybe you remember seeing her steal something from her boss last night.

It might not have been stealing. She could have . . . She might not be mixed up with Dunster either. Nor with Wade. Maybe he doesn't rate a sort of employer's perpetual droit de seigneur?

Suppose he does? She means nothing to me.

Then get clever! Don't let yourself be goosed into passing up a good lead. Where was she when they got killed?

With Wade. He said so.

Wade was so pie eyed he didn't know where he was or who was with him. Where'd she get that wad of bills she had on the train? Salary? If she gets more than forty per, I'll pay it.

I'll make you a promise too. Give me one reason why she'd bump off the Messingers and I'll have Crane pinch her right away.

Cass Harty sloughed through heavier water rounding West Point and straightened out to run before the wind once more, both his inner selves in agreement that the whole argument went a little flat whenever that angle was touched on. There seemed no reason for anyone to intend harm to the father and his son.

A lonely shack, the occasional refuge of duck hunters, stood gloomily amid tattered beach grass a hundred yards from the Point.

The sergeant trained glasses on it, speculating whether it could be a McNiff hide-out. Its secluded position made it seem a little too obvious; moreover, no smoke came from its chimney nor was there other sign of life. Still he decided to look at it later if nothing better turned up. He supposed glumly that it would prove no more productive than the rest of the trip and thought that, aside from having gained the pleasure of handling the boat, he might as profitably have remained at the settlement to work with Stauffer.

Even the business of sailing began to prove more of a chore than a pleasure as the homeward scud wore on.

Jubilee was taking something of a beating from the following wind. She rolled, her bow pounded heavily, and at each dip she buried her nose deeper in the waves.

The san was still nearly a mile ahead, which meant that the club pier was far beyond.

Got to stop that slamming, Harty thought, Ehsod will be madder than hell if I bring her back with a seam started.

He decided to shift some of the iron ballast to help compensate for the pressure of wind on the sail. Lashing his tiller down, he made his way cautiously forward and began to move the heavy pigs to the rear of the cockpit.

Jubilee's response to the change in weight was almost magical. Her pounding lessened appreciably with each brace of pigs moved.

"Glad I thought of it," Harty said as he picked up a final pair from beside the mast step. "These two ought to do the job." He straightened up with one in either hand and started aft, going along the starboard side since the crumpled sail that lay to port of the centerboard trunk all but filled that half with its bulging folds. He set down the pigs against the locker door at the back of the cockpit and unlashed the tiller, holding it momentarily with his right hand while his left dug into a pocket for his cigarette case.

There was a hint of motion behind him, a small scraping sound as if the sail on the floor had been disturbed. His half turn was not swift enough.

A shoulder butted against his side with explosive force. A voice snarled, "Over you go."

Harty toppled sidewise, his arm swinging out in a wide arc. His hand closed on loose knitted material and he growled, "You're coming with me."

They hit the water together.

The sergeant came up first. Jerking his head back to clear his eyes, he trod water easily, surveying the scene.

Her white sail taut, Jubilee was tearing down wind as though a cup were at stake.

Harty said, "What the blue hell," and said it loudly. From his position deep in the waves he found it hard to tell how far off the shore might be.

With a sputter the assailant broke surface. His eyes goggles of terror, mouth open and arms flailing frantically, he beat the water for a moment and then sank from view.

"I suppose I've got to," the sergeant said aloud, "but I'm god damned if I feel like it." He took three slow overhand strokes toward the spot where the face had disappeared.

Bubbles eddied up and the man followed them.

Harty calmly shoved him down again, waited till he rose, and then asked, "In trouble?"

"Help!" The tone was hysterical. "I can't swim."

"And you didn't think I could." The detective got a grip on the man's sweater. "I ought to let you drown."

"Don't . . ."

"I will—next time." Harty's head lifted from the water, looking for Jubilee. The glance showed the situation was not completely hopeless and he ordered, "Turn over on your back."

The fleeing sloop was already beginning to be affected

by the pressure of the water on her free rudder. As Harty watched she responded by coming around into the wind, to hang motionless in stays.

"It's a break for you that I got that tiller unlashed before you jumped me," Harty assured his foe. "Otherwise there'd been a boat and a life lost—neither of 'em mine."

Ahead, Jubilee was drifting very slowly to leeward. Then the drifting ceased as she fell out of the wind and the breeze took her in hand once more.

The sergeant struck out, swimming down and slightly across wind, trending rather out to sea than toward shore. He swam with both legs and his right arm; his left towed the enemy.

The man seemed to have recovered from his panic. He said, "You're going away from land."

"So's the boat. But she's doing it by going through a lot of little half circles, while we're swimming straight across to meet her. At least we are if I've guessed her course right." A wave slapped against his face, filling his mouth with water, and he decided not to talk.

They beat their way along while Jubilee swung around again, spilling the wind from her sails. As before, she drifted briefly, then yielded to the breeze.

Encouraged, Cass Harty fought through the rollers. Once, many years before, he had recaptured a boat in this fashion, but on that occasion he had not been towing anyone with him.

Down the wind, Jubilee continued her antics while the detective battled on, his breath growing shorter and ever more difficult to get. Each pause in the sloop's course brought her nearer, each fill and run drove her at an increasingly acute angle toward the spot Harty had determined on.

"Go for shore," the towee said. "You'll never catch her."

"*I'll* get there," Harty said coldly, "but it's a tossup whether I can swim well enough to drag you along too." With the words, he caught another mouthful of brine. His clothes were like a waterlogged shroud now, and the gun strapped beneath his left armpit felt as heavy as a battleship's mud hook. His second wind came to him like a tardy blessing and then departed much faster than it had arrived. Each torturously achieved intake of air was a hot file rasp deep in his lungs, every thrust of tired muscles an experiment in pure agony.

The man in tow asked, conversationally, "Are we making it?"

Cass Harty was too nearly plugged to waste breath telling him he was damned casual for a person who was so near to drowning. He grunted "Ugh!" and left it open to interpretation.

Across the whitecaps Jubilee's gaff wagged idly against the sky, marking an improbable goal.

The sergeant kept on. He counted strokes, trying to make the distance shorter and his strength seem more. Ten.

He could do ten. He *did* ten, mule-skinned himself for ten more and got them too. Now, just ten more.

No—too many.

He did five, five, five and five; and had cut his hopes to two and then two more when the pounding of defeat in his heart changed to hope. "Rope . . . dragging," he told the man. "Knocked . . . overside. If . . . other . . . end's . . . fast . . . we're . . . good . . . as . . . home."

Harty's muscles were like stale dough but they got him to the trailing fine. As his hand closed over it he did not let himself think of the chance that the end inboard might not be secure. He merely knew that he could not possibly swim the remaining distance to Jubilee's smooth white side.

Wind swelled the sail and she turned about, moving under its power. The tautening of the line meant that it was fast.

"Hang on." Harty put the rope into the man's hands.

"And I wish it was around your neck," he added and rolled over on his back, resting to gain strength to climb on board.

"You do, huh?" The man drew himself a little way toward the boat and kicked at the sergeant's unprotected jaw.

The denseness of the water robbed the kick of power. It took Harty on the shoulder, hurting only mildly.

"You're a nice ungrateful son of a bitch," he snarled. "Anyone who'd pull a stunt like that would . . ." The potentiality he specified was calculated to get action.

"That makes two of us." The man tried another kick.

Harty dodged it. Hs swung his right fist free above water and looped a punch onto the man's nose.

It flattened nicely. Blood mixed with the sea water.

The sergeant waited only long enough to see that his adversary still held the rope. Then he paddled aft and climbed in over the stern.

The hard boards of the cockpit felt incredibly fine to his aching back. One hand on the tiller was enough to keep Jubilee in the wind's eye as he lay there resting until a noise at the bow told him the other had come aboard.

Shoving the jib aside, the man moved along the deck and ducked under the boom into the cockpit. Blood still dripped from his nose as he stared at the detective.

Harty thought: This guy looks familiar. He said, "How 're you doing?"

"Not so hot." The man bowed his head in his hands and shook it twice as if to clear his brain.

I landed a solid one, Harty thought, but he had it coming.

The man lifted his head slowly. As if he saw the detective for the first time, he asked, "Why did you hit me?"

Cass Harty laughed. "What do you think?"

"I don't know."

"What?"

"I said I didn't know why you slugged me." The expression on the man's face was peculiar. "The first thing I recall was being in the water and you taking a poke at me."

"Are you saying you don't remember shoving me overboard?"

"Frankly, I don't."

"Or the boat getting away and almost being lost?"

"No."

"Or trying to kick me?"

"Why would I kick you?" The man chuckled. "I never saw you before."

Harty thought: It's a cinch I never saw you either, but I won't forget you in a hurry. "Remember our swim?"

"I remember I was on the beach this morning—or was it yesterday?—around sunrise," the man said slowly. He seemed to be almost counting his words. "The next thing was you hitting me."

Harty put his tiller over and let the mainsheet belly with wind. "You can't recall any of those things?"

"Absolutely none."

The sergeant did not believe him. "Then," he sneered, "there must be something wrong with your head."

"Yes—there is." The admission came placidly. "At least that's what everybody tells me."

The feeling of familiarity was justified, but to make sure the detective asked, "Do you know whose boat this is?"

"Of course. It belongs to my cousin Randall."

"And you are?"

"I thought everyone on Sand Head knew me. You must be a stranger here. I'm Morgan Elrod."

5

"A Boy Scout you became?" Stauffer grumbled. "Taking Morgan back to the san was your good deed for today, maybe? Now he can bust out again whenever he wants to."

Harty kicked a clamshell out of his path. "Maybe. But

Larsen says he's about over the present attack. He claims, even at the worst, Morgan's not dangerous."

"He proved that when he beat that guy's ears off, didn't he? And I suppose chucking you in the drink was just being playful."

Again Harty said "Maybe." It was emphasized this time, and he added, "I heaved a guy overboard myself, so I can't kick."

Barney dug his feet angrily into the face of the slope above the pier. "Whatta you mean, 'maybe'?"

"Just what I said. How the hell should I know about him? I'm the kind of trustful young fellow who goes around believing everything the people tell him."

"In a pig's *tochus*," Stauffer sneered. "You wouldn't believe tomorrow's Thursday without a not'ry public witnessed the calendar. Come on—why'd you bring him back there?"

"What else could I do? Rev wouldn't arrest an Elrod. I couldn't take him up to his cousin's by the ear like a kid playing hooky. Randall'd thank me and that'd be that. No—the mugg's supposed to be balmy, so where's a better place for him than the san?"

"You mean you're gonna play his game?"

"For a while. I'm a long way from sold on the idea that he's as nutty as they say he is, but by putting him back in the san I make them think I've accepted him as a dizz. It's smarter than forcing a showdown on his sanity right now when we've no evidence against him in connection with the murders."

"Do you think he killed the Messingers?"

"All I know is that he made a very snappy bid to alibi himself for last night," Harty answered. "It was supposed to let him out of explaining how he came to be on Jubilee too."

"He mighta been there since he left the san. Say he saw the sail and picked it for a good thing to hide under."

"No chance." They topped the rise and headed toward the settlement, Harty walking uncomfortably in his soggy clothes. "In the first place, Randall Elrod would never have left the sail in a heap that way. Sails cost money . . ."

"He's got it by the barrel."

"If he owned the U.S. Mint he still wouldn't do it. No real yachtsman treats his sails that way and, as yachtsmen go, Randall's the goods. He'll have a natural pride in his boat that will always make him keep her shipshape. But when I got my first close-up of her at the pier she was a Grade-A mess. Ropes were uncoiled, there were footprints all over her and the jib'd been set the way a suburban handyman would hang an awning."

"What of it?"

"This: I wasn't smart enough to catch it at the time, but that whole setup was a blind to excuse the presence of that sail in the cockpit. What's more, only a crack waterman would have figured out the *need* for that particular blind because no one but a waterman would have seen the need for any blind at all. A landlubber wouldn't see anything out of the way about a sail lying carelessly in the bottom of a boat nor would he expect another landlubber to notice it. But to a yachtsman, that sail meant bad seamanship. If he was going to keep it from sticking out like a sore thumb and drawing attention to itself right away, he'd have to complete the picture of bad seamanship. So he tracked up the decks and kicked the sheets around until Jubilee looked as if she belonged to some slob of a Sunday-afternoon skipper, instead of to the best sailor in these waters."

"Then the sail was there for no other reason than to help Morgan get a whack at you," Barney said. "If he's smart enough to dope all that out, he's no loony. Lucky you could swim!"

"Damned right . . ." The sergeant hauled up short. "Say! there's one guy who thinks I *can't* swim. Thornton, out on the Sad Angel."

"Him?" Barney scoffed. "*He* wouldn't want to hurt you."

"What do you know about him?"

"Not a hell of a lot—but enough to know he don't want no more deaths around this place."

"How'd it bother him if everyone on the Head got killed?"

"Right where it always hurts the most—in the pocketbook. Murders ain't good for business."

"Before I go crazy, Barney," the detective pleaded, "give me the answer. Thornton's not in business here."

"But he's gonna be. He made Rev a offer for the hotel."

"Well, I'm damned." Harty turned down a street of the settlement, making for the general store. "I need some dry clothes anyway; we'll ask Rev about this."

"He'll tell you. It's no secret."

"It was to me. What would Thornton do with a rattletrap old dump like that, even if he did buy it?"

"He'd tear it down. He ain't buying a hotel, he's buying the right to run one. Y' see, Randall Elrod and the Ocean Club control all the land here and it's specified in the deeds to any that's sold that you got to use it for a private home. The idea is to make the place exclusive, keep out the boardinghouses and the riffraff. But the Sea Spray was a hotel before all the restrictions started up, so it don't count. A whole courtful of lawyers couldn't stop a guy from buying it, ripping it down, and putting up a big up-to-date place on the same ground."

"I don't suppose they could." As he opened the door of the store Harty was thinking that it was interesting to know that Good Ol' Chet had not come to Sand Head merely for the sea air.

"Got m' glasses safe?" Rev demanded.

". . . and sound!" Harty handed the binoculars over. "I want to buy a shirt and a pair of pants. Think you can fit me?"

"Reckon so—gents' furnishings over here." Rev threaded a path to a remote corner, slapped a pair of white ducks onto the counter, and asked proudly, "How's these for britches?"

The sergeant inspected a price tag marked $1.19. "I have a hunch they won't make me look much, like the drawings in *Esquire*," he said, "but I'll take them."

"Wrap 'em up?"

"I'll change here. The ones I've got on are damp, and I'm too old a boy to go around that way. Let's see the shirts."

Seventy-five cents bought the best shirt in the store; half a dollar, underwear; a quarter, socks. Rev's clothing prices were conditioned to the permanent residents of the Head, while his charges for nonessentials were aimed at the purses of summer visitors. For a dollar Harty bought canvas-topped sneakers, and, for two and a half, a strange bastard garment, part sweater, part windbreaker, which lacked the comfort of the first and the warmth of the second but which Rev swore was "t' very latest style from t' city."

"From Oil City, Pennsylvania, possibly," Harty chuckled and went around the counter to change in the shelter of the mail racks. He was glad to see that the roll of newspapers still lay beneath the desk. As he switched into the stiff new garments he debated and abandoned the idea of sneaking the package out with him. With this Thornton angle cropping up it was better not to lose Rev's good will.

"Boy, if you ain't pretty." Stauffer guffawed when he emerged. "For a minute I thought Grover Whalen was back in the cops again."

"These pants look more like Heywood Broun." The sergeant bent to fold back dragging cuffs. "Never mind, after Rev sells his hotel and the new place is built he'll have to stock a full line of the latest scenery."

"I don't know as I'll sell t' Sea Spray." Crane wandered around turning off lights, preparatory to going to dinner. "Got a real good offer, but I want more cash down than t'at Thornton feller 'll give."

"You oughtn't to let a deal get away from you just because you can't have everything the way you'd like,"

Barney said.

"I know. But Thornton talked all cash, first off. But now he's having trouble arranging for his backing—so he says."

Harty thought that mildly interesting. "Did he say what bank he was getting the money from?"

"Don't b'lieve it was any bank—seems like he counted on some friend t' swing it for him." Rev killed another light. "Mebbe I'll go inta the deal yet, on his terms. I figger t' Sea Spray 'll lose money this year, lessen we get t' killer. Y' learned anything?"

"I've fixed the positions of the various people—if that helps. Laura Ladd on the yacht, Gresham telephoning from Dunster's house, Tenny working on reports at Elrod's place, and the Albrights safe in their own cottage—they're all pretty certain. Randall Elrod and Melissa Packe are supposed to have been in the water, which may be true. The others are less positive: Dunster somewhere on the slope, Thornton galumphing up the beach—by his own admission, somewhere near the club pier, Wade and Kay Franklin also on the beach—maybe doing a little necking, and maybe not—but there's no one to vouch for them. Where Morgan Elrod was is anybody's guess."

"Then it lays between Wade and t' Franklin girl," Rev said. An eye to trade made him exclude Chet; respect for local magnificoes saved Dunster and Morgan Elrod.

Harty understood perfectly. He used the word that was growing almost chronic with him: "Maybe."

"I stopped at the club this afternoon," Stauffer said, apropos of the Thornton—pier connection. "I talked to the steward—he sleeps there at night—and he says he didn't hear a gun go off last night. Maybe he's a extra-heavy sleeper, and maybe he was paid to say he didn't hear anything—but if we're gonna trust what he says, it means the harpoon gun wasn't fired."

"And the destroyer's guns are out," Harty said, "both by the officer's say-so and the homemade load. Scraps like that would have ripped the inside of a rifled barrel to hellangone. So it's evident that someone's been diddling around with a damned queer gun. It has to be big and heavy to throw the load we know was thrown. Obviously it's maneuverable in spite of its weight because it hasn't been found. And it's got to be fired from some kind of a stand or base."

Rev Crane asked why.

"Nobody could fire a gun like that from his shoulder, not unless he wanted to wind up as a hospital case. The recoil would smash his collarbone to splinters."

"B'George, it would, right enough."

"This Melissa Packe," Harty said. "Know much about her?"

"Just what I told you yestiddy. Why'd you want t' know?"

The sergeant did not intend to dilate on the train of thought roused by Miss Packe and the sturdy little tripod which was so often with her. "No special reason."

"Then why ask?"

"Why not?" Harty rolled his damp clothes into a bundle and tucked it under his arm. "Let's go and eat."

"O.K." Rev locked the door of his emporium. "Hope Gen's got something good."

"Think there 'll be any more of those steamers?"

"Durn seldom seen the time there wasn't," Rev assured them. "A Drink 'll go good, won't it?"

"Durn seldom seen the time it wouldn't," Harty paraphrased.

The hotel kitchen smelled steamy and wholesome.

"We're goin' in the office for A Drink, Gen," Rev said. "You be ready t' feed us when we come out."

"There's aplenty," Gen promised. "Serge-unt, you look on the desk there. A note come for you not twenty minutes past."

The demijohn gurgled while Harty found and ripped the small square envelope. "I'm due to eat a fast dinner," he said when he had read the note. "It seems Poppa's got him a date."

"Who with?" Barney asked. "I bet it's the blonde."

"Not with that blonde—maybe 1937 means she's been around long enough to have dates with the grown-up boys; but I doubt if she's reached the age of consent mentally, yet." He passed the note across to Stauffer. "Read it yourself."

We're still having that sail tomorrow but I do
wonder if you could stop by, tonight. I'd like
to talk with you.
K.F.

WEDNESDAY
(NIGHT)

SECURE in the cape of moonless dark which shrouded all the Head, Cass Harty knelt on the rugose surface of the dune, well outside the ring of flickering light thrown by the barbecue furnace. The spits above the blaze were empty now, but it was hard for him to keep from imagining he still smelled burning meat. He told himself, as he counted heads, identifying each in turn, that Dunster's friends were in a hell of a hurry to have another party.

Thick frame, stretching black trunks and white shirt to their limit, meant Charley Wade. The fat man had a half-empty glass in his hand as he sat cross-legged in front of the fire, gazing listlessly into the flames. Beside him the turntable of a portable phonograph went around and around, bleating the hoopla words of an old song hit, but the sag of Wade's shoulders hinted that he did not hear.

Kay Franklin was half-a-dozen yards back and to Wade's left, still in swim suit and rubber cap. She had a tolerant smile on her lips as she wrote things in the sand and erased them with a tiny stick.

Harty could not guess what the things might be, but the smile was for Ronnie Gresham who sat beside her and its tolerance was more than a trifle obvious.

Across the lighted area, powerful shoulders and near bald Roman-emperor's head showed where Randall Elrod sat as motionless as marble. He was silent, giving no indication that he heard the words of Chet Thornton and Melissa Packe who sat beside him.

From the distance it seemed that Chet did most of the talking, his smooth supersalesman's face fluctuant in the firelight. The Last of the Go-Getters can't lay off his technique for a minute, Harty thought. He's putting himself across with Elrod—or trying to.

Patently uninterested in each other, the last two members of the group sat furthest back, their faces twin burlesques of unrequited emotion. Adrian Tenny was wrapped in an enormous monk's cowled beach robe and his attention was so riveted on Kay that he had no time for Laura, posing stagily on a blanket next to him.

Cass Harty noted that the fireglow lit up her blonde handsomeness magnificently. He thought that not even the cheapness of a too-small red swim suit could keep her from looking like one of the Valkyrie whose horse and armor and great two-handed sword were waiting just beyond the next dune. Something made him recall that Valkyrie meant literally "Choosers of the Slain" and he reflected that she was just twenty-four hours too late.

She sat tense, watching Ronnie as he talked to Kay. Her eyes were narrow and her mouth twisted in jealousy.

As he started toward the fire Harty told himself that she'd get further if she remembered not to let herself look that way too often.

"What's that?" Melissa Packe asked sharply.

The detective said, "Don't be frightened," and stepped into the circle of light. He saw that Kay managed to look as surprised as if she had never written him the note.

Miss Packe's alarm faded. "Oh, it's you, Sergeant," she murmured in relief. "I was afraid . . ."

Loud whoops of welcome from Ronnie Gresham blurred the explanation of her fear. "Well, if it isn't my ol' pal Cass Harty, the man from Scotland Yard," he yammered. "Nobody needsta be afraid of him, do they, Cass? C'mon—join our merry group. The Friendly Society of Sons of Beaches! Haw, haw, haw!"

He's stewed to the hat! Harty thought, as he circled the fire to Miss Packe's side. "Sorry I startled you," he apologized.

"It's quite all right. I . . . I've been panicky . . . since last night. Don't think any more about it."

Wade misunderstood her last words. "How 're you gonna stop?" he demanded. "It's enough to scare anyone—don't feel so good myself."

"C'mon, Charley—hell with 'at stuff! Drink an' be merry, for tomorrer you ... I mean, le's have drink." Ronnie tipped a vacuum jug as big as a carboy, and five ice cubes tumbled like poker dice onto the sand. "You have drink, Cass. Make y' feel berrer, chase all y' woes."

"I'm fresh out of woes now," Harty said, "but a new crop might show up any time. Pour me a shot."

"We're hitting up some rare ol' rye." Ronnie put two of the sand-covered cubes in a glass, spilled whisky on top of them and sloshed in some lukewarm ginger ale. "Here y'are. Drink deep and temme how y' like it."

Harty would as soon have had creosote mixed with his rye, but he sipped the sweetish mess and said, "Swell."

"Better have one yourself, Ronnie," Chet suggested. He took the bottle away and made Gresham a thundering drink.

Harty thought that loading other people's glasses seemed to be a Sand Head practice for, like Dunster at noon, Thornton kept his own drink light.

"Sergeant, I'd like to talk to you about Morgan." Randall Elrod tugged at Harty's jacket. "I want you to know I'm sorry as the dickens about your being thrown overboard."

"Yeah," the detective said, "I can see how you're suffering."

"I meant that." The big man rose and drew Harty a few paces away from the others. "You understand, of course, that Morgan is not responsible for his actions at all times?"

"But you're responsible for yours."

"What? Oh, I see what you mean." Despite the admission Elrod's strong features were still an impenetrable mask, hiding his real feelings. "Well, perhaps I should have told you Morgan was in my house when you stopped to ask about borrowing Jubilee. But I had some idea of letting him stay with me—and I couldn't tell how you'd take to that. I hated to ask him to go back to Larsen's; it's a bit away from being the pleasantest place in the world."

"I gathered that—when I took him back there."

"Then we've no hard feelings? On either side?"

Harty tried another sip of his drink, decided it was hopeless, and spilled it on the beach. "None."

"That's pretty fine of you," Elrod said loudly. "Now . . . h'm ... I haven't my wallet here with me, of course, but I'd like to see you later and square things."

The entire group was frankly listening.

If they're waiting to see how cheap I can be bought, Harty said to himself, this 'll show 'em. "No need for that," he grunted, crossing to sit beside Kay and Gresham. "Everything's squared. Your cousin dumped me in the water and I busted his nose."

Someone laughed shortly with a sound like a champagne cork being drawn. Harty regretted that watching Elrod's reaction kept him from identifying the author of the laugh.

"Good for his soul," Kay muttered. She did not make plain whether it was Morgan who would profit by having his nose bashed in, or Randall from a touch of ridicule.

"Soon's I drink this . . ." Ronnie held up his glass. "I say, soon as I get this down, I'm gonna do per . . . per . . . mmpers'nation."

"It would be an agreeable novelty if he would impersonate a completely sober young man and manage to convince us," Melissa Packe said caustically. "He is the most annoying alcoholic I've ever seen."

Randall Elrod grunted agreement.

Harty said to Kay, "I didn't expect to find a party going on." He used "party" for want of a better word. Actually it seemed more like a kind of gregarious death-watch; eight people drawing meager comfort from one another's physical presence while they waited for the evening to end. With Dunster absent there was no other link to bind them together.

"We had to do something to get our minds off last night. Do you think he'll care?"

"Who?"

"Dunster, of course. The Messingers were his friends."

"I would, if it happened to mine." Laura, maneuvering to get near Ronnie, had overheard. "They told me what happened," she said to the sergeant. "It don't seem right for us to be carrying on, does it?"

"Is that *your* opinion?" Kay turned sharply. "Maybe it'd be better to stay in that morgue of a house till something else happened."

Laura said very elegantly, "I wasn't talking to you, dearie," and moved on.

"What'd you mean about something else happening?"

"Everyone's so overwrought. We had to keep our minds occupied—or begin to scream at each other."

Harty thought that was an overstatement but, in any event, he did not see how a return to the scene of the tragedy could help matters.

Ronnie drained the last of his monumental drink and wabbled to the fire to kneel before it and smudge his upper lip minutely with charcoal. "Tenshun, everyone," he roared. "Gonna do my act!"

"Life-of-the-party Gresham, the boys called him," Harty muttered, "and the boys were right."

"Gonna 'personate the one an' on'y Furrer . . . Firer? . . . Furrier? . . . No, ain't right! Say, how'n hell do you p'nounce Ill Doochay in Dutch? Heil Hitler!"

Chet started applause, then realized the others were not with him. He stopped abruptly and peered at the fire through the bottom of his glass.

"Gresham's condition chronic?" Harty asked.

"I wouldn't know—it's the first time I've seen him really go to town," Kay said. "Apparently it just caught up with him. He seemed to be all right until you got here."

Heiling en route, Ronnie wavered toward the white framework of a lifeguard tower well down the beach. He clawed his way up the ladder and posed dramatically on the tiny platform at the top, giving the musical comedy brown-shirt salute.

"Come down outa there," Laura called. "You'll fall."

"When *I* fall it 'll be for that black-haired bebby in the white suit," Ronnie said. Saluting again at each phrase, he howled, "Heil Hitler! Heil Kay! Heil Gresham!" On the last word he swayed wildly, tried to gain his balance with a lurch in the other direction, and crashed to the sand below.

Chet's shrug disclaimed all interest. He turned from the others and began to poke at the fire.

"Someone should at least determine whether he's broken his neck," Melissa Packe said. "We've already had quite enough disaster for one season."

"Yeah, somebody see if he's hurt." Showing no inclination to leave the lighted area herself, Laura joined Chet in front of the blaze. "He's prob'ly all right, though. Drunks never get hurt much."

"If no one else has nerve enough to go," Tenny stared pointedly at the detective sitting beside Kay, "*I* have."

Kay breathed, "My hero!"

Her suitor gave her a stagy you'll-be-sorry-if-I-don't-come-back look. The monkish robe flapped about his skinny legs as he crossed to where Ronnie lay. He asked, "Are you hurt?"

"No—but *you're* gonna be, if y' don't lemme alone," Ronnie threatened boozily. "I wanna sleep." He got up, reeled a dozen yards further down the beach, and collapsed again.

Tenny did not join in the laugh which went up, but it suited Chet perfectly. Ever the opportunist, he grabbed the triple opening, to have the center of the stage, to remain Gresham's pal, and, at the same time, withhold endorsement of his actions. "Forget him for a while, Tenny," he advised. "He'll be himself when he's napped a bit. The rest of us can have a swim."

"Don't care for a swim." Tenny climbed the tower and

sat down, apparently to sulk in wounded isolation.

"You'd best not count me in either." Melissa Packe's tone indicated she was fed up. "I find I am rather tired. Home looks very attractive. No—please, no one need escort me."

"I'll stay, but I won't swim," Wade grumbled. "Not while the hooch holds out. But don't let me stop anyone else."

"We won't," Chet snapped. Having set himself the job of getting things going he felt he must put it over, even at the cost of making peace with the detective. "How about you, Harty? You won't let the evening go to waste, will you?"

"I haven't a suit." Harty had no intention of wasting any part of the evening, although his definition of "waste" would not have corresponded with Chet's.

"Plenty of them in Dunster's cabana," Thornton said. "Kay 'll be glad to show you. What do you say?"

Glad of the opportunity to question Kay apart from the others, Harty said, "All right."

"Swell!" Chet's enthusiasm was oppressive. "Come on!" he bawled at the others. "Last one in mixes the next round of drinks."

"That's O.K. by me," Harty told Kay. "Maybe I'll get a snort that doesn't taste like old carpet slippers boiled in maraschino."

Ahead of them Melissa Packe had already vanished in the darkness. Behind shrieks rang out: Laura's response to being dragged playfully toward the water by Good Ol' Chet.

"*Cute*, isn't she," Kay said contemptuously. "And Chet's such a great guy too. On land he wouldn't look twice at a girl for fear she'd try to hold him to it; but when he gets Laura in the water she won't know whether she's having a swim or a Swedish massage. I've seen boys like Chet before."

"You'll see him wearing beefsteak on both eyes if he gets cozy with Laura," Harty chuckled, turning to watch them. "She isn't offering anything this side of the altar these days."

Randall Elrod tore past the tussling couple and sprinted with middle-aged vigor toward the white line of breakers. He dove under a tall wave and was lost to view until his bald head appeared, a dozen yards further out. In the lifeguard tower a peaked gray outline indicated that Tenny still nursed his deflated ego. Harty could not see Gresham from where they stood on the slope and he remarked it to Kay.

"I wasn't really making a play for Ronnie," she said. "Hanging around me was his own idea."

"Why tell me? I'd rather hear why you sent the note."

"Do I *have* to say?" Her voice was as phony as the train smile.

"Don't try to kid the old professor," Harty said. "That isn't the way it is."

"No . . .?"

"No!" He clapped her sturdy small rear. "You're figuring on using me. I want to know how."

"I wrote that note because I didn't like the atmosphere around here. I was frightened—and that's the truth."

"And I'm supposed to make a muscle at the bugaboo? Aren't there enough men in your own crowd?"

"Men? Softies! I wouldn't string with any of them in a showdown. They have mush where their spines ought to be."

"Like all sweeping statements, that one has a heck of a flaw. Its name is Randall Elrod."

"Randall's hard, all right—too hard for me. If I'm to get anywhere I've got to get a man interested—even if it's just a little."

Harty chuckled.

"Don't be too sure. You don't give in much—but you're *here*, aren't you? And that's what I wanted."

"O.K." Harty was willing to let her misread his motives for being there—if she was misreading them.

"Randall's hard," she went on, "but Chet thinks he's hard. He thinks he's smooth, too, but if he lived a hundred years he wouldn't be as hard as Randall, nor as smooth as Dunster. Where Randall gets written up in *Fortune* and Dunster wouldn't be interested, Chet would die of joy if they gave him a paragraph in the *New Yorker*—even if they made him look silly he'd still think he was a big shot because they mentioned his name."

"All true enough, but why feed it to me?"

"Simply because Randall is like you . . . and me. Hard inside . . . where it really counts."

He grasped her arm to swing her over an obstacle, dimly seen in their path. "Does that mean hard enough to go after what you want—*and get it?*"

"I'd say it differently." If she thought there was any reference to a roll of newspapers, her answer did not show it. "It's the contrast between that corn-fed blonde and me. Her hardness is terrible grammar and hipwaving in a second-rate clip joint and getting blotto with the visiting firemen afterward. She thinks she's doing a great job in trying to hook Gresham, but she's soft underneath. This is her one big chance and if she muffs it she'll never get another. She'll go back to her floor show, and five years from now she'll weigh a hundred and ninety-two pounds and be working in a call house on Ninth Avenue and telling drunken plumbers on Saturday nights all about the rich man she could have married. That won't happen to me."

"No, I don't believe it will," Harty said. "I wouldn't have thought so even the first time I saw you—on the train."

Kay's loquaciousness ceased abruptly. She walked in silence until they reached the crest, then said, "You weren't on the train."

"But you were. You didn't have to worry about your fare."

She stopped dead in her tracks. "The cabana's down that way," she pointed. "I'll wait here. About that money

... I was bringing it down to my boss."

Harty left her standing there and struck off across the sand toward the Dunster house. As he walked he heard no sound but the crunch of his own shoes and the scrape of the stiff duck of his trousers. He passed the house and entered the cabana, thinking that whether Kay felt she had convinced him or not, she had at least been smart enough not to protest too much.

Three statements, he thought as he stripped off his clothes, and two of them are true! The cabanas are down here, and she's waiting. But that money! Of course, if it really was Wade's it might explain why she didn't get rattled when it was blowing all over the car.

From a shelf he took down what seemed to be a uniform for Dunster's natant guests, a swim suit of white shirt and black trunks. "They must be bought in carload lots," he said aloud. "I'll . . ."

A sudden boom, swelling upward from the sea, smashed against the sergeant's eardrums.

"Can't be another," he muttered, tightening the belt buckle. "That's impossible."

Then, exactly as on the previous night, hysterical screams followed the crash of the explosion, making him know it was all too possible.

2

A faint light from the furnace glowed along the rim of the slope, its paleness unbroken anywhere by the shadow of a waiting girl. Off to the right vague figures moved, obviously cottagers on their way to the beach. Harty was at the brink ahead of them, sweeping the scene below with a single photographic glance.

Pale limbs, red suit, horrorbound at the water's edge, meant Laura Ladd. White shirt, dark arms and shoulders, emergent from slightly greater depth behind her, for Chet Thornton. Gray form, not yet swung down from the lifeguard tower, Adrian Tenny. What was prone before the brickwork could only be guessed at and, with the picture fixed in his memory for all time, Harty asked himself which of the missing three it could be, Elrod, Wade or Gresham.

Directly below him something was suddenly in motion across the face of the slope, trending slightly upward.

It's Kay, copping a sneak, he thought.

He saw immediately that he was wrong. Wind on the fire brightened the scene enough to let him make out the figure of a man.

If it's the screwball, Harty decided, he's put himself in the soup. Three queer stunts in a row can't be charged off to coincidence. "Hold on!" he roared.

The running man increased his speed.

"O.K. We'll play your way." Harty broke into stride, converging on the other's course. Then, as the gap closed, he launched downward in a hard diving tackle. By the fireplace men were yelling.

The sergeant's shoulder crashed solidly home. Captor and captive pinwheeled down the slope together.

On the crest high above them more men yelled.

Cass Harty sat up first. He scooped sand from his eyes and shouted "Right here, Barney" toward the sound of Stauffer's basso query, "Where the hell's the sarge?"

With Rev trailing, the little detective scrambled down. "It's the same stunt," he panted. "Who'd they get?"

"I don't even know who I've got. Someone hightailing it away from the beach. I hopped him—he hasn't moved yet."

"We heard you holler," Rev said. He struck a match with his thumbnail and held it low. "Gawd a'mighty, it's Mr Dunster."

Harty swore fluently—and thought fast. "I figured it was Morgan Elrod. Rev, dust right down to the san and see if he's there. On the way you can stop at Melissa Packe's place and tell her I want her to come here—pronto!"

"B'George, I don't mind going to t' san," Rev said, "but

I'm durned if I see t' sense in butherin' Miz Packe."

"Don't argue! We blew our chances last night by getting off to a scraggly start. Hop it!" Harty watched him start, then turned on Dunster who was trying to sit up. "Weren't you supposed to have left the Head?"

"I *did* leave. What's the idea of knocking me down?"

"I'd slap George the Sixth down, too, if I saw him splitting the wind away from a setup like this," the sergeant assured him. "Everyone else who heard the shot was running toward the fire."

"Which shows nothing but their poor judgment."

The celebrated Dunster aplomb was returning. "I had enough presence of mind to try to get to a telephone to summon aid from the mainland."

"That line of bull will get you nowheres," Barney growled. "When did you get back here?"

"I came down from New York on Number Nine . . ."

"An' I suppose you swam over from Keyesport? The ferry made its last trip around suppertime."

"It always does. I used my own speedboat."

Number Nine and speedboat alike could be checked. "Bring him along," Harty ordered, and made for the fireplace.

Within a circle of horror-sick cottagers Laura Ladd knelt, her body shaking with sobs. Emotion twisted grooves in the faces of Tenny and Chet as they stood beside her, staring at the body of Charley Wade.

In dreadful duplication of the slaughter of the previous night, Wade's corpse was frightfully riddled. His once-white shirt had wetly turned the color of peony shoots in late April.

Tenny peered myopically around. His voice quivered as he said, "Kay—where is she?"

Randall Elrod stooped over the body, his head shaking slowly.

Harty looked for Gresham in vain. "Kay left me a little while ago," he told Tenny. "Where were you?"

"On the lifeguard tower—the whole time."

"O.K." The sergeant risked looking foolish rather than miss a possible chance. Though Tenny had been conspicuous on the tower, the tower itself would not have been a bad place to shoot from. And, as for getting rid of the gun, what could be a better hiding place than the wide locker with which the observation post was equipped? "Barney," he said, "go over and take a look at that thing."

"It's just a platform," Tenny said mildly. "Can I have a drink?"

"Sure. Take a stiff shot—it 'll straighten you up."

"I think I can use one too." Good Ol' Chet moved toward the bottle with pathetic eagerness. Making a poor job of upholding the tradition of the Last of the Gogetters, he looked far from high pressure as he murmured repeatedly, "*Ohmygod!*"

Kay had their numbers—Tenny, Dunster and Chet all look ready for nervous breakdowns, Harty thought. It occurred to him that she had also done a neat job of calling the turn on Randall Elrod.

"What did you do?" he asked the big man.

"I wanted to swim—not to watch this bounder's actions." Elrod's bald head jerked toward Chet. "When I saw I was the only one interested in swimming, I left. I came out on the beach, spoke briefly to Wade, and warmed myself at the fire. Then I lay down to rest."

"Did you see where the shot came from?"

"No. Fortunately, I was in a hollow of the sand; otherwise it would have got me too. However, I have a definite impression that it came from out at sea."

"It did," Tenny said. "I saw it myself."

"Why didn't you tell that before?"

"You didn't ask me. I was afraid I might get into trouble if I volunteered too much."

"The guy must read detective stories," the returning Stauffer sneered. "Go on—tell us everything you got. We'll decide who it's gonna make trouble for."

"I haven't really got anything. Just a flash that I saw

on the water out there . . . near the yacht."

"Yacht, huh?" Harty scratched an ear. "Did you find anything on this guy's perch, Barney?"

"Just the reg'lar junk lifesavers use. Rings and a float with a lotta rope, and a first-aid kit. There's a big box to hold it," he explained. "But there's a guy laying on the sand up that way, dead drunk. He smells like a whole row of distilleries."

"That'll be Sonnyboy Gresham—drag him up here." Of Chet, he demanded, "What do you know about this business of the yacht?"

"Nothing. Miss Ladd and I were facing land, letting the waves break over our backs. We couldn't have seen it."

"See any flash on land?"

"None."

Mention of Ronnie had percolated slowly through Laura's brain. Now she rose and grabbed at the shoulder straps of the detective's suit. Even the sea water had not been enough to kill the heaviness of the carnation scent she wore. "What'd you say about my boy friend?" she asked hysterically. "Tell me! I can stand it."

"Shut up!" Thornton ordered. "That other cop found Ronnie lying on the beach down there . . ."

"Oh, they killed him too," she moaned, and fainted in a heap.

Cass Harty swore like a fleet of cab drivers while they worked over her for minutes, trying to bring her around.

She finally opened her eyes. "The only man I ever truly loved," she mumbled, "and now he's gone."

"Empty that bottle into her and put her to sleep again," Harty advised. He had caught a glimpse of Melissa Packe struggling through the crowd and he went to clear a path for her.

"Rev said you wanted me," she began, then saw the robe Elrod had thrown across the corpse. "Oh! Was that what I heard?"

"Wade," the sergeant said. "Just like the others."

"But how dreadful! The windows of my house were closed—I didn't recognize the noise as another shot."

Harty thought that possible, since her cottage was on the bay slope. "On your way home from here did you notice anything unusual?"

"No." Her bladelike face was thoughtful. "That is . . . No, there was nothing wrong with *that*."

"With what?"

"A man—I couldn't see him plainly. He was a little below the top of the slope. Almost as if he was watching us."

"It wasn't out of the way for someone to spy on the party?"

"I didn't think of it as spying. The natives often watch the doings of summer visitors. I suppose that sandwiches and highballs beside an open fire seem almost Lucullan to them."

"A native—with a clear conscience—would have greeted you?"

"Possibly. That hadn't occurred to me before."

But Dunster wouldn't have spoken, not if he'd been waiting there to slip something across, the sergeant decided. "You were on that slope a good ten minutes before this happened," he accused the man.

"It might have been nine," Dunster smiled cynically, "or it may even have been as much as eleven, but you are approximately correct."

"You saw Miss Packe pass and you didn't speak?"

"Right again. Twice, this time."

"A lot of people might wonder why."

"Why you happen to be correct? I am sure they would."

"Why you didn't speak—why you were there at all."

"My failure to speak was natural. We live so casual a life, here on the Head, and see each other so frequently, that a formal exchange of greetings at every encounter would be ridiculous."

"But not as ridiculous as hanging around in the dark,

watching your own guests. That hasn't been explained
yet."

"It will be—even though I question your right to
demand an explanation. When I returned to the Head
and Towei, my houseboy, told me that a party was in
progress, I was surprised. You have not impressed me as
an especially sensitive man, Sergeant, so, at risk of
puzzling you, I will even say I was shocked. After last
night . . ."

"Only this morning," Harty broke in, "you seemed to
feel things would go on as usual." The hell of it is, he told
himself, all these people seem to have two reasons for
everything that happens.

"I did not intend that to include public merrymaking
—I was fond of the Messingers. When I saw, from up
there, that Towei was correct, my first impulse was to put
an end to the whole thing. I started down and had come
about halfway when it occurred to me to stop and think
the matter over. I sat there, asking myself whether I
might not be acting too hastily and, before I could make
up my mind, there was a flash of light, out at sea, and the
sound of a shot."

"On or near the yacht?"

"To answer that is to come much closer to making an
accusation that I can, with honesty, do. Remember, the
flash leaped out of total darkness and was gone instantly.
If there had been a moon . . ."

"But there wasn't," Harty said wearily.

"Open up!" Stauffer called. "Let us get through."

The ring of onlookers parted.

Supported on one side by Barney, and on the other by
Kay Franklin, young Gresham lurched into view. If Harty
had not seen the cargo of liquor the boy had taken aboard
he would have sworn the lolling head meant a cracked
vertebra.

Kay's eyes refused to meet the sergeant's.

"Whazza marrer?" Ronnie mumbled. "I wanna know
whaz all 'bout. Can't guy get li'l sleep in 'ish damn place?"

"Oke, sister," Stauffer told Kay. He let Gresham sag to the beach and propped him against a roman-striped canvas back rest. "I seen fellas with a can on—but this guy's got a lulu."

"Lulu? Who's Lulu? He means Laura." Ronnie blubbered drunken laughter. "Good Ol' Hard-to-get Laura! If he can make her he c'n keep her. *I* couldn't." His chin sagged on his collarbone. "Now go 'way an' lemme sleep."

"Wake up!" Harty soused the contents of the vacuum jug into the boy's face. "Snap out of it!"

"Wha' for?"

"This." The sergeant yanked the robe from Wade's body.

The crowd made a collective sound like air brakes blowing off. The momentary glimpse before the corpse was covered again told almost as much as an autopsy could.

"Darling," Laura flung herself down beside Ronnie. "I was worried. I'm so glad you're safe."

"Sumbudy get hurt?" The wabbling of Gresham's head slowed. He pawed amiably at Laura with his right hand. "Who izzhit?"

"Poor Charley Wade—he's shot."

"Who cares?" He found her knee and jiggled it like a gear-shift handle. "Whazzat gotta do with me?"

"Plenty!" Cass Harty pulled the drooping head erect and shouted into the boy's ear. "A gun flash was seen out there."

"'S foolish. S'nobuddy onna yacht. Gave crew night off."

"Three different people say the flash was out that way."

"Tellum f'me, they're cuckoo! *I* saw flash, too, an' it wuzzen onna water. Wuz up ... up there." He fumbled with Laura's knee until the enamaled toes of her right foot pointed at the dune Rev had climbed that morning. "Up *there*," he repeated. "I thought it wuz guy lightin' cig'rette—or something. Dunno what I thought; went sleep."

"I lit a cigarette," Dunster said. "But I was over this way."

"You were—if you're the man I saw," Miss Packe confirmed.

Cass Harty tried to decide whether Ronnie had really seen something or if he merely lied to clear himself. Dunster's admission about the cigarette had come too glibly—almost as if he were trying to clear someone. Himself? Possibly, although he had had no time to dispose of the gun. If it had been left on the dune it must still be there and could be searched for directly. Was he helping Melissa Packe? Scarcely, since her time schedule would not permit of her guilt, as she had been at her cottage when Rev called, and such a setup implied an impossible two-way race against the clock. Morgan Elrod ...

"Serge-unt, oh, Serge-unt," Rev's voice came down from the crest. "I got . . ." The rest was lost as he hurled himself down the steep incline, but he was obviously full of tidings.

"Hold them here, Barney." Cass Harty jammed through the encircling vacationists, and went to meet Rev. He did not dare take a chance on the Sand Head officer's tendency to blurt out whatever he might know.

Breathless with excitement, Rev tobogganed to a stop at the base of the slope. "Went down t' san and seen t' doc," he panted. "He says Morgan Elrod's there, all right."

"Well, that's something to know," the detective murmured. "I thought it'd be a little too much like rubbing our noses in it if he was running loose again tonight."

"Wait a minnut," Rev cautioned. "I ain't told you t' whole story. There was something 'bout t' way t' doc said it t'at I didn't like, so I hunted up a orderly and put t' same question t' him."

"Now you're clicking," Harty cheered. "What'd he

say?"

"Him? Oh, he backed t' doc up. Said 'twas true enough t'at Morgan was in t' place right then—but he hadn't got in no more than five minutes before I come along."

THURSDAY

DANK, fiber-wilting heat of a New York summer morning lay heavy upon the concourse of Penn Station and sifted down to the track where the Keyesport train had just pulled in.

Cass Harty was striding along the platform before the wheels had completed their last screeching turn. His suit showed elephant-iron wrinkles from yesterday's ducking, his hat was dusty and his shoes were whitened by brine. Prolonged wakefulness had made his eyes feel like a pair of superheated ball bearings in an unoiled, overworked engine but, as he shouldered through the fringe of redcaps who disdained to ask so shabby a traveler if he had any baggage for them to tote, he hummed gently to himself:

> ". . . that a victim must be found,
> I've got a little list—I've got a little list,
> Of society's offenders who should all be under
> ground . . ."

He thought he could be pardoned for feeling like an occidental Ko-Ko, since the compilation of the list had cost him the nap he had hoped to catch on the train.

Outside the iron railing at the head of the stairs, First-grade Detective Dan Monahan waited. A big, meaty-necked, purple-jawed man in deliberately commonplace clothes, with iron hat shoved back from damp forehead and a frayed matchstick eternally bobbing between lazy teeth, Dan Monahan seemed the archtype of all the stage detectives between Broadway and Hollywood.

The similarity ended with his appearance.

Monahan had a brain which earned him in the neighborhood of four thousand dollars a year, and considerable respect, from the city of New York, and a rigidity of conscience which would not permit him to resign from the department to pick up an assured fifteen to twenty thousand in the mephitic practice of private sleuthing. He was as thoroughgoing as a steam roller, as brave as a pit bull, and as difficult to fool as a demolition bomb.

He said "H'ya?" to the sergeant and they swapped participially qualified comments on the intricacies of the case at hand as they made for the Seventh Avenue exit.

"Wait a second." Harty stopped to buy a paper at the newsstand beside the subway turnstiles.

Monahan shook his head at him. "They didn't get the Wade story in the early editions."

"Wasn't after that." Harty leaned against the change booth and conned the obituary notices. "Here it is: Messinger . . . Blatchford Funeral Home . . . interment private . . . sole surviving relative . . . Miss Pauline Messinger . . . please omit flowers. You talked to Pauline?"

"Elder sister, by about ten years. Didn't know a thing."

Cass Harty waited for more. He knew that one profitless interview was merely a beginning for the big man.

"I saw his doctor, his dentist, his banker, a lawyer named McGann who defended him in some income-tax trouble he had two years ago; the real-estate people who rented him his apartment; the guy who sold him his car; the guard in the safe-deposit vault at his bank and two tellers for good measure. I talked with a Professor Leonard who got his kid ready for the college-board entrance exams last year. I visited his liquor dealer; the minister of his church; the nurse who took care of him when he had his appendix out; and the guy who gave him the anesthetic. I chinned with a fella named Heney who runs a bathing pavilion where Messinger used to go in the summertime."

"A lot of work, Dan. What'd it get you?"

Monahan's thick right fist traced a large zero in the subway murk. "It's about like this: The old man was in good health. Retired from business. Comfortable circumstances. The income-tax thing was a washout. He paid two hundred smacks a month for his flat. His car had only run about twenty-five hundred miles in the six months he had it. He went to the safe-deposit vault about four times a year, and the bank tellers say his deposits and withdrawals never changed much from an average. The kid was a good student, a fair freshman halfback last fall, and took fourth place in the slalom race at the winter carnival. The old man didn't hit the booze much; his receipts show he bought sherries and madeiras, mostly. He only went to church at Christmas and Easter, but he always kicked in nice when the preacher put on a special get-to-heaven shakedown. He never made any passes at his nurse; and the anesthetician told me he didn't say much of anything while he was under the ether. The bathhouse man says Messinger always hired a season locker, wore one of those old-time gray suits with the little sleeves and didn't know how to swim." Dan paused, then added the unnecessary summation: "No dirt anywhere."

"Nothing to show why anybody'd kill him," the sergeant murmured. "But if you say so, Dan, it's oke by me."

"There's always a reason, if you go deep enough," Monahan said humorlessly. He took the match from his mouth, inspected the worn end, and threw it away. Another replaced it instantly. "Always."

Harty's mind leaped from the impeccable Messinger to that other seeming monument of probity, Miss Packe. He believed that when the addition of two and two failed to total four, it was often practicable to chip in another two and arrive at six. "You're probably right," he said.

"Let's grab ourselves a taxi."

2

The cab's wheels slurred against the curb outside the office of the paper Harty had bought. He paid the driver and at a desk inside asked, "Where will I find Paul Chase?"

"He went out ten minutes ago." The eye-shaded man at the desk leaned toward a window. "You might catch him in that restaurant over there."

The smell of giant rolls of newsprint clung in their nostrils as they crossed between moving cars to the little reformed speakeasy where a single customer was absentmindedly destroying ham and eggs while his eyes followed the lines of a technical-looking book he had propped against a sugar bowl. Rimless glasses and somber clothing made Chase look more like a science instructor in a rural high school than the popular idea of a newspaperman.

Cass Harty sat down and introduced the two men, endorsing Chase as "the best damned news photographer in town," before he ordered a double portion of ham and eggs and a pot of coffee for himself.

"You're after something when you appear bearing praises." Chase folded a paper napkin into his page and closed the book. "What's up?"

"Ever hear of a woman named Melissa Packe?"

"Did you ever hear of the criminal code?" Chase grinned. "She's as well known in my game as that is in yours."

"No fooling."

"Not even a little. Every honest-to-goodness bug on photography faces Mecca and bows his forehead three times in the dust when Melissa's name is mentioned. She's *that* good!"

"Well." Harty thought it over. "And I had an idea she might be a phony." He took a later edition of Chase's paper from beside the photographer's plate and found the Wade story in the second column from the left on the front page. "Did you read this?"

"I haven't looked at a crime story since the Elwell case. They're too repetitious. What's this one about?"

"You wouldn't go for it." Harty folded the paper while the waiter put down crockery and a small coffeepot. "It's too repetitious—and I mean that."

Dan and the cameraman watched in respectful silence while the food was attacked.

"Did you"—Harty's mouth was full of ham and eggs but his tone was thoughtful—"ever know her to do any original work in color photography?"

Chase pondered a moment. "No, I didn't—but that doesn't imply she's not doing it. Judged by her past career, she's not the type to sound off about what she's after until she has it down perfect."

"I see." The sergeant put down his fork and tilted the spout of the coffeepot. "Do you know her well?"

"Only by reputation. She's a rather withdrawn person—from what I hear. Aside from photography, her only hobby is European antiques of which she is an amateur of acknowledged standing. I do happen to know that she had a decidedly embittered girlhood. Her father shot a man who had been attentive to her mother. Melissa was requested to leave the finishing school she was attending at the time, and it's possible the scandal and attendant public scorn left its mark on her. I don't doubt that any journeyman psychologist could evolve something from it—her choice of a career, I mean— recording life photographically, sort of playing with the world on a plate, you know; and then there's the seclusion of the darkroom, and all that sort of thing."

"Those psychologists can do a lot," Harty laughed, "but I never heard of one who was able to explain just what there is about their racket that makes it possible for any two of them to give conflicting expert opinions in any case where enough money is concerned." He gulped his coffee, wondering how much it would cost to get an expert opinion about the possibility of a tendency to murder running in the Packe family. Well, tendency or not, the next item on his list would tell whether his sole remaining idea about the woman had any worth. "Thanks, anyhow, Paul," he said, taking up his check. "I'll get in touch with you sometime and let you know how all this pans out. I'll have to—if you keep on refusing to read crime news."

As they climbed into another taxi, to ride to the sergeant's apartment, the restaurant window gave them a glimpse of Paul Chase reaching for the newspaper.

3

Dan Monahan reposed his bulk in a comfortable chair in the living room and gnawed a match while he worked a crossword puzzle. Next door the sergeant shucked out of his battered clothes to shave, shower and dress again. Then he dragged a big kit bag from the closet and began to pack.

Suit; underwear; socks; ties; shirts; a threadbare tweed jacket and a pair of unpressed slacks; two cartons of cigarettes; and three bottles, gin, vermouth and scotch, respectively, followed each other into the bag. Swim suit next; he avoided trunks because they showed the bullet scars on his torso and made strangers come up and ask stupid questions. A beach robe; heelless leather sandals; handkerchiefs and a trench coat went in and, last of all, a small but hard-hitting 38, familiar to the cognoscenti as a "belly gun."

"Things are as tough as that?" Dan asked, from the doorway. "Isn't your regular rod good enough for the job?"

"It's too damned big." Harty patted the powerful weapon in its bulky shoulder holster. "When I'm around down there with no coat on, I might just as well try to hide a French seventy-five in my pants pocket as this thing." He dragged the zipper fastener on the bag shut, carted its leather bulk to the living room, and sat down at a desk. "If this is a bust," he said, sketching rapidly on a sheet of paper, "it means Melissa Packe is out of the case."

"What the hell do you call that?" Dan studied the roughly oblong outline as it took form. "A trial draft for a coffin?"

"Just a gadget." The sergeant began to mark in approximate measurements, basing them on his recollection of the size of Miss Packe's camera. "Ring ballistics for me, will you? Have them put that old billy goat Tramyere on the line."

Dan went into the bedroom and dialed. "Is Inspector Tramyere in his office? Cass Harty wants to speak to him," he said after a moment and added in an undertone, "God knows why."

Carrington Tramyere was a socialite and career policeman who dated back to Theodore Roosevelt's days as commissioner. He was venerable and pompous and almost intolerably scientific in the execution of his job as ballistics expert of the department. Now his voice came over the wire clicking like a well-bred comptometer which had seen service in the Harvard Business School. "Fire away, Sergeant. I understand you want my opinion."

"Yes. First, I'd like to know if a saluting cannon on a yacht, its barrel no longer than . . ."

"Tchah! That Sand Head case, I take it?" Tramyere interrupted. "The answer is *no possibility whatever!* No saluting cannon made could project a killing load the distance required in that matter." A drumming noise indicated the inspector was beating his desk in impatience. "Let me hear what else is on your mind—and keep it short. I'm a busy man, you know."

"The other question is hypothetical. Given a gun which will throw a pattern that's more than a dozen yards wide at its point of maximum diffusion and throw it about a hundred and twenty-five . . ."

"Damme, man, what kind of a load?" Tramyere broke

in again. "Jove! This isn't blackjack police work. You're getting into the field of pure science. You must supply *all* the factors."

"Yes sir." Harty's mouth posed a silent raspberry at the transmitter. "The load is scrap metal—small, irregular sizes. The gun slings it with enough penetrating power to cut a two-hundred-pound man into cube-steak. Now—if this load is thrown in an almost flat horizontal . . ."

"Impossible! No gun ever fires absolutely . . ."

"I know that!" Harty interrupted, thinking: If he can get away with it so can I. "What I meant was that there's no possibility of the high parabola of a mortar. I want to know if such a gun could be enclosed in a space no greater than"—he consulted the drawing—"two feet long, a foot and a half high, and a foot wide."

"Preposterous dimensions!" Tramyere's snort portended a tough day for his subordinates at the bureau. "You've imagined a weapon whose like never existed on land or sea. I advise you to forget it! Leave theory to those of us who have been trained to the scientific attitude— and cultivate a sense of your own limitations before you trouble me again."

Dan Monahan watched the sergeant hang up. "You didn't do so well with this inspector either?"

"To a good hot hell with him! And what'd you mean, 'either'?"

"One of two—the other's Johnny MacIver. This stuff about McNiff getting away sure gave him a bug up."

"I wish it was a turtle!" Harty cut in. "Tootie was free before I even started for the damned place. The boss can't blame me."

"He already has. The word's out that if you're not a good enough dick to find a guy hiding in a sand pile you'd be better off in a uniform, learning something about the geography of Canarsie or the East Bronx." Dan flung his match away, discovered himself without a replacement, and searched, grunting, in the wastebasket for it. "That case is growing angles every minute. Some of the tabs are playing Tootie up big and saying he's a killer."

"That's laughable!" Harty said, and knew its ridiculousness did not ease his position. The longer McNiff stayed free and the murders remained unsolved the more discredit would be reflected on the New York police, even though the island was no part of their job. And Sergeant Harty knew how sorely it galled MacIver to have his beloved department held cheaply. "I'd better get lucky—*fast*," he muttered. "Tramyere cleared the lady snapshot artist."

"Are you sure the gun looked like that?"

"Not at all—but it was a chance." The sergeant looked at his watch sourly. "Haven't time to go to the library and look through their stuff on guns; not if I'm going to clean up the other stuff and catch the afternoon train back. Guess I'd better do the next best thing."

He grabbed his bag, opened the door, and started downstairs.

"And just what is the next best thing?" Monahan asked, as they stood on the sidewalk, beckoning to their third taxi of the day.

"If you can't borrow—you've got to buy." Harty winked, and twisted at the handle of the cab door. "Brentano's, driver. Forty-seventh Street, just off the Avenue."

4

The girl said yes, she supposed it would be all right. They could sit down and wait for the boss if they wanted to. But she really didn't know if the boss would be in at all that day. She had an idea that both the boss and his secretary, a Miss Franklin, were out of town.

Legs dull sleek in gun-metal chiffon carried her in a not precisely straight line toward the outer office. On the glass panel of the door which she did not quite close behind her jet-black backs of gold letters spelled, in reverse, the name of the boss who would not be in that day, nor ever again.

Harty thought that a mildly pie-eyed receptionist was something of a novelty. Not as great, perhaps, as the small victrola in the main office over whose next record a male and a female clerk argued bitterly, nor as intriguing as the crap game in the directors' room; but a novelty just the same.

"I've seen queer layouts in my day," Dan Monahan rumbled, "but this is tops. How could they ever make any money?"

"They did, though—and plenty!" The sergeant had gathered, from things heard at Sand Head, that Wade's business affairs were allowed to reel along in somewhat unbuttoned fashion, but even the brief look he was getting at the situation made that seem like an understatement. "That desk is a sweet-looking mess."

The broad surface was crowded with a weird miscellany. An imported riding crop lay across a wire letter basket which held nothing but an assistant deputy-sheriff's badge, slightly tarnished. There was an autographed baseball; a small, pearl-handled revolver; three pictures of girls; the head of a broken sand wedge; and a coat of arms, of the sort merchandised in thousands by fake research bureaus, which bore the penciled inscription : "Some class to the Wades, huh, kid?"

Cass Harty idly considered a more appropriate crest for the deceased Charley. Something embodying a rampant stallion above moneybags gules, on either side of a leaking wine butt.

A correspondence folder of Spanish leather contained a single letter. It was addressed to Wade by a firm of yacht brokers and furnished prices, specifications and photographs of four fine-looking power cruisers. The lowest price quoted was $22,500. And, on the back of the letter was Wade's notation for a reply:

Kay:

Write these bums and tell them I want some-
thing really hot. What do they think I am, a
piker?
C.F.W.

The loose-leaf calendar beside the inkwell had not been turned since early April and Harty leafed back through it to January without finding any notation more important than a scribbled "Don't forget—lunch with Toodles" in mid-February. "Business wasn't that dull," Harty muttered. "I guess Wade just didn't give a damn."

In the outer office, bickering over the record grew louder. "But if ya use that forra opener," the man shouted, "whatcha gonna have left forra smash atta windup?"

"Annif we don't spot it there," the girl answered, "what 'll get us on stage—a w'eelbarrer?"

"Wade didn't have to give a damn," Monahan said, looking up from investigating a drawer. "Not while he had this stuff and these other things kept coming in regular."

"This stuff" was a packet of bonds; "these other things" checks of assorted sizes and colors.

Cass Harty entered the names and serial numbers of the bonds in his notebook, saying, "Can't tell—it might come in handy." Next, he inspected the checks, noting that a few were drawn to the order of Wade himself, but the majority were payable to Wade Enterprises, Incorporated. Averaging between four and six hundred apiece, their total came to well over nine thousand dollars. "Some of these tabs are over a month old," he said. "If we can get someone to tell us why they haven't been deposited yet . . ."

A red-headed youngster in an alpaca office coat came through the door in a hurry. Looking back over his shoulder, he skidded a one-footed Charlie Chaplin turn and banged against the desk.

"H'ya, son," Dan greeted. "Where to in such a hurry?"

"Anywhere. Got to hide. They're after me."

"Who?"

"Loan sharks—I'm 'way behind on my interest."

Monahan looked a question at the sergeant, who nodded. "Get in there," Dan pointed at the door of Wade's private washroom. "We'll front for you."

Red-head ducked in, and Dan moved a chair against the door, tilted it comfortably back, and sat down.

"Use it then, ya dope, use it," the male debater outside was yielding. "But wait and see—we'll get tha gong."

Past the arguing pair tramped a burly man with a cauliflower ear, followed by a smaller comrade whose nose was almost as long as the rank cigar he was smoking. Looking purposeful, Tin-ear and Eagle-beak shouldered through the door of the private office in time to hear Harty say in salesman tones:

". . . and the old farmer knocked on the door with one hand and waved the automobile license with the other; and when the guy inside the room asked him what was the matter, he yelled: 'If you ain't done it, don't do it— 'cause this ain't for it!'"

Dan haw-hawed dutifully, as if the yarn were new to him.

"I ever tell you that other one?" Harty went on. "About the proctologist and the man who swallowed the glass eye? It seems . . ."

"Excuse me, mister." The cigar filled so much of Eagle-beak's mouth that he found it easier to let speech escape through his nose. "Do you know a fellah named O'Day?"

"O'Day, sorr?" Harty's salesman became a stage Irishman. "That I do."

"When did you see him last? Where is he now?"

"Man, I never saw him at all, at all. Ould Mike O'Day's me granduncle on me mother's side, and he still lives in County Cork, as ever he did. Curse o' God on th' ould miser! But if ye go there to see him, say I was afther astin' for him."

Tin-ear whispered hoarsely to Dan, "Dis guy screwy?"

"You called it, brother," Dan finessed nobly. "Crazier than a bedbug," he added whole-souledly, "and . . ."

Beyond the door the contested record thrummed into action. Stamping shoes and a patter of handclaps accented the music's beat.

"Now, that 'll go big on our entrance," the girl debater's voice approved. "Then when Major Bowes asks me what I do, I'll say I work in an office. And when he asks you . . ."

"I already got my lines pat. I tell him—heh, heh—that I do orifice work, too, that I'm a dentist! Boy, that oughta slay him."

"Y' run up against them amachoors every place."

Tin-ear shrugged hopelessly. "Now, what was you saying about this lug?"

"I said he's crazy—what they call a homicidal maniac," Monahan told him. "He kills people. He lost all his d-o-u-g-h in a bank failure and any mention of m-o-n-e-y sets him off. He's bad."

"Yeh?" Eagle-beak edged toward the door, his cigar bobbing nervously. "Uh—which of you guys is the boss?"

Harty and Dan looked at each other, keeping straight faces while they said simultaneously: "I'm not—are you?"

Tin-ear had enough. "Ev'rybody here's loony," he muttered. "Let's get the hell out. We can write that mon . . . that *you know what* off the books. It 'll be safer than tryin' to collect."

In their exit they were almost trodden down by the prancing amateurs. When the door of the outer office had closed on them, Harty called toward the washroom, "O.K., kid. All clear."

Red-head looked relieved, but his hands were still trembling. "That was close," he said. "The big guy was their persuader."

"And a nice bit of type casting he is," the sergeant said. "Didn't you ever think of going to the cops for protection?"

"That might save me a beating, but I'd lose my job. Those moneylenders make a habit of squawking to a guy's boss when he can't pay."

"I'll guarantee they don't squawk to Wade." With a canny eye to the future, Dan tried to make a little sound like a lot.

"Bighearted Dan, the boys called him." Harty laughed. "And the boys were right." He realized that if the kid could be made to open up, the time spent in clowning with the Shylock and his muscle man would not have been wasted. "You owe us one, kid," he said, "don't you?"

The boy misunderstood. "I do—but don't get me wrong. I don't play the way the rest of the crowd around here does. I wouldn't have those sharks after me if I did. Wade may be a girl-crazy old rummy, but I don't rob him and I won't sell him out."

"No one's asked you to do either. We want information."

"About the process? You won't get it from me."

Harty knew nothing about any process. Gambling, he said, "No—not about that." He took a small leather case from his pocket and let the boy see his badge. "What's the answer to the whole setup of this place?"

"That's a city cop's shield—you're not from the income tax?"

"Call Centre Street if you don't believe us."

"Then"—the boy seemed to feel he could be frank—"the answer's easy money."

"Let's have a little detail."

"Well, whether you know it or not, Wade's success is fairly recent. Five years ago he was dubbing around at whatever he could do, some of his lines shady, and some on the up-and-up, but none of them making much dough for him. Then he stumbled onto this old chemist who'd worked out the process but didn't have enough sense to see its commercial value. Wade arranged for backing and bought it for a song, and ever since . . ."

"Just a second, son," Dan cut in. "What is this

process?"

"It's a formula that about ninety nine and nine tenths of the paint and varnish and lacquer makers in the world need in their business. Wade sells them yearly licenses to use it and they pay him royalties. It adds up to more money than he ever thought existed."

"This stealing you said was going on," Harty said. "Does Wade's secretary have any hand in it?"

The boy would not name names. He said, "I wouldn't know." But his face showed that he did.

"Dan! Go outside and look through her desk," Harty ordered. Of the boy, he inquired, "How was the gypping handled?"

"Nobody's ever made up any rules for it—everybody just cabbages whatever's handiest. The big shots draw contracts for less than regular scale, present 'em to Wade for approval when he's stewed, and get a juicy kickback from the manufacturers for their trouble. The ones who aren't so smart dig into the office cash. Believe it or not, I've seen a petty cash sheet for three thousand bucks O.K.'d for one week—Wade never knew he signed it—and there wasn't a thin dime in the drawer on Friday morning." Once started, the boy did not stop at half measures. "And everyone, smart and dumb alike, helps themselves from Wade's premiums."

"How come 'premiums'? Does Wade sell toilet soap or a paint formula?"

"Premiums is just office slang. Actually they're presents that Wade hands out to his customers and girl friends. Some of the stuff is good, and some is junk, but he always pays a lot for it. He buys up whole collections at a crack or walks into an auction and bids in half the catalogue, and if you were to ask him the next day he wouldn't be able to tell you how much he bought or what it cost. Why, the first year he was in the heavy dough, he had a folio Shakespeare and gave it to his bootlegger for a Christmas present. The guy sold it for fifty bucks in a secondhand bookstore and ran out of the place hellbent for fear the storekeeper'd change his mind."

Cass Harty said flatly, "I don't believe you." It was his way of asking for proof.

"There should be some stuff here now." O'Day crossed the room and opened the door of a tall cabinet.

Cass Harty said, "Gooooood God!"

A fantastic assortment of objects was in view.

The sergeant took conscious note of only two, a sculptured abstraction by Brancusi and a camera study of Calvin Coolidge; then he rushed back to the desk. Snapping up the phone he demanded that the operator put him through to Rev Crane. Scruples notwithstanding, the roll of papers could not be left undisturbed any longer.

The operator was murmuring, "Hold the li-yun. I yam ringing Say-und Hay-ud," as a new clamor began to rise in the outer office.

A hatchet-faced woman was brandishing a folded copy of an afternoon paper in her right hand as she tussled with a pair of clerks and shouted, "I can so go in there. I know my rights, I do. You can't keep me out!"

"She knows her rights," Harty said, and had to apologize to the telephone girl. "Not you, sister." He covered the mouthpiece with his hand and told O'Day to go outside and see what the woman wanted. He was beginning to feel that a state of frenzy was a normal condition in the offices of Wade Enterprises.

When O'Day came back his lips were pale. "She says she's Wade's wife," he said. "She claims he's been killed . . . It's in the paper."

"The last part of it's right," the detective told him. "I wouldn't like to bet on the rest."

On the wire a girl's voice said, "Go ahead, New York," and was followed by Rev's, "Hello, who's callin'?"

"Harty! Listen, Rev, things are moving. I want you to get over to the store and open that package that Kay Franklin mailed. Yes, that one. Do as I say. I'll take any blame."

"I'd like t' help, but I just don't dare." Rev went on to mumble obscurely about regulations.

"I'll go to bat for you no matter what happens," the sergeant promised. "I don't care if Jim Farley himself squawks. I'll take the grief. Yes . . . I'll hold the line . . . hurry!"

Beyond the door three clerks were now fighting a losing battle with the woman as she shouted, "I'm going in there, I tell you."

Dan Monahan shouldered past the wrestling quartet and reported, "Nothing in the Franklin girl's desk. Either she's on the square or she's smart."

"We'll know in a minute, Dan," Harty explained. "Crane's opening that package."

With a drive like a Minnesota fullback, the woman broke through the weakening clerks, shoved the door back on its hinges, and was suddenly before the desk. She thumped its glass surface with her paper and mouthed unintelligible claims.

A madhouse would seem quiet as a chess tournament after this place, Harty thought. Above the phone, he asked, "What do you want?"

"I want all that's due me. I'm Charley's legal-wedded wife. I won't get out and you can't make me."

"It will take time to study Wade's affairs." Harty tried to pacify her. "There's no use in getting excited. If you can prove what you say you'll be treated justly."

"Justice? Don't make me laugh! Justice don't mean much where the rich are concerned. Those people buy their justice!"

"Madam," Dan began, "we are police officers . . ."

"Then you'll be the first to be bought—if you haven't already. Randall Elrod won't leave a stone unturned to get his hands on this business. But I'll stop him. I'll stop him if it's the last thing I ever do. I'll expose him. I'll . . ."

"Just a minute, please!" Harty's patience thinned as the woman's wild statements outpaced any evidence that might support them. "What has Elrod got to do with this company?"

O'Day said, "His firm got some of Wade's investment business."

The far from stricken widow was too mad to answer Harty. "Where's Charley's bankbooks?" she screamed. "Where's all his dough? Who's got the key to the vault where he keeps the process? What's become of that collection he bought last month?—stuff worth thousands and thousands of dollars."

But not to me, Harty thought, I'm not that strong for either Coolidge or Brancusi.

"Y' there, Serge-unt?" Rev's voice came through. "I . . . uh . . . you might say ... I looked into t'at little matter. Ketch on?"

"Yeah. What was inside—anything important?"

"Not s'far's I can see. Just a old letter. Paper's so durned brown and t' ink's so faded, 'twas all I could do t' read it. But I copied down t' name of t' feller wrote it. I figgered y' might want t' look him up in the telly-phone *dee*rectory while you're in t' city. It's spelled capital B-u-t-t-o-n and a capital G-w-i-n-n-e-t-t. Button Gwinnett, I guess y'd say it. Funny-sounding name, huh? I hope y' locate him."

Sergeant Cass Harty could only say "Good-by!"

The office was silent as the phone clanked down upon its cradle. Monahan stared owlishly.

"I tried to ask you a moment ago," Harty said to the woman. "I wish you'd answer now. Why are you worried about Randall Elrod?"

The fury of her glance faded into cold astonishment that anyone could have failed of understanding for so long. "He has his chance to get control of this business now," she said. "He was in on it with Charley right from the start, but a share wasn't good enough for that fellow. Randall Elrod's never satisfied; he's the kind of hog who wants the whole trough."

THURSDAY
(NIGHT)

THE TRAIN WHISTLE flung its banshee yowl like a challenge toward the twilight-wrapped roofs of Keyesport. In the smoking compartment Cass Harty tore a sheet of paper into confetti sizes and let the bits flutter down toward the polished brass ring of a cuspidor. When the last one had settled to rest he picked up his bag and swayed to the door to be the first one off.

At the end of the line the car would get a hurried cleaning before starting back to town, but no jigsaw expert would reconstruct that sheet of paper to read:

1. M. Packe. No assurance her feelings Ms' & Wade . . . can get none. Bad background, but whole case against her hangs on camera. Tramyere says: No can do. Packe app'ntly clear.

2. K. Franklin. Her story of money being for boss, a phony . . . No such sum found in Wade's room. Gwinnett holograph letter one of rarest of specimens of signers of Declaration of Independence and, therefore, prob'ly three times as valuable as the dough. Makes her look bad. Excuse for leaving last night, "I was frightened and I ran. Where? Oh, just anywhere," makes her look worse. No motive Ms'. Strong motive, Wade . . . he might have threatened prosecution for thefts. Free to pull Wade job, possibly free to pull M. job. So?

Dunster. Puzzle of them all. No motive Ms' or W, but queer actions. Question: Do his two introductions of yacht and his alibiing of flash on land mean he's protecting someone on land? And who?

Randall Elrod. Dunster protecting him? Kay hinting at him with that talk on hardness? Mrs Wade accusing him directly. Motive: Ms', weak. Wade, terrific.

Opportunity: Ms', almost none. Wade, slightly better.
Strong enough, physically, to handle a heavy gun. Strong
enough, emotionally, to carry through a risky stunt. But if
motive killing Wade was get control business, why in hell
were Ms' killed?
  Gresham, Laura, Tenny, Chet . . . No motive. Ms'
Laura, Tenny, Chet . . . No opportunity, W.
  Laura, Gresham, Tenny . . . No opportunity, Ms'.
  Morgan Elrod. Opportunity, Ms' & W. Bad record of
violence. But motives, Ms' & W, doubtful.
  Mrs Wade. No motive Ms'. No opportunity W, since
Monahan's check-up proved her at work last night at time
of death.
  One best bet: Morgan Elrod? Randall Elrod? Aw, nuts!

Across the yard a man in a blue striped, mattress-
ticking jacket was wrestling a crate onto a small stake-
sided truck.

Cass Harty crossed between departing station wagons
and roadsters to ask, "You the agent?"

"That's me." The man got the crate aboard and
climbed in after it. "You looking for some baggage?"

"No. I wanted to learn if you were here when Number
Nine came in last night." Harty was checking the "queer
actions" note. "LeMoyne Dunster, from over on the Head,
lost a wallet and he thought he might have dropped it
when he was getting off."

"Yeah?" The agent straightened; hostility, almost to
the point of preparation for combat, was in his manner.
"Just who do you think you're kidding, mister?" he
snarled.

"I didn't know I was kidding anyone," the sergeant
said easily. "But it's possible I've been kidded. I was
asking about Dun . . ."

"Y' can stop right there. I don't know who you are, and
I don't know if Dunster lost himself a wallet like you
say—but he didn't lose nothing getting off Number Nine.
I was right here when she come through last night and

there wasn't ary a Keyesport passenger aboard."

"You're sure? Positive?"

"Course! Didn't I ketch hell from the old lady when I got home. Nine was late last night, y' know. Freight train run into a auto t'other side of Wantagh an' tied up the whole line."

Nice going! Harty thought. "What time'd she finally pull in?"

"After midnight. Prett' near ha' past!"

"O.K.," Harty said. "I guess I was wrong about Dunster." He meant it two ways. As he strode toward the ferry he congratulated himself upon the ease with which Dunster's story of being on Number Nine had been dynamited. It was not much after eleven o'clock when he had been captured racing across the face of the slope.

Cap'n Somers collected the fare with an unfriendly, "Humph! 'Nother two minutes and we'd 'a' sailed without ye."

It gave the sergeant a chance for an extra check-up. He said, "Just like you almost sailed without Dunster yesterday?"

"Dunster?" The captain looked puzzled. "Oh! You mean *Mister* Dunster. He had plenty o' time to make the Editha—I seen him hanging around town all afternoon — but he didn't sail with us. Had his own speedboat tied up right at the next wharf there."

This is the damnedest case I ever handled, Cass Harty assured himself. Every time I get set to go to town on one angle, a new one bobs up. As soon as I get my sights pretty well trained on the Elrods, pal Dunster has to stick his neck out and practically beg me to swing the ax. But why . . . why . . . why?

The sergeant bent to pick up his bag, wondering what crazy new turn the case would take next. It had taken many, but, as he straightened up, the Fates gave him a quick preview of the latest in the string.

A competent-looking man sat alone on the Editha's portside. He wore a double-breasted blue suit, a far from memorable dark tie, lightweight black shoes, and a soft gray hat with a snap brim. The thin lips holding a cigarette were like a two-em quadrat, between a strong chin and a hawk nose. He had large-knuckled, very white hands; an intelligent face; and, at a snap judgment, a disinclination ever to rate his own general worth at anything less than A-plus-plus. Fifteenth-century Spain would have seen him a first-assistant inquisitor under Torquemada, and Ireland of 1916 would have known him as a dapper and extremely efficient lieutenant of the hated "Tans." The United States in the nineteen-thirties offered only two openings to people of this man's particular bent—and the gentleman whom Cass Harty recognized as the celebrated "Nemo" Noone was not a gangster.

"Oh, oh," the sergeant murmured to himself. "And how did you boys get asked to the party?"

"If y'r coming," the captain snorted, "y' better git aboard."

"I'm with you," Harty laughed. "You may not know it, Cap'n, but I wouldn't miss this for anything." He stepped to the Editha's deck and walked forward, balancing himself with fake caution. Opposite the blue-clad man he contrived to trip against the coaming, lurched once, and dropped into the cockpit.

Noone's killer eyes gimleted through him.

"Almost had a swim ahead of time," Harty said.

"I noticed. You need to be careful of boats if you're not used to them." Noone's tone implied he was used to boats and practically anything else he might encounter.

"I will be—before the summer's out." The sergeant stuck a cigarette between his lips and patted three pockets in succession in apparently fruitless search for a light. All three held little paper books of matches. "You down for long?"

"It depends." The man offered a lighter initialed with a big "N." "I'm here for business, not pleasure." He toed at a large black case on the floorboards beside him.

It really did look something like a salesman's sample case, but Cass Harty could have enumerated its contents, one by one. "Business should be lively," he said, as the Editha chugged along. "What's your line?"

"Heat—oil burners and air-conditioning apparatus." With a little double entendre of his own, Noone added, "You see, our outfit covers the entire field." He accented the "our" slightly.

The New York detective pretended not to get it. "You're in luck," he said. "I don't believe there's a burner on the island."

Noone showed small inclination to talk during the journey, a not particularly convincing way to impersonate a traveling man.

The sergeant spent most of the trip studying his famous adversary. Perhaps, he guessed, one of the reasons MacIver is so sore is because he knew these birds were coming down here to put on their regulation quick-trigger act. Still, it was hard to see what had brought them in. Nothing in either the McNiff or the murder cases was properly under the jurisdiction of Noone's bureau.

The stuttering of the Editha's kicker died at last as she slid through slack water to the Sand Head dock. Harty dropped the last of a chain of cigarette butts overside and prepared to debark.

Noone was staring at him fixedly.

"So long," the sergeant said. "Luck in your job—of selling oil burners."

"And in yours." Noone's expression did not change. "I hope you learn a lot—about boats."

It looks, Harty decided as he trudged up the slope, it looks as if neither of us got fooled.

Far behind him, Noone made his way upward, lugging the bulky "sample case." If it had actually contained all the parts of an oil burner it could not have been much heavier.

In the lobby of the Sea Spray Rev bustled from behind

the desk. "Got good news for ye," he greeted. "Y' partner thinks mebbe he's found McNiff."

"Swell," Harty approved. "Where's he at?"

"Mr Stauffer? He's up to his room having a shave."

"I meant Tootie."

"Down West Point end of things—least t'at's what y' friend thinks. He'll tell ye about it."

The sergeant continued upstairs and shoved open the door of their room. "Take it easy, Barney. Saturday's the day after tomorrow. Yom schabess, yom menucho, you know."

"No rest for us," Stauffer growled. "Not 'll we get Tootie."

"We may have to do it in a hurry." Harty went to the window and pulled the shade aside. "Take a look at what's coming."

Barney took the look. "That makes four," he said in disgust. "Three of 'em have been working the Cottage Line all day, pretending to be canvassers of some kind and giving every house a pretty good once-over."

"This one's game is air conditioning." The sergeant chuckled. "Looks as if we're in for a run for our money."

"What's all this?" Rev demanded from the doorway. "Them fellers crooks or something."

"Far from it—but they've got about as much fondness for city cops like Barney and me as any crook you ever heard of," Harty told him. "They're the dashing daredevils from Washington. The two-gun heroes they make all the movies about. And from the looks of that case, they've brought their pretty little cap pistols and firecrackers with them."

2

Four pseudo salesmen might be ranging Sand Head from end to end, but not even the whole Federal Bureau of Investigation could have kept the sergeant from doing a two-fisted job on the meal Gen had made ready. The amount of food and the care she had taken in preparing it indicated definitely that she no longer considered the two detectives as untrustworthy city smart alecks, but had come to accept them as people of good will toward her brother. After the ritualistic Drink, Gen opened fire with an even dozen clams on the half shell, each one drowned in her own version of stinging cocktail sauce. Followed next a magnificent fish chowder of a specific density so great it could almost be eaten with a fork. Then, Tuesday's entire meal, demoted now to the status of a single course: steamed clams, a mountain of them, sozzled in liquid gold of melted butter and washed down with alternate drafts of their own broth and foaming beer. After that: lobster, lordly as a chief justice of the Supreme Court; roast chicken; a platoon of vegetables; and a salad whose dressing was as oily as a stock promoter's approach and which held just as much concealed bite. Marching in the rear guard with the coffee came a half watermelon and a buxom gobbet of old-fashioned strawberry shortcake, both of which the sergeant declined on the plausible grounds that he was already fed fat.

Barney grunted, "Hand 'em across to me, then," and tore into both desserts, grunting a little from sheer joy of greed.

Smoking a cigarette, Cass Harty leaned back in his chair and made book with himself on just how soon the little detective would burst. "Rev told me you've got a line on McNiff," he said. "You think he's up west of here?"

"'Ink? I 'ould be as 'ure of a mi'yon bucks," Stauffer mumbled through a faceful of shortcake.

"You'll have to try that one over, Barney—the mind-reading act doesn't play the supper show."

"I said I wished I could be as sure of a million bucks. People up there say food's been swiped, clothes've been swiped, all kinds of junk is swiped." Barney took a toothpick, inspected it to make sure the point was serviceable, and stabbed at a hollow molar. "They don't usually have one robbery here in five years. How would you add it up?"

"Tootie'd need to eat and keep himself warm," Harty admitted. "And even if he didn't—it'd be like him to steal, just to keep his hand in. Did you get anything else while I was away?"

"I was at Dunster's, chinning with anybody that'd talk to me, just like you said to," Barney reported. "Servants and all. I asked whose idea it was to have that shenanigan on the beach last night."

"What diff'rence it make who wanted the party?" Rev asked. "We know already t'at they had one."

"It may make no difference at all," Harty explained, "and it could make a great deal. Figure it this way: Both shootings took place on the beach. Suppose, for some reason, the murderer could kill no place but on the beach. Then he'd have to get his victim down there —and suggesting another beach party'd be the easiest way to do it. See?"

"B'George, I do! Who'd they say put up the idee?"

"Near as I could make out," Barney answered, "it was that young Kay Franklin."

"Huh! That makes things look bad for her."

Harty went on to give a rapid sketch of the situation as it had revealed itself in the offices of Wade Enterprises that afternoon.

"Then she kilt him t' keep from getting arrested." Rev slowfreighted up to one of the conclusions the sergeant had played with. "We better get her under lock an' key right away."

"Not in too much of a hurry." Harty skipped the minor difficulties in the theory of Kay's guilt. "We still don't know a damned thing about what kind of weapon was used, nor where it is now. It wasn't one of the destroyer's guns; it couldn't have been the saluting cannon or another little hunch I had, according to Tramyere; and, if we can believe the club steward, it wasn't the harpoon gun. So what was it?"

Murder trials and the antics of high-priced defence counsel were unexplored territory to Rev Crane. "There's three people deader than pickled eels," he exploded. "Ain't t'at enough, 'thout bringing a gun into court?"

"Not even Tom Dewey could get a conviction in this case without producing the gun," Harty assured him. "There's enough iron in those bodies to sink a battleship. You'll never get a jury to believe the killer slung that load with a beanshooter." He turned back to Barney. "You get that other job done?"

"Yeah—I went through the san from cellar to basement."

"And . . .?"

"Morgan Elrod's lammed again."

"I almost expected it," Harty grunted. "It'd never do for us to be able to work on one line at a time. Unless there's five or six things popping all together, we might get bored."

"When I got through sizing up the dump," Barney said, "it didn't surprise me that he's able to come an' go as he pleases."

"What d' you mean?" Rev's local pride moved him to defence. "Larsen's got a mighty fine, up-to-date plant up there."

"But it's largely a phony, just the same," the sergeant explained. "Barney and I've seen layouts like that before—there are lots of them around. A family with a rum-pot brother or a hop-head uncle can file him away there and the doc 'll see that he gets his stuff, just as long as the home folks lay the dough on the line. That way, everybody's happy and nothing gets in the papers. It's a great racket! Before this present business blows over Larsen will probably have worked out a standard fee for supplying certificates of mental irresponsibility to those that need 'em."

"Aw, Rev!" Gen stuck her head in through the doorway. "Feller out here t' see you. He's one of the summer crowd and he's all worked up about something."

Rev looked at the two detectives. " 'Nother killing?"

"More of Tootie's work, most likely," Stauffer guessed. "Let's go see what the guy's got to say."

A man stood in the lobby, his back to them as they entered. The neck of his tweed jacket fitted badly, its disarrangement apparently caused by some lumpy wrappings beneath it.

"All right," Rev said. "What seems t' be the trouble?"

Adrian Tenny turned stiffly around, wall lights glinting on the double thick lenses of his eyeglasses. He was sputtering in rage.

Cass Harty saw that his throat was swathed with bandages.

"Great Gawd A'mighty!" Rev gasped. "What happened you?"

"I'm trying to tell you! I want to lodge a complaint, although I don't know what good it will do me." Tenny's voice was hoarsely weak, like that of a third-degree victim whose Adam's apple has been rubber hosed. "Nothing's safe around here any more, not even going down to the beach for a swim. It's bad enough when they shoot people, but when they start going after them like animals, with traps and deadfalls . . ."

"Just a minute," the sergeant interrupted. "What traps are you talking about, and who rigged them?"

"It was a rope across the path from Dunster's house to the beach," Tenny croaked. "It was fastened to one of those scrubby little trees and he was standing back off the path and tightened it as I came along. Kay Franklin saw the whole thing. I ran full tilt into it and it caught me right across here and damned near tore my head off. Now! What 're you going to do about it?"

"Plenty! Tell us who pulled this stunt and we'll do the rest." Harty was half prepared to hear Ronnie Gresham's name. The stunt seemed a logical follow-up to practical jokes with dribble glasses.

"I don't know what they call the fellow," Tenny said surprisingly. "But Kay told me he's staying at this hotel.

He wears a blue suit and I heard he sells vacuum cleaners."

Cass Harty swore in metrical cadence. He took a step forward and tilted the man's head back, easing the bandages away from the flesh.

Beneath the layers of gauze and sterile cotton pads, Tenny's neck was abraded to beafsteak rawness.

Harty swore again, more briefly but with greater color. "I think that salesman's going to have to do some high-powered talking to make this look good," he murmured. His feet thudded across the lobby to the stairs. "What room is he in, Rev?"

Crane looked at the register. "Fourth to t' right on t' second floor."

Barney Stauffer followed at a jog trot as the sergeant made for the fourth door to the right, one flight up. The flimsy woodwork was vibrating under Harty's fist when the little detective reached the hall.

"Hol' on, Bud," a voice responded. "Ah'll be right theah."

"Hold on, hell!" Harty thumped the door again.

A man who was twin to the Editha's passenger in dress and bearing opened it. "What can ah do for y'all? Ah expect you'd like to see a demonstration of ouah product."

"Sure. You can . . ." Not even the writing psychopathologists of Vienna ever recorded encountering such a demonstration as Harty suggested.

"Now, now, brothah . . ."

"Don't give me that stuff," the sergeant snapped. "I'm not having any. I know your crowd—and if you wonder boys are half as good as you're supposed to be, you know me."

"Ah do." The pose was abandoned. "And ah reckon ah know that Jew boy with you."

"Just to keep the classifications straight," Cass Harty said, "I am a mick, my friend Barney is a Yid, and you, I am happy to say"—he smiled engagingly and moved three paces into the room—"are a shoeless, hillbilly bastard.

And now that we've got everyone identified, suppose we get down to business."

"Theah's some names ah don't stand foah," the man said through slitted lips. "Yo' just used one of them."

"You know," Harty grinned, "I can hear every word you say—but since your pals aren't here and I don't see a machine gun handy, I can't picture you doing anything about it. But swapping compliments isn't going to get us anywhere. I want to know what you thought that rope trick was going to get you."

"That was practical crimuhnology. We look at things a bit different from you city flatfeet."

"Yeah," Stauffer sneered. "We found that out during the Milne* case. Our whole department's laughing yet!"

Stauffer's reference was to a kidnaping hoax, perpetrated for publicity purposes, during the fall of 1935. New York City police diagnosed it correctly and immediately, while federal men made vigorous and well-publicized efforts to locate the kidnaper.

"Thuh first thing we did when we got heah"—the man affected not to notice Barney—"was to go ovuh that hahpoon gun with thuh silvuh-nitrate process to bring out latent fingerprints."

"Then you probably found about ten thousand of them." The sergeant chuckled. "My own included. Didn't it occur to you that nine out of ten people who see that gun can't resist taking hold of it and swinging it around, aiming at everything in sight? It'd take a dozen years to track down every print on that handle."

"Theah was right many," the agent admitted. "But this othuh job was different. Tenny was assigned to me foah investuhgation and ah had to find out if his eyesight was weak, like they said. Ah had to make suah—it'd call foah one mighty good mahksman to do whut's been done heah!"

Harty did not bother to mention that between his stop

at the bookstore and his call at Wade's office he had managed to sandwich in a visit to an oculist whose name he had obtained from Kay. He was completely convinced that Tenny's eyes were as poor as report had them. He said, "So . . ."

"So ah gave him thuh ol' ahmy test." The agent's tone showed pride in his own cleverness. "Back in '17 felluhs would try to dodge thuh draft by claiming they had bad sight. They'd misread thuh eye chaht on puhpose; but thuh ahmy doctuhs found a way to stop 'em. Ol' doctuh'd say: 'Youah eyes are bad. You can leave by that doah, please.' And theah'd be a wire strung across thuh doahway. Thuh fakers would duck thuh wire ev'ry time—couldn't keep from doing it—and thuh next thing they knew they'd find theahselves in khaki." He laughed unpleasantly. "When Tenny was due to go foah a swim, I put a rope across thuh path. I pulled it up when he got near; that's all theah was to it."

"I suppose it was a good-enough way to find out about his sight," Barney admitted grudgingly. "But you didn't have to cut him half in two, did you?"

"Mistuh," the agent said defensively, "you know good an' well you cain't make a omelet without breaking eggs. It wasn't none of my fault he was coming downhill so fast."

3

Shroudlike dust covers on the furniture and an absence of ash trays, magazines and other small impedimenta of day-to-day living made the first floor of Randall Elrod's house seem oddly bare.

"I'm rather roughing it a bit here, you know," he apologized. "The servants won't be down until the end of next week."

"You came unexpectedly?" Harty asked.

"Yes—mainly because of my cousin, poor chap." If he knew of the "poor chap's" latest move, nothing in his manner betrayed it. "But I'm glad to say he has been improving steadily."

"Glad to hear it." Harty was on a more intricate trail than that of the vanishing cousin. For an opener, he said, "I was in Wade's office today."

"Were you?" Elrod's voice was thicker than normal, clogged with the beginnings of a summer cold. "Did you come to see me on account of Wade?"

Barney said, "On account of *Mrs* Wade."

"I knew Charley had a wife—a relic, I believe, of his less prosperous days." Elrod's heavy brows drew slightly together. "But that is the sum of my knowledge of her. I never met her."

"I did." The sergeant smiled reminiscently. "She's an aggressive old girl with a lot of funny ideas."

"Why bother me about her?" The great bald head tilted back, then snapped forward in an explosive sneeze. "Damn this cold! I should have known it's too early in the year for night bathing."

With what was, for him, an extremely rare ineptness, Barney played his hand poorly. "We wouldn't bother you at all, only some people say Wade Enterprises is a big money-maker."

"That's fairly well known. But where do I come in?"

"Mrs Wade said you are in," Harty urged. "She claims you've been in since the beginning."

"Oh *that!* It's true I put a little money into the firm when Wade was getting started."

A little, huh? Harty remembered hearing twice that Randall Elrod would not be satisfied with a little. The all-or-nothing attitude fitted him better.

"Take a guy who's got a piece of an outfit like that—making heavy sugar right along," Barney said. "He'd be lucky if he could get control of the whole shebang, wouldn't he?"

The cold germs had Elrod's eyes watery and red, but they could not drown his glare of controlled fury. "Are you men trying to accuse me of killing Wade?" he demanded.

"I don't accuse till I'm ready to make a pinch," Harty said.

"Then you will do well to postpone such a move indefinitely. Dunster and I helped Wade get started, and I have had some excellent returns on my investment . . ."

"All the more reason for wanting the whole pie instead of just a slice," Stauffer broke in.

"Ridiculous." The bald-headed man made an effort to conquer his wrath. He eyed them speculatively as he said, "How would it look to you if I proved you wrong about my interest in the Enterprises? What you considered a motive would disappear, wouldn't it?"

"Yeah," Barney answered, "it would—if we believed you."

"Aside from the notoriety and inconvenience of having Wade's name linked with mine in the newspapers, it would be a matter of indifference whether you believed me or not. It would almost be worth that unpleasantness to see your faces when I proved in court that there is not one share of Wade Enterprises stock listed to the credit of Randall Elrod. Not a share! And now"—he moved into the hall and opened the front door—"I see no need to detain you longer."

Behind the detectives' backs the door closed gently. Elrod's temper was up, but he would not permit himself the luxury of a slam.

"We bulled that one, didn't we?" Barney grumbled.

"I guess so—but it's hard to see where we went wrong. That is one leathery old bird; he doesn't rattle worth a hoot. I thought he was damned sure of his ground when he disowned the Wade outfit."

"We got something out of it anyway. I mean about Dunster being in on the gravy with His Nibs and Wade. Nobody peeped about that before."

"Nobody did." Harty reviewed rapidly. "Dunster was out of sight both times. He's acted funny all along, and the financial motive could fit him. If you want to circulate around with an eye peeled for Morgan Elrod, Barney, it might help. I'm going to take myself by the hand and see what Dunster's got to say."

"That ain't the question," Barney muttered. "Weasel-puss will say plenty—but how good will he say it?"

4

The porch seat was trickily designed, equipped with tongue, hood and wheels to resemble a miniature covered wagon. It made for a cozy Chet and Kay. Across from them Laura Ladd perched lovingly on the arm of Gresham's chair, and Melissa Packe and Tenny, upright on metal bridge chairs, faced each other across an inlaid chessboard. Drinks were within reach of all except Miss Packe, and the portable was grinding out a wailed subchorus of the "Saint Louis Blues":

> *"Oh, let me be your little dog,*
> *Until your biiiig dog comes . . ."*

"I'm looking for the big dog now," Harty called. "Where is he?"

"What the . . ." Laura jumped, knocking the ash from her cigarette. "Do you always go around scaring people?"

"Didn't mean to—I want to see Dunster." Noting cocktail and cigarette, Harty wondered why her struggle for demureness had been abandoned and whose was the victory.

"He's upstairs, changing." Kay assumed the job of hostess. "Will you have a drink while you wait for him?"

"Thanks, I'm thirsty," Harty said, and thought: But I'll mix my own! He climbed the steps and took a chair near enough to the source of supply to forestall Ronnie's attempts at bartending.

They watched him pour rye into a tall glass and pale it to the color of India tea with syphon water before anyone spoke.

Then Chet grimaced and said maliciously, "Don't you

think it would be a nice gesture if you congratulated Ronnie?"

"Yeah!" Laura held up her left hand, waggling it vigorously to catch the lamp's rays in a very young diamond. "You oughta."

"Huh?" Surprises were like breakfast food to the detective, but this one almost made him drop his glass. He looked to Gresham for confirmation.

The Lucky Man wore an expression like a professional pallbearer attending his own wake. "That's it," he said dolorously. "We're engaged."

"Not just engaged, Ronnie Pet," Laura said firmly. *"We're gonna get married!"*

"Local . . . girl . . . makes . . . good," Kay said slowly. She spaced her words like backfield men waiting for a kickoff.

"All the best of it, of course," Harty mumbled. He lifted his glass toward the cuddled pair and wondered what could have altered Ronnie's views on the marriage question.

"I'm sure you wish them every good thing," Miss Packe said.

"Huh?" Harty snapped out of a reflection that it did not make sense to see Laura getting her own way in the matter. Now, if she had something on the poor slob . . . "Oh sure. For years to come."

The record ended and the repeating gadget caught the tone arm and swung it back to the beginning.

"I hate to see—that evenin' sun go down . . ."

As if he had read the detective's thoughts, Chet decided to take himself out of the center of things. "It's a major crime to let that swing tune go to waste, Kay," he said, getting to his feet. "What do you think?"

Kay said she thought he was right. She ducked from under the star-speckled hood and slid, almost too eagerly, into his arms.

Sipping his drink, Harty thought she, too, was glad enough to avoid questioning, although not necessarily the same set of questions which would have embarrassed Good Ol' Chet. "Thornton," he called, "how is the backing of your hotel deal coming on?"

"Just fine, old man." Chet posed briefly with Kay in a deep corte. "I expect to close the deal in a day or two."

"It must be an awful job to get a loand out of a *bank*," Laura said, "but we wish Chet lots of luck . . .all of it bad," she added in a lower voice. Tipping the silver shaker above her cocktail glass, she murmured, "I guess another one of these won't hurt me—even if I'm not used to the hard stuff."

If Gresham made them even one is too many, Harty thought.

Melissa Packe was not fooled. "But my dear child," she said, "the habit might grow on you."

Across the chessboard Tenny's eyes followed Kay.

She danced extremely well, her tanned stockingless legs twinkling accurately through the too-intricate steps of Chet's devising.

"Nice hoofing," Laura approved. "Goin' to town!"

Upstairs water glugged in a bathtub drain. Apparently the truth had been told for once: Dunster was dressing.

"Do you mind?" Ronnie said peevishly. He boosted Laura from his lap. "I'd better mix another shakerful . . . darling."

"O.K. by me . . . darling." Over her glass Laura framed a provocative smile at the detective, a smile that seemed badly remembered from an old-time movie. She had another nip at the sickish pink cocktail and sang with the record:

> *"If you don't like my peaches,*
> *Why do you shaaaaake my treeeee?"*

When Ronnie did not look up from the rolling bar she

tried to give the smile more meaning.

Might as well string along, Harty decided, it's my only chance to find out! It had occurred to him that there were no jewelry stores on Sand Head. Getting up, he said, "Shall we?"

"Y' betcha ... I mean, I'd be delighted." She folded to him and caught the rhythm quickly. The drumbeat of the record became immediately superfluous.

Kay, deftly keeping pace with Chet's circus-pony steps, looked across his shoulder and flattened her lips at the sergeant in a moue whose significance he missed.

He shrugged and grinned back at her.

The watching Tenny noticed. He was so annoyed that he moved a minor piece in slovenly fashion.

"Chess is a game which should never be given less than complete attention," his opponent said sharply. "It is almost impossible to tell what square that one is on."

"Oh, sorry." Tenny centered the little ebony figure meticulously and murmured the conventional, "*J'adoube.*"

"Huh?" Laura swayed around to look at him. "What was that?"

"He said he was adjusting his bishop," Harty explained. "But from the way things look, she's going to grab it."

"Imagine that." Laura sniffed. "And she acts so high and mighty all the time." She hummed with the record: "They say a black-haired woman made a gooooood man leave the town!"

"You do all right with a man yourself." Harty wanted to know more about the engagement. "Don't you?"

"I told you I would, out on the yacht."

"Sure. But where did that ring come from?" He guided her beyond Gresham's hearing. "It wasn't bought here."

"No, it wasn't." The lovely vacant eyes clouded with amateurish guile. "It was Ronnie's grandmother's. It's a reg'lar heirloom—I think it was real sweet of him to give it to me."

The sergeant had a view of her left hand on his shoulder. "Sweet," he said, "is only approximately the word."

"But a red-head gal can make a boy—" She broke off her crooning abruptly. "Say! You looked at the ring kind of funny. What's the matter with it?"

"Nothing. It's an O.K. ring. But your story about it is all wet. That type of setting is comparatively new—nobody's grandmother ever wore it."

". . . woman makes a freight train leave the track," she sang. "What'd you say about it?"

"You heard me." He steered back toward the others. "Frank and honest Laura, the boys called her—and the boys missed that one."

"Okey-doke," She made a physical persuasion of her resistance to his guiding and kept their course still further down the porch. "You're right," she giggled. "I brought the ring down with me. What's wrong with that? I hadda hunch we'd get engaged."

"I know *you* did. But Ronnie came over to that idea in a hurry."

"There's no law says a person can't change their mind. Besides, it makes a man feel good when he does something brave."

Something brave? The sergeant thought about it while the record ended with an outburst by amok tympanists. "If it's not too much to ask: what did Ronnie do that was so heroic?"

Laura hoisted almost-plump hips onto the porch rail. "He saved me from drowning."

We've been getting nearer to it right along, Cass Harty assured himself, and now we're in the realm of sheer fantasy. "How did you come to be drowning?" he asked. "Did you dunk yourself on purpose, so's Ronnie could rescue you?"

"I did not." Her voice was genuinely indignant. "I wasn't even in the water. I was in a boat, the yacht's ding . . . What do you call it?"

"Dinghy?"

"Yeah. I was waiting for Ronnie at the club pier, and this fella come along and untied it. I thought he was fooling with the ropes of another little boat—but all of a sudden I was drifting away. B'lieve me, I hollered—I was plenty scared. Ronnie got another boat and came after me. He saved my life."

"Who untied you?"

"How do I know who he was? He didn't dress like they do here. He hadda blue suit on and a gray hat."

"Excuse me! I'll get the rest of it later." Harty felt he already knew the rest. It seemed obvious that the same brain that had devised the test of Tenny's eyesight had also wanted to learn whether Laura knew how to handle small boats. The reasoning was evident: shots from out at sea . . . gun on yacht . . . yacht moored too far from shore for murderer to swim there and back in time available . . . boat next best bet.

"Where you going?" Laura called after the departing detective.

"In here." He continued around the corner of the building, making for the door of a room through whose window he had just observed Dunster's entrance. "I've got to see a man about a corporation."

The master of the house was seating himself at a large desk as Harty came in. He said "Good evening" and said it coldly.

"Busy?"

"Not if you've anything important to say." He looked past the detective, half-polite detachment gauze thin above contempt.

He acts as if I'm just another guy named Gus, Harty thought. Is it because he doesn't want to play square with me, or does he know the federal boys are here? "It's important, all right." He sat down, uninvited. "I want to talk about Wade Enterprises. Mrs Wade . ."

"Will have to wait until the entire corporate picture is analyzed," Dunster interrupted. "I dare say some competent underling will be able to supervise office routine in the meanwhile—from what I've heard the business practically ran itself. We shall have accountants go over the books and find out what shape the firm is in before we concern ourselves with Mrs Wade. As a matter of fact she and Charley had been separated for some time; I question greatly whether he would have cared to see her profit by his death."

"That 'we' who'll hire the accountants—who's in on it?"

"I am and Randall Elrod. Wade came to us when he needed backing to acquire his formula. We had no great faith in it, but we advanced certain sums and received shares of stock to secure our investment. When you recall Wade's way of managing his personal life, it is perhaps too much to hope that the shares will have any worth other than as voting power to determine future policy."

Sergeant Harty sat back, feeling like a man groping through a tunnel. Didn't Dunster know how profitable the company was? Or did his words express a doubt that any of the profits could have survived Wade's wild spending? Or was he out to disguise the strength of his own interest and, consequently, his motivation toward murder? Trying a carom shot, Harty said, "Randall Elrod won't do much voting."

"He will cast the same number as I. We were given identical allotments of stock."

"Is that so? Half an hour ago he denied to me that there was a single share of the Wade stock to his credit."

On the porch a new record began. It drove a torrent of swing in through the window and, for a long moment, there was no other sound in the room. The sergeant stared at Dunster and Dunster stared back.

"Well," Harty said, "what about it?" His tone meant plainly: "If you're going to call Elrod a liar, hurry up and get it done!" No use to ask why Elrod, who admitted knowing the Enterprises was a success, should deny owning stock; while Dunster, who was frank about his participation, should profess ignorance of their fiscal standing.

"Sergeant, I hardly know what to say." Dunster passed an almost surgically manicured hand down his smooth-shaven jowl. "I dislike casting doubt on the word of a friend, but, for our money, Elrod and I each got one third of the company's fifteen hundred shares of stock— Wade keeping the remaining third. And I never heard of Elrod's getting rid of his shares."

"You didn't hear of the train wreck last night, either, did you? The one that kept Number Nine from getting into Keyesport until half past twelve?"

"No." The answer was startled out of Dunster before he realized what it did to his account of his previous day's actions. Enraged, he slammed the desk with his fist and snarled: "It's nothing to you if I never left Keyesport. You're washed up here, whether you know it or not."

FRIDAY

"THERE SHE IS." Cass Harty pointed down from the brow of Sand Head's most westerly dune at the little shack. "Just like I saw her on Wednesday."

Barney shaded his eyes against the setting sun. "Tootie better be here," he said without much hope. "After all the hiking we done today, my dogs are killing me. And what've we got to show for it?"

Harty's "Not a hell of a lot" could as truthfully have been, "Slightly less than nothing." It was a discouraging admission.

Since breakfast time the two detectives had beaten every inch of the island between the settlement and the western tip. Under a blazing sun they had plunged into tiny hidden gullies and scratched their way through scrub-pine thickets of a barbed-wire denseness. They had struggled up the near side of countless sand hills and found nothingness at the top; they had slid, sweating, down the far to hail disappointment at the bottom. They had feloniously entered and carefully searched twoscore of boarded-up cottages and they had talked with the occupants of more than a dozen tenanted ones.

The cottagers had been even more discouraging than the empty houses and the vast reaches of sun-baked sand. No—very ponderously—they hadn't seen any strangers about; but what with that fellow breaking jail, and all, they were a little afraid he might be in the neighborhood.

Had anything been taken from their homes? Any supplies missing?

Well, that'd be hard to say. You know how it is when you're opening a house for the summer. You're not sure where half your stuff is, and you wouldn't really want to swear just how much you had in the first place. But at a time like this it was wisest to play safe.

In the time-honored manner of the good citizen made jittery by a crime scare, even the householders who had actually reported thefts to Rev Crane were beginning to hedge now. They couldn't say for sure, but it seemed like some things must be missing. Oh yes; if the stuff should be found, they thought they could identify it.

A little of that sort of thing went a long way with the sergeant, and slightly more than a little constituted an overdose. He was in a fine welter of stored-up surliness as they descended from the dune and started across level sand toward the shack. There was no hint of cover for them; if a man in the hut had a gun, they would be easy targets.

But McNiff won't have a rod, Harty grumbled at himself. And if he had one, there's nothing in his record to show he'd use it. Still . . .

"Makes you feel funny, don't it?" Barney said. "Walking up here and not knowing if you'll get plugged."

"I felt like it once in France." The sergeant reminisced. "Four of us rushed a machine-gun nest, figuring all the way that the gunner'd cut loose any second and blow us all to hell. When we got up to the damned thing . . ."

"They were all dead inside?" Stauffer anticipated.

"No. There was one alive—a kid about sixteen. He was sitting in the saddle of the gun and looking at us the way a guy who's run through a red light sits in his car and looks at the traffic cop while the old summons book is coming out. There wasn't a single bullet left in the ammunition belt. Poor cuss! One of the boys let him have it with a bayonet, just out of nerves. We all got medals afterward, but I never liked mine somehow. I traded it to a guy in Brest for a quart of vin rouge."

Barney thrust the door open. "No bayonets here," he said. "Nor McNiff either."

They stepped through the doorway, appraising the one-room building's emptiness with hasty glance.

A sour-smelling blanket, riddled like Switzer cheese with moth holes, was crumpled on the foot of a miserable bunk along the north wall. In the center of the room an enormous potbellied stove, its sides red rusted and cracked with age, lifted a leaky pipe toward a hole in the roof. A poker hung from a hook, and a huge bundle of firewood, enough to last for a week, was heaped untidily on the bare floor to the left of the stove.

Cass Harty lifted the lid and rammed a questing hand deep into the bed of gray ash. He fumbled about, currying the mass from side to side, before he was content. "Very faintly warm," he said at last. "And ashes will hold heat for a hell of a time. I'd guess there hasn't been a fire here in the last twenty-four hours."

"Without the ashes we'd still know somebody was here." Barney was scraping something from a rickety table into the palm of his hand. "Here's bread crumbs — stale too."

Harty rubbed the tiny scraps to powder between thumb and forefinger. "But not too stale," he said. "It checks with the stove. And look at this." From a pail beneath the table he lifted a twisted sardine can, reeking of rancid olive oil. "Tootie wasn't living precisely like a king."

"It all adds up—he's been gone at least a day," Stauffer said. "Well, what now?"

"Back to the Sea Spray, I guess, and then search from the settlement to East Point tomorrow."

"You don't figure Tootie 'll be back here?"

"No. There's no food around, and if he'd intended to come back there'd be some. Before the locals started to crawfish on their statements about what was stolen it added up to more than a loaf of bread and a can of sardines. Tootie must have taken the rest of the grub with him to a new hideaway."

2

A pair of yellow envelopes were waiting for Cass Harty at the Sea Spray House. He ripped the flap of one, read its contents, and whistled.

"Trouble?" Barney asked.

"Read it yourself." Harty handed it over. "Root . . . tee . . . toot!"

UNDERSTAND YOU VISITED CITY YESTERDAY IN DIRECT CONTRAVENTION MY ORDER TO REMAIN SAND HEAD UNTIL MCNIFF CAPTURED STOP REPETITION

THIS DISREGARD FOR INSTRUCTIONS OR FURTHER DELAY APPREHENDING ESCAPED PRISONER WILL CONSTITUTE GROUNDS FILING DEPARTMENTAL CHARGES

STOP

HAVE LEARNED FBI INTERESTED THIS CASE

STOP

WILL HOLD YOU PERSONALLY RESPONSIBLE ANY DISCREDIT ATTACHING TO THIS DEPARTMENT

STOP

MACIVER

"Hum!" Rev grunted. "How'd he know you was up t' town?"

"The departmental grapevine most likely."

"He'd hear it t'at soon?"

"Soon?" Barney said. "Hell, the cop on the beat can walk past my house while I'm eating my breakfast and before noontime every precinct in the city 'll know if I've had a scrap with the wife."

The sergeant opened his second telegram.

THE WORD IS OUT THAT THE BOSS WOULD BE TICKLED SILLY IF YOU CAN MANAGE TO SLIP THE BOOTS TO THOSE OTHER BOYS STOP MUST DO IT WITHOUT MAKING ANY HEADACHES FOR OUR OWN CROWD

STOP
CATCH ON
STOP
DAN

Cass Harty's broad face was thoughtful as he crumpled both slips of yellow paper into a pocket. It was the old army game, from away back, he realized. With the usual nonchalance of superior officers, Inspector MacIver was offering him the chance either to make a ten-strike or to get his tail most beautifully caught in a crack. "Rev," he asked, "did a package come for me?"

"Yee-op, it's out in t' trunk room. It's heavy as all get out."

"Should be. It's full of books."

"Booze, you say?"

"I wish it was. These are books—every damned volume the store had on the subject of firearms, and they had plenty."

"Oh yeah?" Barney's curiosity was highly practical. "Who's gonna pay for all this reading matter?"

"I'm counting on the city to pick up the tab—if we catch McNiff and the killer. If we don't, I guess you and I'll split the bill."

"That's a smart idea! I can just hear my missus: 'Reader-schmeader you became, already; ain't the *Sat'day Evening Post* big enough for you?' And how much of my month's pay would splitting the cost leave me?"

"We'll worry about that when we have to," Harty said, and silently promised himself he'd dislocate a vertebra trying not to have to.

"But whatcha gonna *do* with the books?" Rev asked.

"Read 'em—it 'll improve my mind."

"Y' won't have time t' read 'em all. T' package is as big's this." Rev spread his arms. "Y'd do better t' be out looking for t' killer."

"I'll make time—if I have to sit up all night," the sergeant assured him. "And while I'm going through those books I'll be looking for the killer. Dammit all, no matter how amateurish the load was, I don't believe the killer improvised the gun. There's sure to be a background for it somewhere, and right after dinner I'm going to get to work and find it."

3

It was well past midnight when Barney Stauffer climbed to the little upstairs room where, since dinner, the sergeant had been pursuing the will-o'-the-wisp hope of a clew to the mysterious gun through a maze of detail about culverins and hackbuts, Prussian needle guns and muschites, petronels and bombardes and blunderbusses.

A pile of hastily scanned books lay on the floor. Tobart's *Guns: A Comprehensive Study* was in the washbasin where it had been flung; *Artillery,* by Captain Allan Archibald Lewis was under the bureau; *The Story of Firearms* was in a remote corner; and *A History of Sporting Guns, American and European,* by one Horatio Bott, lay open on the table in front of the sergeant. To the right of the Bott opus, a fifth of scotch was almost empty; to the left, an ash tray overflowed with burnt-out butts in mute testimony to the aid alcohol and tobacco had given the research work.

Cass Harty sat slumped in his chair, a grin on his face and a darkish scotch and soda clasped in his right hand.

"You getting much?" Barney questioned.

The sergeant had a belt at the scotch and murmured something to the effect that there was nothing under forty registered at the Sea Spray and, anyway, he hadn't been out of the room.

"I meant from the books."

"We'll see what you think." Harty spun the book around to face the stocky little detective. "I hate to go off the deep end—but this looks so damned good I'm almost afraid to admit it. Run your eye down this page "

. . . originally indigenous to Europe and used, as the name implies, from a punt, or flat-bottomed rowboat. Wealthy planters imported them to the colonies as a means of supplying duck and other game as food for their vast numbers of slaves. The punt gun was admirably adapted to this purpose, since it harvested enormous quantities of birds with every shot.

Its barrel was frequently more than nine feet long, and the weapon weighed in the neighborhood of one hundred pounds. According to the predilections of the individual gunsmith its bore varied, sometimes approaching two inches; and it carried a charge of ten ounces of powder and a pound and a half of shot. It was a powerful weapon and capable of projecting this amazing load a distance of better than one hundred and fifty yards.

Nor can it be said that this unique and valuable arm was always restricted to its original purpose. There are recorded instances of several of these guns being carried westward from Virginia and the Carolinas by early settlers and employed, from a fixed mount within the primitive stockades, to repel Indian attacks with devastating losses . . . .*

*An historically accurate fact.

"A punt gun, huh?" Barney muttered.

"Yeah—now don't get me wrong." Harty emptied the last of the scotch into his glass and held it between his eyes and the light. "After all it may only be this stuff — it's done funny things to me before. But I think that punt gun fits in. Its history on this side of the Atlantic goes back to colonial days; it throws a hell of a load of shot a long distance; it's been used to kill human beings in the past; and it was originally designed to be fired from a boat. That takes care of every angle we've got to face."

"Damned tootin', it does." Barney liked to show outward caution but his tone gave away his real excitement. "This sounds like the gun they used, all right;

now all we got to do is figure out where they keep it and who's been shooting it off."

"I've got something that 'll help me with that job." The sergeant ripped the pages containing descriptions and diagrams of the punt gun from the book and folded them into his wallet. No snooper was going to stumble on that lead if he could help it. "Do you remember I said Dunster had told me about a man whose family tree ran 'way back to the days of the Virginia Colony?"

Stauffer stood with one foot on the rung of a chair and scratched at his head. "Doggone," he said, "I ain't sure."

"I'm sure about it," Harty told him. "And I remember who the man was—Randall Elrod!"

SATURDAY

RAGGED shreds of fog and batlike veils of flying spindrift rode the offshore wind a swirling steeplechase along the beach in the dead morning light. The air was full of sharp needle points of sand which drove like Spandau bullets against the faces of the two detectives as they tightroped along the creaking boards of the tiny pier where Randall Elrod's dinghy was customarily moored.

"Do you think this thing's safe?" Barney asked.

"Probably—until the storm gets here. We won't wait for that."

Down wind at the end of a long painter, the dink danced an eccentric nautical cancan to the saxophone whine of the gale.

"She looks like a Central Park rowboat to me," Stauffer muttered. "All it needs is a couple sailors and their girl friends."

Cass Harty hauled in on the painter until the dinghy came alongside. He swung down into its rocking hollowness and told Barney to come on.

"Me? In that peanut shell? Say, Gen Crane didn't feed us that swell breakfast so we should throw it to the fishes."

"Quit clowning. It 'll only take a minute to see if we're right." Harty steadied the dink beside the pier. "This is important."

"I don't see why." Barney climbed in and perched squarely upon the long coiled rope that was made fast to a cleat at the stern. He braced his feet against the middle thwart and growled, "I wouldn't know one of these scows from another."

"Well, if a punt gun was used at all, I'm betting it was fired from this baby."

"Does it have to be a boat? How about shooting from

on land?"

"They'd have needed a solid base to rest it on; that kind of gun couldn't be fired from anyone's shoulder. The gun's traditional mount was a boat."

"That don't say it's gotta be *this* boat."

"It comes damned close. Outside of a dink at the club pier and some fishermen's dories down near East Point, I doubt if you'll find any other small boats on this side of the island. They're all around on the bay."

"It 'll still be tough proving all this in court."

"Not too tough." Cass Harty had been inspecting the inner woodwork of the dinghy closely as he talked. "Look at this."

Stauffer examined a forward thwart. "It's cracked!"

"Right! And here's how it probably happened. We know the punt guns had a terrible kick. Now, if you'll look at this picture from the book, you'll notice that there was a deep notch in the butt of each gun. The idea was to pass a rope through that notch so as to take up the backward thrust when the gun was fired."

"So . . ."

"Then, when the other end of the rope was fastened to something *nearer* to the target than the gun's butt, the recoil would be absorbed, being distributed over the entire framework of the boat and passed off into the water. That way, the shooter, who stood by and fired the gun with a lanyard, was perfectly safe. But it seems to me that the thing the forward end of the shock-absorbing rope was fastened to needed to be stronger than this thwart. That's the reason the thwart is split now." The sergeant slid forward to the bow, almost causing Barney heart failure as the dink responded to the change in weight by trying to nose under a huge wave.

An instant later the attack was made nearly fatal when he said, "Shove up here, will you? This is something worth seeing."

On a certain memorable occasion Barney Stauffer had walked coolly into a Brownesville cellar where a pair of hop heads, who had sworn to get him, waited with drawn guns. A little later, with knuckles bleeding, a furrow above one temple, and the dark leather of his blackjack redly stained, he had walked out again and summoned an ambulance.

But now, as he edged forward to a place beside the sergeant, his face showed he would gladly have taken a twirl at a dozen similar cellars rather than have any such intimate traffic with a frail boat on a bucking sea.

The weight of the two men made the little craft ride perilously low. Waves washed almost over the gunwale as Barney studied the indicated spot. Then he worked his way back to the stern and sat gratefully down, letting his breath go in a long "Whoooosh!"

"It adds up nicely," Harty said. "What do you think?"

"I think you're nuts," Barney growled. "You take a chance on drownding the two of us, just to show me a hole in a piece of wood!"

"And a nice new hole it is!" Harty exulted. "You can see it was bored recently. And there could only be one reason for boring a hole right there in the stem."

He reached back and plucked an oarlock from its socket beside the center thwart. "The killer had to have a rest —preferably a swiveling rest—for the barrel of his gun, and"—the oarlock was stabbed into the hole, filling it snugly—"I think this was it."

"You win!" Barney said. "Can we get the hell out of this?"

"We can—the boat's told all it has to tell." Harty hauled in on the painter, let Barney scramble onto the pier, and then followed.

As he stood on the slippery boards, measuring distances with his eye, the sergeant felt that he had the entire process worked out. The night tide would have a slight run in the direction of the barbecue furnace, permitting the killer to cast off from the pier and, sculling with one oar at the stern of the dink, bring himself opposite the furnace very rapidly. Somewhere off there,

possibly between the buoy and the float, he would be
ready. Erect in sculling position, he would have the finest
possible view of the fire and the prospective victim before
it. A quick alignment of the gun, a tug on the lanyard,
and the job would be over. Then, with the beach a scene
of frenzy, and all attention focused, not on the sea, but on
the horror in front of the flames, he would have had
ample opportunity to beach the dinghy and rejoin the
others.

"This figures to be the boat, all right." Barney broke in
upon his reasoning. "But who used it?"

"Well, Randall Elrod put money into the Enterprises.
People keep saying he'd like to own the earth. He gave us
a pretty odd story. The background of the gun matches up
with his background—and this is his boat."

"So . . ."

"So, I'm making no promises—but let's go see Randall
Elrod."

2

Barney was shivering from the unseasonable cold as
they climbed the steps. "This," he grumbled, "is what you
call weather."

"I've got a hunch it's only the beginning," Harty said.
"The real storm will probably be riding on its tail."

The appearance of the Elrod home indicated that its
occupants were expecting something extra fancy in the
way of a storm. All porch furniture had been moved
inside and every window and door was tightly closed.
From the mast in the center of the green square of lawn
out front, flags snapped like bull whips in the wind, blue
over red, yellow beside blue, and blue stripe, white stripe,
blue stripe, overtopping all.

Cass Harty crossed the porch and bumped urgent
knuckles down the panel of the door. He let a moment
pass, then rapped again, and more loudly.

After tho door had been whacked a third time, Barney

ventured, "Maybe they're asleep."

Harty looked at his wrist watch. "If they're not up now, I feel sorry for them." He tried the door, found it locked, and rattled it enthusiastically. "Damned sorry for them—because Elrod's going to answer a few questions if I have to yank him out of bed to do it."

"We'll bust in?"

"If there's no other way." Harty abandoned the front door as too solidly constructed for what he had in mind. He followed the broad curve of the porch around to the lee side of the house. "Sometimes you can do this if the frame's warped a little," he said. "It saves kicking a window in."

Stauffer watched him grip the doorknob and jiggle it smartly. One, two, three—hard forward shove. One, two, three—another thrust. Four times he repeated the effort and on the last try the lock hopped out of its slot.

A wide sunroom, bright with bold-patterned chintz and wicker furniture, was before them. A hall and the arch of heavy-balustered stairs could be seen through an inner door.

"I'll go up," the sergeant said. "Barney, you might sort of have a look around." His gaze slanted toward a secretary in the living room beyond. "In an entirely legal way, of course, in case Elrod should come downstairs in a hurry."

"I get it." Barney's tone implied that his snooping would be conducted with all the circumspection of Sir Basil Zaharoff arranging for a border incident.

At the top of the stairs a broad hall ran the length of the house. In it chairs were squat ghosts in their pale linen covers, and a grandfather's clock, whose hands showed eight minutes past four of an unidentifiable day, gave the impression of having gone unwound since the previous fall. Six bedrooms, each with attached bath, and one with sitting room as well, opened off the corridor.

Each was empty now, though two had been slept in.

That'd be Tenny and Randall Elrod, the sergeant

thought. Morgan the Dizz must have dossed somewhere else.

A climb to the third story revealed that the walls of the chambers originally on that floor had been knocked down to form a huge aerie which was half game room and half cocktail lounge.

A bar duplicated the line of the wall at the detective's right and a postage-stamp dance floor spread its meager, polished surface immediately in front of him. A ping-pong table and layouts for roulette and bird cage were at the room's further end. Against the wall opposite the bar, tiny chromium tables and chairs were incongruously near an old-fashioned glass-doored bookcase which had been converted to serve as a trophy rack, and, to provide music, a combination radio and phonograph bulked large between the two wide windows that looked out to sea.

There were pictures over the bar, waggish in intent and leaning heavily upon the alimentary for their humor. Above the pictures, a row of sturdy iron pegs currently held nothing. They looked solid enough to have once supported something heavy—possibly a punt gun.

Cass Harty helped himself moderately from a bottle of Irish whisky and leaned against the bar, looking at the pictures and reflecting upon the importance of locale in humor.

The Irish was good, and when it was finished he found and snapped an electric switch to supplement the gray light from outside.

Immediately, the gleam of silver in the trophy case attracted him.

The well-stocked wide shelves were evidence that the Elrods went in for pothunting with considerable success. Guerdons of assorted size and importance were placed with seeming carelessness; a carelessness which had not, however, been carried to a point where it would prevent the more notable winnings from being recognized.

Without pausing to catalogue, Harty noted a second place in the North and South Open at Pinehurst, taken in the late '20s; a blue for a Welsh terrier which had gone best of breed at the Westminster; a win in the five-gaited division at Rye; and a cup from the annual Moth regatta at Daytona among others on the top shelf.

Monotonous as a column of infantry, Jubilee's winnings were ranked on the ledge below. The dates engraved on the small chalices made it apparent that the trim sloop had romped off with the Labor Day races of the Ocean Club, year after year.

Older and less valued garnerings were haphazard on the lowest shelf. A varsity letter, ringed by bronze and silver medals. A football, bearing on its grass-stained surface the India-inked score of a long-ago fall struggle. A picture of a youthful-looking Randall Elrod in the center of a jerseyed group captioned: "1913—Unbeaten, Unscored on." A black rubber hockey puck, mounted with a silver band. Two smallish cups, like outriders, guarding the ends of the shelf.

More in curiosity than thoroughness, the sergeant inspected the medals and discovered they had been won by Morgan Elrod in dash and hurdle events of college track meets of a bygone day. The cups, likewise, were souvenirs of intercollegiate competition; one for the free style championship, the other for the plunge; also his.

"Hell!" Cass Harty muttered. "*Morgan* Elrod!"

He returned one cup to the shelf and, with the other jammed beneath his arm, went down the stairs.

Barney was innocent-faced beside an apparently undisturbed secretary. "Not a damned thing in it," he said from the side of his mouth. "What'd Old Baldy have to say?"

"He wasn't up there," Harty said. "But this was."

Stauffer studied the inscription on the cup. "So the loony was kind of an athalete in his day," he murmured. "A swimmer too. Say! Waaait a minute—I thought he *couldn't* swim!"

"So did I. But it turns out he's a champ."

"When he went overboard with you, he hadda be

saved. What's the matter—did he forget how to swim?"

"I know three things nobody forgets, once he's learned to do them right. Two of them are riding a bicycle and swimming. When you catch the knack it's with you for life. But that bird hung onto me and damned near wore me out. It means that he's either as crazy as they say he is and doesn't know he can swim, or else the son of a bitch was trying to kill me in cold blood."

"If that's so," Barney demanded, "what's to keep all the stuff we worked up against his cousin from fitting him?"

"Nothing! Yes, there is something. Morgan wasn't in on the business end. He'd have no motive against Wade —and nothing in the world to tie him up to the Messingers. Damn it all, here we are with a swell case against Randall, and Morgan has to butt in. Aren't we ever going to get a clear trail?" In his exasperation he slammed the cup to the floor.

It split into three pieces.

A smaller crash sounded like an echo behind them. It was made by Kay Franklin closing the door of the sunroom.

"I saw you trying to get in," she said, loosening the belt of the man's polo coat she wore. "So I came over to see what you wanted."

Cass Harty's temper was still up. "We wanted to get in," he snapped. "And we got in."

Kay grinned. "I imagine you also wanted to see Randall Elrod," she teased. "And five will get you ten if you did."

"You'd take my five." Harty matched her grin but only with his features. "Do you know where he is?"

"Um-hum!" Her head bobbed pertly as she turned to face the rear windows. "Out there somewhere—in Jubilee."

"You're crazy." Barney rushed to the end of the room and peered out, trying to locate a sail somewhere on the dark turbulence of the bay. The *Editha*, wallowing laboriously toward the island, was the only craft in sight. "People with sense don't take boats out in this kind of weather."

"Elrod and Dunster did—a couple of hours ago," Kay answered. "And I'm not crazy, but you look as if you were."

Harty said, "Maybe *I* am." He could see no reason for the two men to sail out into the start of a storm. Unless . .
.

"Why pick a day like this?" Stauffer asked. "Don't they get enough of boats in nice weather?"

"The answer to that is the same as why Randall sits for hours fishing—he likes it. I argued with him and told him he was foolish to go. He had chills last night —and he's got a dreadful cold. But you can't sway him. First he asked Tenny to go along, but Adrian begged off. He said he couldn't find his glasses, but I think he hid them when he saw Randall taking three reefs in the sail. So then Moy said *he'd* go, and Adrian looked a lot more cheerful."

"Did they say how long they'd be gone?"

"Not to me. What on earth are you getting so excited about? Randall takes Jubilee out every day he's down here—no matter how rough the water is—" She broke off suddenly as Harty moved toward the door. "Why, where are you going?"

"Who, me? Down to Crane's store. I have to send a telegram," he said—which was an understatement.

3

In Rev's emporium the sergeant dictated not one, but three telegrams over the wire to the operator on the mainland. He sent the first with his eye on Rev's clock and not too much hope in his heart, since the hands of the clock were drawing near to twelve and the detective was well aware of the penchant of government employees for quitting work exactly on time. The message which he hoped would get to Albany before noon was a request for

all available data on the papers of incorporation issued to
Wade Enterprises at the time of its organization and for a
summary of its income-tax payments during the last year
or two.

The second wire went to Police Headquarters, New
York City, and was longer than the first. It had to be, for
it cited the names and serial numbers of the bonds found
in Charley Wade's investment portfolio and asked that
they be checked to see if any were listed by the Stolen
Securities Division.

Message number three was the shortest.

"Things," Harty read into the phone. "Yes, sister, t as
in terrible, h as in half-wit, i as in idiot, n as in nerts, g as
in godhelpus, and s as in stupidity. That's it: Things . . .
getting . . . hotter . . . here . . . stop . . . what . . . is . . .
delaying . . . you . . . question mark . . . stop . . . shake . . .
the . . . lead . . . out ... of . . . your . . . uh . . . shoes. Yes,
the last word is 'shoes.' And the message is signed H-a-r-
t-y." He listened while she read it back to him, fed coins
into the slot, and hung up, lamenting: "More damned
routine work. If I get one good answer out of the three,
I'm a fool for luck."

"T'at Roscoe Bennet t' last wire went to," Rev said.
"Ain't he t' feller y' sent those nails and stuff to on
Wednesday?"

"Same guy. I can't figure what's holding him back. I
thought he'd finish the comparisons the same day the
stuff reached him." The sergeant did not leave the phone,
for one more angle had to be covered. "What's the phone
number of that sour-puss little cop over in Keyesport?"

"2-4-5. Why?"

Money clanked in the coin box and Harty told the
operator "2-4-5," before he shoved the receiver into Rev's
hands and ordered: "Tell him Jubilee's been stolen."

"Her? Stole?" Rev's chin dropped. "Y' durn fool, if she
puts inta Keyesport with Elrod aboard they'll know she
ain't."

"Sure. And the first thing they'll do will be to call you

up to have the laugh on you—and then we'll know where
Elrod's gone. But if they knew we needed the information,
all Rockefeller's dough couldn't buy it from them. Do as I
say." To shut off argument he turned away from Rev and
walked out of the store.

Sea mist was rolling along the sandy slope, whirled on
the bitter wind; and below the sergeant the surly gray
Atlantic lunged and beat upon the shore and gathered
itself to lunge again. He looked at it listlessly and was
hearing, with even less interest, Rev's endless wrangling
with the dour Frosty Davis when, improbable as
something taking shape beneath a magician's wand, the
figure of a little white-haired man limped out of the murk
of the bay slope.

Cass Harty blinked his eyes. He could not believe that
he was seeing Inspector John Kennaston MacIver, his
boss, and big gun of the Detective Division of the New
York Police Department.

The thin small figure limped on. Product of damaged
motor centers on the right side of the brain, the limp
dated back to the previous October when an improvised
blackjack, wielded by a homicidal undergraduate at
Cardaff University, had splintered MacIver's skull. But
even the club of Hercules, swung by the Fourth
Horseman of the Apocalypse, could not have extinguished
the chill vitality of MacIver's icy gaze, nor crushed the
fanatic devotion to police work from his soul. From
October till February, he had been flat in bed in the
Uptown General Hospital, and in early March he had
embarked on a six-weeks period of torture in the effort of
relearning how to walk. Now he was making up for lost
time.

"Sergeant!" The inspector's voice was not old. It bored
like a gelid diamond drill through the yards of fog and
cracked against Harty's eardrums. "Where is Stauffer?"

Rev responded to the voice like a doll on a string. He
popped out of the store, asking, "Who's t' little guy? Never
saw him before."

"Barney's up the Line, sir." Harty finally began to credit the presence of his chief. "He's keeping an eye on the home of a man who's missing?"

"Tchuh! Still doing things the hard way, aren't you? Sitting at ratholes may work when you've the men for it, but down here . . ." He made a short, controlled gesture indicative of complete hopelessness. "Is this the man who allowed McNiff to break jail?"

"Didn't let him," Rev defended. "He bruk out while I was busy tending store."

"Well, I want him. We've got to have him. If getting him means catching the person responsible for these murders, well and good—but *I want McNiff.*"

"Those gov'ment men say they'll get him soon," Rev offered. "They tol' me it'd be t'day or t'morrow."

"*They'll* get . . ." The federals missed a blasting only because someone shouted up from the crest:

"Hey, Rev Crane! Trouble!"

"Guess it's McNiff, swiping more stuff," Rev said, as a boy in khaki pants stumbled toward them.

"The kid's from the west half of the island," Harty said. "Barney and I've covered that. I doubt if it's about Tootie."

Rev steadied the trembling boy. "What's up, sonny?"

The youngster looked sidewise at Harty and MacIver. "Well," he drawled in contrast to his former excitement, "there's a boat in trouble off West Point. I seen her through m' gran'pop's spyglass."

"T'at's a job for t' Coast Guard; not us. How big is she?"

"Little twenty-one-footer. She's the one wins the race every year—the Jubilee."

"An' y' run down here t' tell us 'stead o' lending a hand?" Rev raged, his instincts less those of cop than waterman. "B'George, I don't know what's the matter with t' young folks nowadays."

"They didn't need no help." The boy sounded aggrieved. "I seen the two fellers swim ashore. They made it all right and went for the shack at the Point."

"Then why 'n the name o' goodness did y' come at all?"

"I'll tell you if you'll walk over here." The boy moved away, his eyes proclaiming distrust of city folk. "I won't say nothing in front of them fellers."

"This one's a cop." Rev endorsed Harty. "Y' can talk out."

"Well, then." The youngster drew a deep breath and blurted: "It was on account of them killings."

"Killin's?"

"Yep—the ones on the beach. I seen Jubilee go over and—and I know good and well it wasn't no ord'nary knockdown."

"Take it easy, Bud." Harty patted the boy reassuringly on the shoulder. "What was wrong with the way she tipped over?"

"A whole lot. I know the feller at the helm done it on purpose!—Scout's honor, he did. I had Gran'pop's glass right on 'em. They was sailing along with three reefs and that ol' Jubilee's right seaworthy—they needn't have gone over. Course it was blowing hard, but it was blowing steady and I've seen her sailed in worse weather. Anyhow, feller owns her is supposed to be the best sailor on the Head. Nobody's telling me he'd of held her that close on the wind if he didn't want a knock-down."

"No sense t' t'at," Rev muttered, " 'less'n . . .'"

MacIver snapped, "Unless what?"

Cass Harty said nothing. He saw no sense to such a move in any case—but he was wondering how swiftly he could get to West Point.

"Less'n he wanted t' drownd Dunster an' himself," Rev ended.

"I seen 'em *both* get on the beach," the boy reminded.

Elrod deliberately turns his own boat over in rough weather, Harty thought, and then he swims to a lonely headland with the *only other surviving partner* in Wade Enterprises!

". . . and corruption!" he concluded a tripartite

category. "We've got to make the Point. Who's got the fastest boat around here, Rev?"

"Mr Dunster, I reckon." Rev looked off at the angry whitecaps, calculating the weather. "But his speedboat 'd founder, like as not, in this kinda sea. Don't b'lieve my old Lily C would, though."

Without knowing the situation MacIver sensed its importance. He grabbed Rev's shoulder and swung him around. "Where's this boat of yours?" he demanded. "We're starting now."

"Down thisaway." At the foot of the bay slope a battered Seabright dory bobbed, riding the rollers like a merganser duck.

Harty discerned true and sturdy lines beneath the superficial shabbiness of worn paint. He said, "She looks as if she could take a beating and come back for more."

"What do you care?" MacIver rasped. "You want those men."

"Don't worry 'bout my boat, she's safe as a church," Rev boasted. "Ride any sea a Coast Guard boat will, and she's got a geared-down auto engine in her that 'll move her right along."

The inspector looked glacially furious that anyone could think him capable of worry about his personal well-being. "What are you after these two for?" he asked Harty.

"They're partners with Wade—at least Dunster admits he is."

"And Elrod?"

"Says ixnay—but Wade's widow and Dunster both claim he's in."

MacIver snarled, "Get that engine going!"

"Yes *sir!*" Rev yanked a tarpaulin from a husky-looking eight-in-line motor and kicked her over.

She caught like tinder and Harty said, "Sweet job!"

"Right there when y' need her." Rev threw in the clutch and shoved the tiller over. The motor drummed like the hoofbeats of a troop of Don Cossacks, and they roared westward, their wake vanishing instantly in the heavy seas.

The inspector wiped liquid salt from his eyes with a coat sleeve. "How do they tie up with the Messingers?"

"They don't," Harty said. "Nobody does." The Lily C bucked across the top of a hill of water, making him grasp a thwart for balance. "I've been going nuts, trying to figure out why."

A succeeding wave which would have sunk Dunster's speedboat smashed itself powerfully upon their bow and dissolved into sheets of spray.

MacIver kneeled, gray faced, on the floor boards, grease from the engine staining his decent dark suit. "And with McNiff?"

"One of the Dunster crowd put the finger on him—it's hard to say just who." Harty crouched beside his boss and wished for a spray hood. He was wet to the skin, from shoes to haircut.

The Lily C raced magnificently across Himalayas of tumbling brine while Rev did things to the throttle, feeding his eight big ones more and more gas. Seasickness settled down on MacIver and agonized retchings shook his spare frame in endless sequence, but between them he managed to gasp, "Haven't you made any progress at all?"

"Some," Harty said, and gave his chief a precis of his activities. Thankful for the motor's roar that walled Rev off from the confidences, he even explained his theory of the punt gun; but when he had finished the outline it seemed to him that the results of his work boiled down very small.

"You're making a good try—but in this game trying's not enough." MacIver's voice was muffled by the arm on which his head had slumped. Spray formed a tiny puddle in the hollow at the back of his thin neck. "We've got to win every time we leave the stable."

Harty knew that—he had been hearing it long enough.

"We'll hafta tie up there." Rev began to round in toward an old dock well short of the Point. "No landing nearer."

MacIver raised his head and swept the bay with his gaze. "Their boat must've gone down," he said. "I don't see her."

"She might have drifted. Funny an experienced waterman like Elrod didn't get an anchor over."

"Make no never-mind if he did," Rev said. "Anchor'd drag in this kind of sea. Rougher now than I've ever seen her in summer." He fended for the landing while MacIver scrambled out.

The old man's face was like the mask of a corpse but Harty knew him too well to dare to offer aid. "You said summer?" The words burst from the inspector like an imprecation as he stood on the pier, wringing ice water from his clothes. "Is that the shack?"

"Yeah." Harty made for it. "We were in it yesterday."

Ahead of them, smoke of a dirty yellow oiliness curled thickly from the length of rusted pipe that served as chimney.

"Anyway," Rev said, "we can get warm."

Cass Harty's sodden windbreaker felt like the upper half of a refrigerated shroud, but he stilled his chattering teeth long enough to say, "Good thing! I'm colder than a politician's heart." He reached the shack a step ahead of the limping inspector and smashed at the door with his fist.

An echo, dull as the sound of a punctured drum, was the only answer.

He turned the knob and thrust the door open.

Acid foulness billowed in a cloud, enveloping them.

"Pee-yew!" Rev snorted. "I'd 'a' durn sight sooner freeze."

"They must be burning the old blanket to make a smell like that," Harty guessed. With the others he stood well back, waiting for the ocean blasts to vitiate the smoke and give them a glimpse of the interior of the hut.

"Mist' Elrod—Hey! Mr Dunster, you in there?" Rev called.

He got no response.

Through the thinning cumulus of yellow vapor Cass Harty could see the old cracked stove glowing cherry red. He covered his nose with his handkerchief, still soggy with brine, and stepped inside.

Randall Elrod lay face down on the dingy cot, covered from feet to the middle of his back by the moldy blanket. From a broken-runged chair his clothes dripped sea water onto the bare floor boards. His right hand, cramped like the talons of a condor, gripped his neck; and drifting curtains of the vile-smelling smoke swayed and hovered above him.

Cass Harty said, "Hell!" Grabbing the chair, he punched out the panes of both the windows.

Sea air rushed through in a perfect draft, clearing the place rapidly. But even as the smoke thinned, the scarifying penetration of its reek still outraged their nostrils.

Rev touched Elrod's naked shoulder. "Wake up," he said. "Are you all right?"

Under the whistling gale from door and windows the fire hummed like a blast furnace.

Cass Harty looked at the fuel remaining beside the stove—small broken bits of dead-black stuff.

"Inspector," he said, "something's screwy. Yesterday there was a big pile of ordinary driftwood here."

Examining the drab things, MacIver coughed deep in his chest. "This stuff has been machined," he said. "It looks to me like that casing they have on storage batteries."

Cass Harty thought so too. He looked at the figure on the cot and tried to remember whether he had heard or read about something like that before. There'd have to be a post—that would show.

"Wake up, Mist' Elrod," Rev urged again. He turned to the city men, complaining, "I can't get him woke."

The inspector touched a pulseless wrist. "Who'll have jurisdiction in this godforsaken place?"

"They've got a coroner over on the mainland who wouldn't make a good veterinarian," Harty said. He took a turn of the blanket about Elrod's middle, got an arm beneath the unresisting form, and heaved it onto his shoulder.

"Local cops?"

Bending with his burden to clear the doorway, the sergeant explained in crisp, few-lettered words how the local cops were even worse. "I know this is cutting corners," he added, "but there's something about this business that just misses connections with my memory. I want a post-mortem on Elrod as fast as possible. Larsen at the san, is a long way from being the world's best doctor, but he ought to be able to tell us what happened here."

MacIver's head wagged as they started back for the Lily C. "You're still doing it the hard way," he muttered, "but it's still a good try."

4

Evening was shutting down on Sand Head as Cass Harty and Inspector MacIver came through a door and looked, for the second time that day, at Randall Elrod lying face downward.

There was a notable difference this time, for the man's scalp was pulled down across his face like the husk of some obscene fruit, and the heavy bony structure of the skull had been sawed away, exposing the brain.

The wrinkled grayish mass of the cerebrum looked cold and soggy.

"You two may come in," MacIver said, "—if you can stand it."

"I think *I* can." Kay Franklin stepped firmly over the threshold, her glance challenging anyone to deny she was as good a man as any present.

Cass Harty thought she looked more of a man than her pallid suitor who followed.

Stauffer came in after them and looked bored. "Couldn't find the others," he reported. "Crane's still trying."

The sergeant asked himself if the others had deliberately made themselves scarce.

"I didn't have you brought here to witness a chamber of horrors," MacIver told the man and girl. "I wanted all the members of the house party to appreciate what is happening—so that they may be on their guard." His words told less than half the truth. "We are ready, Doctor."

"It is my opinion that this was a natural death." Larsen took an instrument from a tray and posed it above the spilt-melon of Elrod's skull. "A very usual thing," he added. "I will let you see for yourselves."

"Interesting." Harty rested his knuckles on the cold cleanliness of the table and leaned toward the corpse. No use admitting he lacked knowledge enough to be certain.

"This is typical of cerebromeningitis," Larsen went on. "A very evident inflammation of the cortex, you see . . ." The shiny steel hovered back and forth above the kneaded-looking coils. "Such inflammation is always to be found, post mortem, in cases of cerebrospinal fever."

"It was meningitis, was it?" Harty was picking at an association of ideas which stubbornly refused to come full focus. "For an apparently well man he went out damned fast."

"That is not, of itself, extraordinary," the doctor said judicially. "I have seen people linger many days with it— and I have also seen them die in a few hours. It all depends: some forms will be of malignant character from the outset and, when they are, death comes very rapidly."

"Then you'll certify his death was caused by nothing other than meningitis?"

"It most probably was that." Larson had the typical medico's reluctance to give a straight answer. "I wonder if he had shown any symptoms?"

"He'd been feeling badly since Thursday," Kay said promptly. "Isn't that so?"

"He complained a little," Tenny agreed. "We thought it was just a cold coming on."

"A common error." Larsen's tone implied that that settled everything.

"You *will* certify it as meningitis?" Harty persisted.

"Ah . . . I'd feel much more certain if . . ." The instrument moved across the brain once more. "Or rather, as I've said, the condition of the meninges makes it look very much like a true meningitis. But with that, it is customary to find serum in the ventricular and arachnoid spaces." The steel pointed in turn to almost microscopic tubes and tiny triangular areas. "Such serum is not apparent in this case."

Harty's mind was made up. "I guess those things will happen," he said largely. "It must have been meningitis."

He would cheerfully have bet his future it was not.

"Oh," Kay said, "I hate to think he suffered so."

The sergeant thought her face wore a rather good imitation of concern. "Tell the others about it," he said, "when you get back."

"Ronnie and Laura and Chet are due at the house. The yacht had to stand further off shore on account of the blow."

"Well." MacIver turned to the two detectives. "There's nothing more for us here."

"Nor us." Kay was obviously proud of having gotten by without wilting. With an air of See-what-a-brave-girl-am-I she took Tenny's arm. "We'll be going."

"Wait." He blinked at the three policemen. "Shouldn't something be done about notifying Elrod's relatives?"

"Of course. Outside of Morgan, who are they?"

"An uncle, Pendleton Elrod, in Charleston; a brother, Devereaux, in Grosse Pointe; and two nieces on the Coast, Santa Barbara, I believe. But Morgan alone inherits."

Cass Harty's face remained expressionless, but he

raged inwardly. Again he was face to face with the old problem of double complications that cropped up at each new turn of the case. With Elrod dead and Dunster missing, a pat and simple hypothesis presented itself. But Morgan's status as his cousin's heir made things tougher. "Wire them," he told Tenny. "Or get them on the phone."

"I'd offer to let you call from here," the doctor said, "but, unfortunately, our phone is out of order."

"That suits me." Tenny looked pleased. "I'd sooner let Dunster tell them anyway. He knows them better than I do."

"On that basis, it's a good idea—but there's a catch in it," Harty said. "We don't know what's become of Dunster."

"Oh." Kay swayed slightly. "*He* can't be dead too."

"Now, Kay, darling," Tenny murmured encouragingly, and slipped an arm about her. There was more of weak amorousness than support in the gesture.

Kay knew it. Her hand slid beneath his, moving it away. "But Moy was so alive this morning. I can see him laughing as he started down the hill."

Harty thought: He was laughing the first time I ever saw him. He said, "What's all this about?"

"I—I can't help it. Another death would be too much."

"The ones we've had already have been too much for me," Tenny said nervously. "But he didn't say Dunster had . . ."

The sergeant's glance stopped him. "Why are you so sure Dunster is dead?" Harty asked Kay.

"Didn't you . . . I mean, I thought that was what you were going to say. Hasn't he been drowned?"

"Possibly," Harty said. "But I haven't seen his body." He stepped through the door and followed MacIver and Barney down the long hall.

"Funny play for her to make," Stauffer grunted. "Was she leveling when she figured Dunster dead?"

Harty threw his hands in the air. "Don't ask me to tell you if a woman really means what she says! But this

stunt of looking at a skull full of fresh-killed brains
without batting an eye, and then getting all goose flesh
over a mere drowning, doesn't ring true. Maybe the first
used up all her nervous strength—I wouldn't know.
Maybe she knows what's become of Dunster."

"What a life," Barney groaned. "Have we got three to
look for now? Morgan Elrod, Dunster and Tootie."

"No more than two," MacIver said brusquely. "Three
aren't hiding out on one small island . . . not alive. I think
Dunster's killed Morgan Elrod, or Morgan's killed him.
The business angle would fit, either way. Forget Tootie in
connection with this—he doesn't match up anywhere."

"Serge-unt!" Rev darted at them out of the waiting
room near the front door, "I located t' folks from the
yacht. They was at my hotel all t' time. They said
straight-out they'd be durned if they'd come out in any
such storm t' look at a dead man. Claimed he'd keep till t'
storm went down."

"Didn't it occur to you to make them come?" MacIver
asked contemptuously.

"Don't know's I'd 'a' felt just right doing t'at," Rev
hedged. "Not whilst they was my paying guests."

Johnny MacIver said, through gritted teeth, "God in
heaven!"

"No call t' git annoyed—business is business, y' know."
Rev reached inside the heavy sheep-lined coat he wore
and brought out two folded bits of paper. "Tellygrams for
y', Serge," he said. "They phoned 'em over from t'
mainland. Eben won't make no more trips with th' Editha
till t' storm's done." He passed both pieces of paper to the
detective. "Gen wrote it down just like it came over."

The first of the two was from the lieutenant in charge
of the Stolen Securities squad. It acknowledged Harty's
wire, informed him that the requested check-over had
been made, and reported that six of the bonds were red
hot. The message closed with a request that Harty
impound the certificates for more complete identification.

"I'd oblige, if I could," the sergeant said. "But the

bonds are still in Wade's office."

The second sheet of ruled notepaper bore a shorter tale:

RETURNED TRIP YESTERDAY AND FOUND YOUR PACKAGE
STOP
NO LEAD IN MY SHOES
STOP
SPECIMEN NUMBER FOUR MATCHES MASTER SPECIMEN BEYOND ANY DOUBT
STOP
ADVISE GETTING LEAD OUT OF MY OWN SHOES OR SOMETHING
STOP
REGARDS
ROSCOE BENNET

"Boss," Harty handed the note to the inspector, "it sure looks as if you hit it right on the nose with that crack about it being between Morgan Elrod and Dunster. This master specimen Bennet mentions was a nail-head that I took out of Hubert Messinger's body."

"Smart work, getting Bennet in on it." MacIver looked as near to being pleased as his nature would permit. "And what's this number four?"

"That's a nail too. A nail that I pulled out of the wall of LeMoyne Dunster's brand-new cabana!"

SUNDAY

SERGEANT CASS HARTY sagged tired shoulders above his empty coffee cup and stared morosely at a stain in the center of the tablecloth.

MacIver was upstairs in bed, his slender strength exhausted by a fruitless all-night prowl of the island which he had insisted on carrying out in spite of cold and storm.

Rev Crane had not been seen since late the previous evening and nothing was known of the whereabouts of the quartet of self-declared salesmen.

Across the table, a hollow-eyed Barney Stauffer eviscerated a doughy roll and dabbed butter into its husk while he muttered something about the storm growing worse.

Sheets of water splashed opaquely down the window-panes of the Sea Spray dining room to back up his statement. Sunday noon was more than making good on the promise of Saturday night.

Sometime between the fall of dark and the coming of the tenebrous gray that currently passed for daylight, the sea had invaded the beach and made it its own. The lifeguard tower was gone, reduced to its component boards and scattered on the tide; and the barbecue furnace was scarcely awash in the thrashing waves. Barely visible offshore through rifts in the fog, the float leaped and bounded at the end of its chains, as fantastic as a drunken aoudad. At the front windows of the lobby a little group of guests watched its antics and organized a pool on how much longer it could remain in place. All up and down the Cottage Line little knots of vacationists in oilskin armor peered down from the ridge at the unending ranks of waves which battered the face of the dunes with the aimless, unrelenting fury of a crowd-pleasing slugger in an armory bout.

Cass Harty pushed back his chair and damned the island, his luck, the case and the storm. Ordinarily he would have stayed for more coffee, but since the storm had kept the supply boat from coming from the mainland there were no newspapers; and the sergeant was, when he had time, a confirmed two-papers-for-breakfast man who held his twin journals as necessary to starting the day right as plenty of bacon and eggs and the first luxurious smoke.

Stauffer followed him into the lobby in time to see shoes come into view around the turn of the stairs, shoes of a styling that could only have been worn by Laura Ladd.

She tripped into view and smiled at the detectives, flicking a left hand which now showed a wedding ring besides the engagement stone. Ronnie Gresham followed her, not at all trippingly.

Harty supposed she must have brought the wedding band with her, too, and thought her a decidedly fore-handed young lady.

"Oh, Sar-jant," she trilled at him. "Did they tell you what happened? Ronnie and I got married last night."

"I heard about it." He felt that offering congratulations would present certain difficulties since it was hard to say which one deserved felicitations and which sympathy. "Great idea," he compromised. "But why was I left out?"

"We looked for you after . . . after we decided to get married," Ronnie said. He had the vaguely bewildered look of a man who has reached an objective via a rather different route than that by which he set out —and who is wondering like the devil how he can ever get away from it again. "We wanted to round up everyone."

"Yeah, it was so thrilling. We almost hadda double wedding. Adrian wanted to, but Kay backed down," the happy bride chirruped. "We came up and banged on your door but you di'n answer."

"I must be a heavy sleeper," Harty apologized. He was a distinctly light sleeper, but there was nothing to be gained by telling them that when they were at his door he and Barney and MacIver had been far down toward East Point on the all-night search.

"You missed a swell party," Ronnie informed him. "We'd brought some champagne in from the Sad Angel before she left, and everyone got good and sous . . ."

"We did not get drunk," Laura interrupted. "It wouldn't of been respectful to the dead. But we hadda have champagne for the wedding."

"I hear one's not official without it," Harty agreed. "Did everybody have a good time?"

"Yeah," Laura said fondly, then amended, "All but Chet—he's a pain in the neck anyway. He acted last night like he did'n want to see us get married. But we don't care—we're too happy."

The sergeant said that that was nice and thought he might as well see Thornton. He watched Laura clasp Ronnie's limp hand cozily under her arm and go swing-hipped through the door of the dining room. "I hope Ronnie eats a good breakfast," he told Barney, and added the old tag-line, "He can't carry that schedule on mush and milk."

They located Good Ol' Chet in a huge wicker bath chair in a sheltered corner of the wide veranda.

The Last of the Go-getters looked glum. He was slumped deep in the chair, knees higher than his chin, and had the polo coat Kay had worn yesterday turned up about his ears as he stared out at the storm. A few scraps of legal foolscap and torn blue contract binder lay in a fold of the coat; the rest had been whirled away on the wind.

"Do too much celebrating last night?" Harty hailed him.

"Huh?" Thornton awoke from his grief for the lost cause. He looked at the detectives sourly for a moment, then grumbled, "I didn't celebrate at all."

"That's not the traditional way to act when your pal is being made The Happiest Man in the World." The sergeant chuckled. "It's a time for hoisting glasses and all that stuff."

"What a laugh!" The high-pressure boy had never looked less like laughing. He leaned forward, a crooked forefinger beckoning them nearer. "Haven't either of you birds sense enough to ask what's behind this business of getting married?"

"Well, I saw a set of Levantine drawings one time," Harty said, "but I've always had too much delicacy to inquire if that stuff happened in real life."

"This isn't any time to wisecrack," Chet snarled. "You ought to ask yourself why they got married."

"Why should I?" The sergeant led him on. "I'm a romantic sort of a guy who believes that love is beyond logic."

Thornton said bitterly, "The hell you do."

"All right," Stauffer said. "So it's foolish. But we're used to seeing crazy things happen down here."

"Then start getting used to this: A husband can't be compelled to give incriminating testimony against his wife! Is that news to you?"

"You'll kill us with that stuff. It's bad for the digestion, to laugh so much right after a meal." The sergeant kicked a chair into position facing Chet and sat down on its arm. "What gave you the notion I wanted him to testify against her?"

"I know what you did on the Sad Angel. You were snooping around that saluting cannon."

"What of it?" Harty had too much hope in the punt-gun theory to be sidetracked by an already discredited weapon. He had an idea Chet was merely trying to pay off a grudge.

"It had been fired—and Ronnie and I were ashore that night."

"Sure you were! And Laura was aboard—and I suppose she shot Wade, capsized Jubilee, drowned

Dunster, and fed Randall Elrod meningitis germs in his martinis." Mention of meningitis stuck in Harty's craw, for irritating little half memories of something involving small bits of wood and a diagnosis of meningitis still frolicked just outside his reach.

"I was talking about deliberate murder—not accident nor illness," Chet said disgustedly. He hauled himself out of his chair, preparatory to going into the hotel. "Remember what I said about a husband not testifying against his wife—that's all."

"You've got hold of a swell idea there," Harty said, "and there could be more than one way of looking at it. Suppose you try remembering that a wife can't be made to testify against her husband—and Ronnie changed his ideas on matrimony damned fast!"

2

Ahead of them the Elrod and Dunster homes loomed like strange castles of some half-world of fog and rain. Offshore the buoy clattered its melancholy bell in protest against the buffeting of wind and sea. Somewhat to the left of the two detectives, three men and a woman hurried by muttering something about hoping they would not be too late for it.

"Of course the marriage could work out two ways," Barney said thoughtfully. "Did you have something else in mind?"

"Yeah! What I came down here to see . . ." The sergeant aimed a forefinger, as stiff and straight as a Luger barrel, upward through the murk. "That string of flags."

"Nobody took 'em down?" Stauffer approached the tall mast and squinted aloft where, their brilliance dimmed by the storm, flags, blue over red, yellow beside blue, and white between two stripes of blue, whipped in the gale.

"They're still up," Harty affirmed. "And, like everything else we run into, there's two possible answers to that. Either the guy who's supposed to take 'em down let the job slide—or else *he wants* them to stay up . . . maybe *needs* them up."

"I don't get it."

"It didn't hit me right away, either—about the flags having more than one use. But here's what I was after: Why were they run up in the first place?"

"For appearances, I guess. They kind of pep the place up and make it look sporty."

"Well, that's one answer." Harty jiggled the dripping halyards slightly. "And, according to custom, they'd be taken down at night and run up again in the morning."

"So what?" Barney said. "They're up now."

"I'm not trying to go mental on you," the sergeant went on, "but it seems to me that if the flags were hoisted merely to decorate the place, they'd be flown in the same order every day. After all, it calls for quite a little effort to knot them in sequence to the main halyard. A guy wouldn't take the trouble to change them unless he had a damned good reason."

"Sounds sensible! But ain't they in the same order?"

"I'm fairly sure they're not."

"Don't tell me you remember how all them flags were located," Stauffer said incredulously. "Nobody could."

"I'm not talking about the little triangular ones on the side lines. There's 'way too many of them. But the center halyard has never carried more than three and they're flown right up at the top, above the yardarm where they'll stand out plainly. And, unless I'm wrong again, when I sailed Jubilee past here on Wednesday, the flag up there where the blue-and-red one is now was half white and half a blue fork." He scratched at the stubble on his chin. "I can't remember the others—I wish to God I could."

"What difference would that make? You don't know what they mean."

"They're marine signal flags—standard the world over!"

"Someone was sending messages with them—"

Stauffer broke off abruptly as more people streamed past, too remote in the fog for their numbers to be clearly reckoned.

On the outskirts of the hurrying group a woman pointed at the two detectives and said to her companion, "There they are now. Why do you suppose they're not going."

"Aw," the other answered, "they're prolly afraid."

"What is this?" Barney demanded. "Where are they going?"

"That ought to be easy found." Harty moved into the path of an oncoming man, blocking his progress. "Where to, big boy?"

The man's wife galumphed ahead, calling back over her shoulder, "Now don't stop to gossip, Mervin. You mightn't ever get a chance to see a thing like this again."

"Lemme go, will ya?" Mervin gabbled. "I'm in a hurry!"

Cass Harty put out a broad hand and took a reef in the man's coat. "Why?" he shouted above the gale. "What's it all about?"

From far down the ridge, half-blurred by the blanketing fog, a ripping racketing sound came to their ears, explaining what it was all about. A sort of typewriter taca-tac-tac-ataca-taca-tac—the distant crepitation of a machine gun.

"Y'r making me miss it." Mervin screamed his frustration. "They got him cornered!"

Harty thought: They can't have! The significance of the flags overhead slipped from his mind.

"Who's got who cornered?" Barney roared.

"The G-men are here! The word just came down the Cottage Line that they've located the guy who's been doing all the killing." Mervin tore loose and began to run toward the sputtering sound. "I heard he swore they'd never take him alive. They say he's got a suitcase full of Mills bombs in the house with him. Boy! Do I want to see this!"

"Not half as much as I do." Harty lit out on the trail of the scuttling Mervin, passed him, and with Stauffer pounding at his reels, raced toward where the taca-taca-tac-ataca-taca-tac was breaking out again.

Pinpoints of fire pricked the dull veils of fog and then where a downward dip of the long crest of the ridge began, they saw a spitting gun.

Its operator lay bellydown on the sodden sand, pointing the nozzle of his chattering black tube at a tiny cottage, halfway up the next rise. His soft gray hat was flung on a clump of beach grass beside him and his shoulder moved in time with the bursts of fire. Gaping cottagers stood in a half circle behind him.

Directly across the hollow, another gun stuttered into action. Sand flew up in tiny flurries along one side of the cottage; then, as the gunner got the range, chips of wood spun into the air to an accompaniment of tinkling glass.

Off to the left a man crept on hands and knees, shoving a tear-gas projector ahead of him.

They'll smoke him out and then gun him down, Harty thought.

Mervin excitedly repeated his Mills-bomb rumor to a friend who topped it with a: "No, you got it wrong. He wears a flask of nitroglycerin around his neck on a string. If they close in on him he'll blow the whole place to hell-and-gone. This here McNiff is one tough guy."

McNiff?

Sergeant Harty mentioned a barnyard by-product and mentioned it explosively. He shouldered past a man who remonstrated "Look out who you're pushing—there's room enough for all" and walked around a woman who was busy lifting a four-year-old on high, that he might have a better view, while she urged: "See, Junior! Look at the bang-bang. Just like Jimmy Cagney does it in the movies."

Rev Crane started up from beside the gunner as Harty broke through the group. "Where you going, Serge-unt?" he demanded.

Harty did not answer. Instead, he broke into full stride and sprinted for the cottage.

Startled at the move, the gunner on the opposite slope ceased firing.

The sergeant galloped on, his mind outspeeding his flying feet. *McNiff's my prisoner,* he thought, *and more than that, McNiff can be a key. The tip on him came from Dunster's home and Wade was a guest in Dunster's home. There were hot bonds in Wade's office, which meant a professional crook was in on that end of things —even if the murders were done by an amateur. Tootie may be able to link up the whole thing—if they haven't killed him already.*

In front of him the cottage door was a flimsy obstacle, its panels honeycombed by machine-gun fire. A crash of his shoulder sagged it back upon its hinges.

Coming up behind him, Noone murmured, "Watch yourself now." A massive automatic was in the agent's right hand.

"Don't be in too much of a hurry with that thing," Harty warned. "The job doesn't call for it."

"I'm used to it," Noone snapped. "Better get yours out!"

"I . . ." Harty had forgotten to pack even the small belly gun. "I'll leave the soldier-boy stuff to you birds," he said, and stepped through the shattered doorway calling, "Hey! Tootie!"

A tiny patch of plaster, chunking down from the bullet-pocked ceiling, was the only sound.

"The kitchen, probably." Noone sloshed through water from a blasted jardiniere as his three assistants crowded in. "Come on."

"While you're there, I'll have a glom at the bedroom." The sergeant spoke out of the fullness of his knowledge of Tootie.

Glass was gone from the bedroom windows, and pictures and wallpaper alike had been punched full of round black holes. The mattress from the double bed lay in the center of the floor, quivering slightly.

Cass Harty said, "O.K., Tootie."

The vibrations of the mattress increased. A pair of green-socked ankles projected from under its edge. Harty nudged the nearer ankle gently with the toe of his shoe. "Come on out."

"Don't kill me," a scared voice pleaded. "I'll go quiet." A pinched face turtled into view. "Oh, it's you, Sarge."

"Sure! And I'm ashamed of you—turning into a gun fighter at your age."

"I ain't even got a rod, s' help me." Some of the terror ebbed. "What's the idea of all the shooting? I got a slug through me leg."

"Youah lucky, fellah." The room was suddenly full of agents, the machine gunner in the lead. "Last man ah laid a gun on didn't have no forehead when they picked him up."

"No kidding?" Harty said. "Was that where your bullets came out?"

"Nevuh mind that. We got this felluh."

Tootie was yanked from beneath his shield and handcuffed with the speed and precision of a magician's stunt.

"Now," Noone said, "we'll take you down to jail and—"

"Where does that 'we' come from?" Harty interrupted. "This punk was Rev's prisoner and now he's mine. I'm taking him back to New York."

"Ah wouldn't be too suah about that." The machine gunner was joyously getting even for having been down-faced in the hotel room. "Ah heah it don't pay."

"Rev, you're the local authority," Harty said. "How do you stand?"

Crane stood sidewise and looked uncomfortable about it. "Now, Serge-unt," he crawfished, "don't git excited . . ."

"You knew this was coming off and you froze me out," Harty snapped. "What do you do now?"

"What can I do? This feller's just told you. He's got McNiff—and what's t'at about possession being nine points to t' law? Got t' let him keep him," he added righteously. "Honor's honor and't wouldn't be square o' me t' act otherwise, after they planned the capture an' all."

"Mistuh, it looks like you been told!" Grinning, the machine gunner stood in close to Harty, a revolver in his hand. He spun it twice, with forefinger through the trigger guard, and looked the sergeant over slowly. "Were you figguhing to do somethin' about it?"

Cass Harty stared back in equal deliberation. With Rev selling out and himself unarmed, he had only two fists to back up his case. Against five guns . . . Never make it! "No," he said thoughtfully, reassuring himself that he had just begun to trade punches, "as a matter of fact I'm not. At least not right now."

"Get moving, then," Noone said. "We've got to talk to this rat about some killings."

"So long," the sergeant said, and managed to make it nonchalant. He moved through the door at a leisurely pace and circled the house to where Barney waited in the storm. To an air vaguely like "The Old Oaken Bucket", he was gently singing a hymn of obloquy to Judas Crane.

"How'd it go?" the little detective asked.

"They have McNiff," Harty said, and went on with his song:

> ". . . the old-fashioned bastard,
> The bible-backed bastard,
> That . . ."

"They got Tootie? What 're we gonna do about it?"

"He can't be taken off the Head until the storm ends. We'll let them keep him a while, if they get any fun out of it. In the meantime, you and I are going after bigger game than Tootie. We're out to show those birds up pretty—and the first move is to see Melissa Packe."

The door of Miss Packe's cottage closed behind a grinning sergeant.

"What do you feel so good about?" A wait of nearly two hours in the dubious shelter of a garden arbor had left Stauffer peevish. "Did you get a confession?"

"I didn't go there for one."

"Then why grin?"

"I put something up to her, asked her if she's game to help. We talked the whole thing out, and she said she'd try."

"I think you must be going soft. That dame's supposed to be up on antiques, and that punt-gun thing sounds like an antique to me. You're crazy to trust her."

Harty shrugged. "I'm willing to risk it."

"But how in hell can she help you?"

"I'm not sure she can and neither is she—but she promised to do her best. The whole idea sounds too silly to let you in on now. If it pans out, you'll know the story as fast as I will."

4

In his years in the department Sergeant Cass Harty had managed at one time or another to get himself rather thoroughly bawled out by varying types of superior officers, many of them experts in the technique of giving a subordinate a whole-souled raking over. But now, as he stood and took it, he could not recall anything one half so blistering as the needle spray of verbal vitriol which MacIver turned on him the moment he finished reporting about Tootie.

Usually the most laconic of men, the scrawny little inspector spat barbed-icicle words while twenty-five and then thirty minutes passed. Bellowing would have bounced unheeded from Harty's consciousness and cursing would only have roused his resentment, but the white-haired man was too smart to fall into either error.

Never was he profane and not once did his tone rise above the conversational. His arctic fury simply flowed on and on, each separate word sharp as the sting of diamond dust.

". . . incompetence and blundering are unpardonable, but they can at least be comprehended. But you're not incompetent and you haven't blundered. Not Sergeant Harty! He's the man who eats his head off and drinks his kidneys rotten. He goes junketing up to the city in defiance of his orders. He sails a little boat and visits a yacht and drinks in an exclusive club. By his own admission he attends a beach party and sneaks off into the dark with some little tramp just in time to let a murder be committed! Sergeant, you haven't even the excuse of incompetence to offer. *You, just aren't trying!*"

"Dammit," Harty roared, "that's more than I'll take from the commissioner himself." No use to cite the reasons for every item MacIver had listed; the boss knew all that. "You're sore over McNiff—you want him and you'll have him. If it comes to a court showdown, those feds can't hold him with one of the Queen Mary's cables. As to the murders, they're so damned close to being sewed up now that the killer might just as well start having his head shaved. I'm waiting for word on just one angle—from a woman."

"*A woman!*" Johnny MacIver's scorn would have withered wolfsbane on the bush. "The sergeant wants the New York Police to lean on the courts to get a prisoner back for them and on a woman to solve a murder case. Stauffer! Go downstairs and get me a knife from the kitchen, a big one."

"A knife? Yes sir. Uh . . . why did you want it, sir?"

"Because if Harty goes on talking that way, I'll cut his heart out and chop it in little . . . tiny . . . pieces."

The sergeant understood well enough just how much of this was his chief's way of jacking him up to more successful effort; but he could have done very nicely with less of the iron ration. "O.K.," he snapped. "You want

McNiff back?"

"Do I want ... Of course! Anything that will keep those feds from having the laugh on us."

"*Anything?*" Cass Harty was not yet sure what that "anything" would turn out to be; but he had an old predilection for keeping his own chin covered. "You'll play ball—and there 'll be no kickbacks?"

"None! Say . . . just a minute . . ." The inspector had suddenly remembered that the chins of ranking police officials needed protection too. "You're not going to leave me up a tree. You make out a detailed report, covering the matter up to the time the government men took charge of Tootie. That will complete the formal record. What happens after that won't concern Headquarters— and if you get yourself in a jam it's strictly your own private headache!"

"Boss, you've made yourself a bargain!" Cass Harty's smile was as wide as an Olympic broad jump. "I'll make that report out for you right after dinner."

5

Sergeant Harty stopped near the Dunster cabana, cupped hands shielding the fourth match in a row. This one got the butt going.

"Who's that?" a voice called from the darkness near the house.

"Harty."

"Oh." Porch steps creaked and the owner of the voice became visible as Adrian Tenny. "Are you looking for anyone?"

"Yeah." Harty had seized on the interval before dinner as a chance to check up on the Morgan Elrod-Dunster situation and find out if either had returned, but to annoy Tenny he said, "I wanted to see Kay."

"She's in the house." The man's answer was less grudging than Harty had expected. "I'm on my way down to the san. Got to see Larsen about shipping Randall's remains."

The detective said "Well, don't let me keep you," and waited until Tenny had scuffed away in the murk before he went toward the house.

Beyond the unlocked front door a hall opened on a living room where Kay sat, staring into a dying fire. "You back already?" she said without turning around. "Who was it?"

"Don't look now," he cautioned, "but I think it's the cops."

"I thought you were Adrian." She whirled around, seeming pleased. "Didn't you meet him outside?"

"Yeah—starting out for the san."

"The call of duty." She yawned. "Adrian is so conscientious."

Harty thought the embers of the fire looked warm, the settee looked comfortable, and the girl all right too. "He'd have to be—to leave this for that."

"You're a swell one to talk—you never give a girl a break."

The sergeant grinned. "I thought we covered that Wednesday night—just before you ran out on me."

"There's always more to be said. Will you stay for a drink?"

"I usually do." He moved toward a glass-sided cellaret. "What do you like?"

She lounged back on the cushions. "You name it. I haven't enough will power to decide . . . anything."

"So?" Harty thought it should take Tenny at least an hour for the round trip to and from the san. He mixed a brace of short scotch and soda and carried them across the room. "Have you heard from Dunster yet—or Morgan Elrod?"

"No. Do you think we will?"

"The sergeant asks the questions." He lifted his glass and toasted, "Luck!"

"Well, please don't ask any now. I'm not up to it."

"That's one of the things I like about you, Kay, a guy

can always count on you for full co-operation."

"Aw." She faked a Gracie Allen accent. "I bet you tell that to all your suspects. But seriously, I'd like to forget the whole business. The lady is tired"—she patted the cushion beside her for him to sit down—"and lonesome."

Tenny's trip should take more than an hour but, as a concession to his own official status, Harty said, "I made these drinks short purposely."

"Make them longer—the glasses are tall enough." She handed hers back. "Don't you *ever* relax?"

More than an hour for Tenny? Hell! It ought to be nearer to two. Harty set about filling the order for a bigger drink and said, "Sure. But in a job like mine I have to pick my spots."

"I think you need someone to help you pick the right ones," Kay told him. She nipped at her drink and set it down on the coffee table, then stared up at him. "I might be just the girl you've been looking for."

There were two meanings to that; but, for the present, Cass Harty was willing to let her construction on it stand. "Perhaps you are," he said, putting his glass on the coffee table beside the one already there. "We'll have to find out."

6

Barney Stauffer was almost finished with his dinner when the sergeant entered the Sea Spray dining room to the accompaniment of half-suppressed snickers; a round of small laughter that was only slightly less irritating than the spattering of handclaps that paid tribute to Noone and his three hoplites when they came in a little later.

The federal men walked down the long aisle and, for the first time, sat together at one table. There seemed to be a general feeling of dissatisfaction that the radio in the lobby was bringing in a dance tune instead of a fully orchestrated rendition of "Pomp and Circumstance."

"You're late," Barney said as the sergeant dug into the meal. "What kept you?"

Harty shrugged. "I got talking—with Kay Franklin."

"Talking? This long? She must know something."

"I guess she does," Harty agreed. "It'd take quite a while to add up all the things she knows."

"Yeah? Look at that." Stauffer pointed across the room where guests, with a great deal of handshaking, were congratulating Noone.

"I don't grudge those birds their Roman triumph— while it lasts," Harty said. "But I hate like all get-out to look as if we're chained to their chariot wheel."

"What the hell?" Barney groused. "We can take it."

Fate immediately gave him a chance to make good his boast. In the lobby someone twiddled a dial of the radio, and music yielded to a breathlessly frenetic voice whose trick of phony excitement would have made a simple "Good evening" sound as melodramatic as a cry of rape.

". . . deserves awkids for her new flicker, which is a superwow. Swellegant work, Joan!" the broadcaster panted. "*Flash!* Sand Head, Long Island: America's latest Public Enemy Number One was taken into custody here this afternoon! At the risk of their lives, Uncle Sam's daring G-men seized Tootie McNiff after a thrilling gun battle in which hundreds of shots were fired. Although it may be denied, your correspondent has it on excellent authority that McNiff will shortly confess to the series of murders which horrified this beach resort and the entire nation. With you, Mr and Mrs America, I say: Goody! and a scallion to that New York City detek*tuff* who is kno-unn to have put obstacles in the way of this bri-yant capture."

Dance rhythm thudded as the dial was twitched once more.

In the dining room a bubbling sound of derision for the two New York men floated fruitily up from a rear table.

Stauffer crushed out his cigar furiously, but Harty grinned.

"It's up to us to take a bow on that, Barney," he said, bobbing his head in mock acknowledgment. "They're laughing too soon, and I'm willing to let 'em do it; but I'm damned if anybody can razz me out of here before I've finished my dinner."

"Or me." Barney knife-tapped his glass for service and ordered a second helping of everything. "We'll sit 'em out if it takes all night."

<h1 style="text-align:center">7</h1>

Waiting out the diners was no part of an all-night job, but composing the report for the inspector sized up as considerably more than that. Python torpid from the double meal he had defiantly consumed, Stauffer tumbled into bed with a conclusive, "I'm gonna get some shut-eye," and left the sergeant to his labors.

Time dragged slowly by while the old-fashioned wallpaper looked down on Harty's woolgatherings at the table and Barney snored like a transport plane's port motor and the weary clapboards outside creaked everlastingly in the wind. The sergeant played with two bits of black wood, brought back with him from the hut at West Point, and belabored his memory, trying to recall where he had heard of something similiar. If he could even think of the name of the town where the damnfool thing happened, he was sure he could get the rest of it. He flung the wood from him in a rage and took up his pen. Circles and curlicues spread themselves across the paper of the report form; a death's-head, a ticktacktoo frame, and the words Police Department, City of New York, done in fancy scroll, blossomed beneath them, but the report itself made almost no progress.

No special difficulty of the story he had to tell delayed the sergeant; it was simply that the murders weighed too heavily on his mind.

If Melissa Packe would only come through!

The queer little designs on the paper multiplied while

his brain fanned over the evidence he possessed. Flowing smoothly from the split gold of his pen point, a perfect triangle spread inky arms upon the report blank and, out of his preoccupation, the detective labeled its corners "Furnace," "float," "Elrod's pier."

Sitting back to study it, he said, "Would that fit?"

"Would what?" Stauffer asked sleepily.

"You awake?" Harty swung his chair half around to the bed.

"How the hell could I sleep with the wind howling and that damned buoy gonging and you talking to yourself? I been awake a half-hour. What are you doing?"

"This." Harty traced and labeled another triangle, then passed the paper to Barney. "It's not some kid's geometry lesson—just a couple of ideas diagramed to make 'em simpler."

Still drowsy, Barney grumbled, "Simple like Einstein."

"The first one." Harty said "Furnace, here; pier, to which the dink was tied, here; and the float out here. Elrod's gun, Elrod's pier, Elrod's boat and Elrod is dead . . ."

"And his cousin's missing," Stauffer cut in. "Maybe he toted the gun down to the little scow and rowed apast the fire to knock 'em off, and then stayed out on the float till the excitement died down. What about number two?"

"Furnace, dune and water," Harty explained. "That dune gave a possible angle of fire at the party. Now—when Rev climbed that sand hill on Wednesday morning he reported that there was nothing up top but an old broken post. It occurred to me just now that a man could have braced the shock-absorbing rope of a punt gun on that post and if the wood was rotted enough the kick of the gun could break it off. And the 'water' corner of the triangle means the surf. He could have slipped in there unnoticed and come out after the others and looked as innocent as a roomful of babies."

"No soap, Sarge." The little detective had spotted the

flaw in the theory. "If that post was already busted on Wedn'sday morning, it couldn't have been used that night Wade got killed."

"Damn! I missed that completely." Harty slapped his forehead. "What a boner! Triangulation's supposed to help mariners find their course, but it hasn't done us much good. Maybe we'd better buy a couple of sailor hats."

A tap on the door preluded Gen Crane's entrance with a steaming pitcher. "I seen your light on an' figgered y' might have trouble getting to sleep," she said timidly. "So I made up a batch o' toddy." She put the peace offering on the table and looked first at one, then at the other. "I'm right sorry 'bout the way Revelation acted this afternoon. No hard feelin's?"

"Not enough to keep me from having some of this." The sergeant put a spoon in a glass to keep it from cracking and poured it brimfull. "By the way, how is Rev?"

"Struttin' like a sandpiper, the big fool! They're letting him take spells guarding that McNiff, just t' make him feel good, I guess."

Harty tried a less personal topic. "Storm easing any?"

"Looks for worse. Guest come in just now and says Elrod's float carried away and's getting washed ashore. It 'll serve Revelation right if he don't get the job o' putting her overboard again. It pays ten dollars, every time."

"Ten bucks?" Barney said. "That's a lot of dough for just putting a big hunk of lumber in the water."

"She's more 'n a piece of lumber. Heaviest float ever *I* saw. Why, look how high she sits—there's a good two feet o' space between the top o' her pontoons and her planking."

Cass Harty recalled that Kay said something about that too. He was thinking of his first triangle as he bade Gen good night and closed the door behind her. When the sound of her footsteps had died at the base of the stairs he moved toward the closet.

"Where you starting for?" Barney demanded as the sergeant began to shrug into a well-worn trench coat.

The coat's fabric bore two skillful patches, one at the side, the other dead centered between the double row of buttons and about belt high. To the sergeant it seemed a long time since a pair of bullets had made those patches necessary. "I'm going out," he said, turning up his collar. "All this thinking's got me down. I need practical stuff— and fresh air.

8

With the scream of a million turnduns the maniac gale howled in from the broad Atlantic and twisted opaque draperies of mingled sand and spray about the trench-coated figure of the sergeant as he plodded along the crest of the ridge. His face and ears were drilled raw by flying grit, but after the stuffiness of the hotel room it was good to feel the champagne sting of cold wet salt in his nostrils and better still to wade through the thick violence of the night.

Two oblong surfaces of light, windows in the Dunster living room, glowed like the eyes of a cubist cat ahead of him in the darkness. He approached them cautiously, going just close enough to identify the people behind them.

Chet in an armchair, sipping glumly at a highball, the defeat wrought by Laura's marriage written plainly on his face.

Adrian Tenny was beside the piano, leaning wishfully toward Kay who sat at the keys. He was talking intensely to the dark-haired girl, probably, Harty thought, in another proposal of marriage.

Ronnie and Laura were bent above a double solitaire layout on the chess table; the card game being simpler than chess and, besides, you got a chance to talk more.

They shifted the cards inattentively: Laura looking like a handsome blonde composograph of all the Northwest Mounted Policemen in pulp literature; the man she had gotten, somehow, managing to suggest the lowest common denominator of their captives.

There was no sign of either Morgan Elrod or Dunster, and Harty noted with pleasure that Melissa Packe was also absent from the group.

"I guess she's doing her best to make good on her promise," he murmured to the storm as he turned away from the house.

Squinting down from the top of the slope, Harty saw that even here, at what was normally its widest point, the beach was all but gone. Waves as wild and endless as files of spahi horsemen raced across the expanse of inundated flat, spraying into whitecaps above the submerged brickwork of the furnace, then rallying again to crash at the foot of the dunes. Offshore, a vague shape, less than half-seen in the gloom, was probably the float.

The sergeant looked once over his shoulder to make sure no one had followed him, then started down the steep incline. Midway to the bottom he checked his slithering descent, braced his feet in the sand, and reached inside his coat for the flashlight.

It was an enormous affair and, as Harty strained his eyes against the dark, he hoped the promises about its long-range beam had been something more than sales talk. Aiming the long metal tube out to sea, he pressed the button.

A narrow finger of illumination prodded oceanward, riddling the folds of murk. It flicked lightly across the surging wave tops and made the gaunt spars of the float stand out in bold relief.

"Gen was right," he said. "It's coming ashore."

While minutes passed, he watched its rocking progress and tried to calculate how long it should take the float to come aground. He had every intention of being on hand when it did.

Somewhere out there in the darkness the clanging bell buoy sent its steady hammer beat toward shore, celebrating a brassy requiem for the float. Harty moved his torch slowly from side to side in the hope of picking up the cross-braced ironwork, but the storm was too dense and the distance too great.

"Funny . . ." He spoke again, realizing he had failed to take the width of the flooded beach into account, "that float must've drifted further inshore than I thought. It and the buoy were almost on a line." But it was only natural, he reflected, that the buoy's moorings should be more staunch than the chains that held the float in place.

His light beam shifted back to the tossing wooden platform once more. Masted by the carpentry of the high springboard, it was yards nearer now.

"Another twenty minutes ought to do the trick," he concluded. He had another job to do and he hoped the delay would not imperil it. To avoid being discovered, he snapped the flashlight's button back again and darkness, complete and impenetrable, closed in as he sat down to wait.

The first little triangle he had drawn gave him faith in his vigil, since it pointed meaningfully at the float and the words of Gen Crane and Kay actively reinforced the meaningfulness of its pointing.

It was queer, Harty thought, how he could have noted the dimensions of the float without thinking very much about them. If he . . .

A distinct change in the trip-hammer banging of the storm-tossed buoy broke in upon the detective's thoughts. All rhythm was suddenly gone out of the anvil notes; they sounded irregularly and by lunatic chance.

Getting to his feet again, Cass Harty reached for his torch. The change could mean only one thing: the buoy had broken loose.

A snap of the button made light fingers across the waves, confirming his judgment. Leaping and quivering with each surge of the waves, the buoy moved into view.

Below where the sergeant stood, the heavy float ground to a stop while his flashlight's ray was still convoying the buoy in. He watched its tall metal frame respond eerily to the drive of the seas, first pausing in a hollow to waver deliberately, like a tipsy but dignified specter, then lurching wildly in toward shore on the crest of the following wave, its brazen echoing a leper bell to warn everything from its path.

There's more underwater structure to it than the float has, the sergeant thought regretfully. It 'll ground further out and I won't be able to look her over till morning. If I try to swim it, the water 'll douse my torch.

In any event, the float was a better bet.

Cass Harty stripped and stacked his clothes in a neat pile, covering them with his trench coat. With flashlight in hand, he descended to the beach level and waded through hip-deep water to the great wooden square.

The float was high, just as Kay and Gen had said. It seemed even higher now, since sand, rather than yielding water, was beneath its pontoons.

Harty worked his way around the wooden structure, inspecting it minutely with the aid of his flash.

A trap door in the first side, large enough for a man to get through, and presumably built so that minor repairs might be made without hauling the float from the water, was opened and showed nothing inside.

The detective struggled along its seaward lateral without finding anything and, as he turned the corner to the third side, the last inshore thrust of the waves slammed his back, staggering him against the barnacled wood. He cursed and rubbed a hand across the scraped washboard flatness of his belly. His palm showed wetly red in the electric glow when he took it away.

Sea water smarted the wounds and he was still cursing as he undid the catch of the trap door on that side. The wind whipped the door open and his lamp sliced the blackness within.

A circle of black metal stared at him.

It looked menacing in the concentrated brightness, this business end of a long heavy gun barrel.

The cross braces of the float's understructure made a

perfect rack for the gun, and lanyard and recoil rope were looped twice about a wooden strut to hold it in place.

Cass Harty said, "Come to Poppa!"

Untwisting the ropes, he drew the gun toward him. Its weight strained the muscles of his arm in the cramped space. He balanced it across his shoulder, bumped the trap door shut, and waded to shore.

A comfortable warmth of partial success cheered him as he knelt beside his stacked clothes, examining the gun at leisure. From deep-notched butt, on through trigger lanyard, flintlock, and nine-foot-long smoothbore barrel, the weapon corresponded in every particular with the description he had read.

"Well, it's nice to know I can't be wrong all the time," was as much congratulation as he would permit himself.

A small silver plate, well tarnished, was visible on the carved cherry-wood of the butt.

Cass Harty rubbed it clean with his handkerchief and read, "Randalle Yllrodde, hys gunne." Below, in smaller letters, was engraved the name of a famous Cheltenham gunsmith and the date "a.d. 1648."

He dressed rapidly, thinking that the very nature of the gun tended to clear Kay. Her physique was not adapted to rapid maneuvering of so bulky a weapon. It was Elrod's gun, he recounted, and the ammunition came from Dunster's cabana—Johnny MacIver wasn't any part of a sap when he left the choice between Dunster and Morgan Elrod.

The sergeant tightened the belt of his coat and told himself that he had completed one half of a good night's work. The remaining part was merely a matter of conversation. If he got the right answers, and if Miss Packe came through for him in the morning, he would be off to the races.

Humming to himself, he scratched a long narrow grave in the sand at the foot of a blasted beach plum. He set the smoothbored tube of death in it, replaced the sand, and tramped the site well over to conceal his

operations. Then, rivaling the clamor of the storm with a
chanted rendition of a verse about an "Old Monk from
Thibet," he headed for the Sand Head jail.

9

Having dealt, en route, with the varied cases of the
"Old Maid in Pawtucket," "The Lecherous Chap in
Bombay," and the "Old Fellow from Wheeling," in
happyhearted hoarse-voiced song, the sergeant had
reached "Whose morals we sternly disparage," in the epic
of a certain gentleman named Harridge, when a crisp
"Stick 'em up!" stopped him in his tracks.

"And get 'em high," the challenger added, emerging
from the shelter of the jail's wall.

Cass Harty damned his luck. He had reckoned on Rev
being on sentry duty. A federal man would be tougher to
deal with.

"Who are you?" the same clipped tone rapped out.

"Harty." Hands remained high to reassure the guard.
"It's O.K."

The shadowy figure moved a trifle nearer. "What the
hell are you doing down here?"

It was dark, but not too dark to let Harty see the
outline of a pump gun, held at the ready. "I want a word
with that stooge in there. It won't take long." There was
no way to tell how the story might be going over, but
Harty chanced a move forward. "Noone didn't say I
couldn't."

The pump gun stayed level, aimed somewhere
between his breast and belt buckle while a minute
passed.

"Well," the sergeant asked, "how about it?"

Triumph had made the agent magnanimous. "We'll
see," he said. "What have you got on you?"

"Flashlight and a gun—I'll drop 'em both here." He
put them on the sand at his feet. "O.K?"

"O.K." The federal man stepped close, patting him

over. "You have two minutes—don't try to do anything but talk."

"What else'd I come for—to play post office?" Harty moved past him. "Keep an eye on the gun, will you?"

The agent puzzled him by saying he'd watch more than the gun, but a sudden glare from the flashlight, focusing on Harty's back, explained his meaning.

It left no more chance of overt action than if he had been on the stage of the Radio City Music Hall under a giant spot, and the detective was glad he had intended only to talk. Through the window, he called, "Hey, Tootie!"

"Who's that?"

Harty identified himself.

"Where's the other lug?"

"Out here—waiting to give me a load of buckshot the way the Irishman got his soup, in case I get funny." The sergeant's voice went lower. "*I've got a deal for you.*"

"Talk louder," the agent ordered.

"I'll come over there. Me leg makes it tough to move." McNiff complained hoarsely. "*What kind?*"

"The prop hurt much? *The only kind that 'll help you.*"

"It ain't too tough. *They got nothing on me. I never killed nobody.*"

"Has the wound stopped bleeding?" Harty tried a long shot, the only possible link between three otherwise unrelated facts: the hot bonds in Wade's office, McNiff's presence on the Head, and the tip on him emanating from the house it did. "*I know you didn't. But by the time they find it out they'll be so sore they'll go after you on those bonds.*"

"Yeah, it stopped right after they brung me in." Tootie tried to make his prison-yard whisper defiant as he said, "*What bonds?*"

"Then I guess you'll be all right. *Bonds I saw in a New York office. You know what ones they are. If the feds stick it to you on that rap, you'll be away for longer than you're slated for in Sing Sing—and in a tougher stir too.*"

"I warned you to talk loud," the federal man insisted. "If you can't—clear out!"

"He's on'y astin' me about me leg," McNiff said.

No Napoleon of crime, he was still able to choose between a short stay up the river, and a long term in Alcatraz. "*What's your deal?*"

"He's right. I wanted to know whether he'd had a doctor," Harty told the agent. Swirling winds helped to cover his, "*I fix it so you take the New York rap instead of this one. You give me the story on those bonds—and give it straight!*"

"Yeah, sure—they had a croaker in. *It begins last year when I hear about how a guy can do himself some good peddling hot paper if he ain't too particular about getting a big price. This ain't no fence, y' unnastan', it's a respectable jernt, Elrod and Company.*"

"I can't hear you," the agent called. "Speak up!"

"It's not our fault there's a gale blowing," Harty told him. "Anyhow, you can see we're not doing anything."

He was thinking that the stunt Tootie's description led to was not particularly new. He had heard before of unscrupulous company officials stuffing their firm's permanent investment portfolios with stolen securities, purchased at a discount. The difference between that and the market price, of course, had gone into their own pockets. And that kid in Wade's office had said Elrod, Incorporated, had handled some of their investment business.

"The croaker took out the slug." Tootie howled to be sure of being heard. "*I don't have nothing like that on hand at the time,*" he continued. "*But one day I lift a keister out a a car parked on Madison Avenya and there's these bonds in it. Honest, I near bust when I see what they was worth. I seen to it that the word got to the right spot in a hurry.*"

"Who was the doc? Larsen?" Harty asked. "*Make it fast!*"

"I think that's his name. *A guy meets me. He hands*

me a phony name, but his dough ain't phony. A week later we make the swap, his dough, my bonds. They're worth six Gees, but I get three."

"Larsen's a smart doc. Where'd you meet this guy?"

"That's what they say. *In a gin mill over on Nint' Avenya. I get the word he'll be waiting for me at the las' table in the back and he is—both times."*

Wariness of having a grab made for his gun would keep the agent at a safe distance, and Harty had enough faith in the roar of the storm to abandon his effort to make the sentry hear innocuous nothings. He whispered, *"What brought you down here?"*

"Nemmind that! How you gonna spring me?"

The sergeant's half-developed plan for that depended entirely upon Rev Crane being on guard duty. *"It 'll have to be at night. When you hear a ruckus out here, you dive under your bed and stay there, out of sight. We'll do the rest! Now, why'd you come here?"*

"When I go on the lam I'm broke, see? I know this crowd hangs out down this way so I jigger I'll look up my man and ..."

"Shake him down?"

"Why the hell not? It's worth something to him to keep my trap closed, ain't it? But I don't have no luck. Before I can find him the constabule grabs me."

"Your man put the finger on you. Who was he?"

"I told you he gimme a phony name. But I'd know him again if I seen him."

Harty determined to arrange that. *"What'd he look like?"*

"Just a guy—average looking. I dunno how to describe him."

"Was he big, little, bald headed, fat? Wear glasses, carry a cane, walk with a limp, have red hair?"

"He wuzzent fat and he don't wear no goggles neither," Tootie said. *"I dimno if he gimped; he sted after I left so I never seen him walk. I disremember about the cane, but,"* he added helpfully, *"he might of had red hair."*

No character under active suspicion had red hair. Cass Harty sighed. "How . . ." he asked, no longer bothering to whisper, "how did you know the name he gave you was not his own?"

"Haw-haw! That was a cinch." The little crook roared in appreciation of his own acumen. "Here's the two of us in a *fee*nancial deal, mind you, and what does that mugg tell me his name is? I ast you."

"No, Tootie," the sergeant corrected gently. "I asked you."

"He says . . ." McNiff took time out to laugh again. "An' if it's the truth, then my name must be Rockey-fella—he tells me that his name is Morgan."

MONDAY

BRIGHT morning sunlight beat strongly down, warming the faded flannel of the beach robe across Cass Harty's shoulders. Heelless leather sandals were on his feet, his hair was darkly wet with brine, and his hopes were riding high as he rounded a corner of the Sea Spray House and made for the rear door. The back stairs were empty and he went up them, three steps at a time.

He bolted the door of his room on the inside and took a cigarette case from the pocket of his robe. He dropped the case into a drawer of the bureau and left the drawer locked while he was puddling in the tub and scraping an agonizing razor down his salt-bitten jaw line. He patted lotion on his chin, put the lotion bottle away, and got out a small brown-glass vial of iodine. With a little rod he retraced the outline of the belly cuts sustained the night before and spread new patterns of the stinging stuff upon a series of smaller, fresher wounds along his arms and chest, wounds suffered when the waves had bounced him against the harsh metal of the grounded buoy, the objective of his morning's swim.

When the iodine was dry, he began to dress. Because his mood of the night before still held, he was humming cheerfully as he pulled on his clothes. He did one verse about a "Young Miss from Montclair," and another about an "Old Man from Cambodia"; a singularly untrustworthy old man whose attempt to welsh on the terms of a commercial transaction was justly, but rather uniquely, punished.

His dressing complete, the sergeant unlocked the bureau drawer, took out the cigarette case, popped it into the pocket of his windbreaker and buttoned the pocket flap securely down.

There was no neat row of firm-packed butts inside the metal case.

It held, instead, an even dozen strands of damp, quite new rope. The strands had been pulled from a joint of the metal arms of the buoy and they matched very perfectly, both in texture and in color, the lengthy painter which was coiled at the stern of Elrod's dinghy.

In a room down the hall Harty told MacIver of his find. He listened without annoyance to the inspector's information, gained through a phone call from New York, that the charges against Morgan Elrod in the night-club matter were about to be dismissed, and heard, without embarrassment, his superior officer's low opinion of his scheme for freeing Tootie McNiff.

"Hell! It's the simple things that work best," he said confidently. "The complicated stunts are liable to get all boxed up and backfire on you. Anyhow, you gave me your word you'd back me up—no matter what. Crane won't be on guard until tonight, so we'll have to wait. You've got your report; and you'll get your signal—then do your part."

MacIver's face showed he still did not think much of it, but he grumbled something about no one ever needing to worry about him keeping his word or failing to do his share of any job.

Even such grudging assurance from the white-haired man was better than a government bond as far as Harty was concerned. He went downstairs in search of coffee.

"Y' must like your swim, Serge-unt," Gen greeted him in the kitchen, "when y'r willing to delay breakfast for it."

"The sunshine looked so good I thought I'd have a splash," he alibied. "But the wind's pretty high and the water's almost as rough as it was during the storm."

"I wish it'd go down. They phoned word over t'at there's a bunch of reporters and suchlike waiting to come 'cross from Keyesport. It 'll be good for business when they get here."

Between gulps of coffee, Harty agreed with her. He

was not at all sure just whose business it would be good for.

Barney Stauffer was in the lobby, chewing an unlit cigar when the sergeant came out. "Did you get what you went after?" he demanded.

"I overlooked something when I was drawing triangles." Harty showed him the hairlike strands in the cigarette case and told him whence they had come. "I should have moved the point of that first one over, just a leetle bit."

"What are you gonna do with 'em?"

"Nothing—until after I've seen what Melissa Packe's been able to work out for me. I'm heading over there now."

"O.K.," Barney said. "Guess I'll go along." The subsurface meaning of his words was that she would not have worked up anything.

2

Their reception at the little white cottage on the bay slope made Barney look like a dependable prophet. Summoned from her work-room by her maid, the thin-faced Melissa had said, "I think everything will turn out all right, but I'd rather not raise your hopes too soon. They're in process of development now. Please sit down and wait."

In the garden arbor the detectives sat and waited while the morning wore away and the early afternoon followed in its tracks. Barney smoked gloomily while the sergeant, fretting at the waste of time, got up at half-hour intervals to pound on the door and beg the maid to please see Miss Packe again and ask her to hurry. It did no good, for each time the maid returned with the message that her mistress knew no way to speed up the action of the chemicals she was using.

Cass Harty's wrist watch showed almost three o'clock, and he was considering another trip to the door when it

opened and Miss Packe emerged, carrying a huge
envelope in her hand. "There are seven perfect prints,
Sergeant," she said. "I do hope they'll help you."

"I appreciate what you've done." He lifted the flap and
peeped inside at the gloss-finished, ten-by-twelve prints.
What he saw made him add, "I'm pretty sure they will
help."

Stauffer took a look also. He waited until the door had
closed on Miss Packe before he asked, "What the hell is
this?"

"Pretty pictures." Harty slid them out of the envelope
and spread them fanwise. They still felt a little damp.
"She knows her stuff, doesn't she?"

Colors of sand and sea and weathered wood were
almost miraculously reproduced.

"Yeah," Barney agreed. "But what good does it do?
They all show the same place."

"Exactly—that's what I asked for. I told her to give me
anything that showed Elrod's house. It's a break for us
that the changeable weather of the last few days gave
different color values to the same scenes. Otherwise she
mightn't have taken so many of it."

"Rev said she'd shoot the same scene over and over,"
Barney recalled. "But seven's a lot of pictures."

"Five," Harty corrected. "These two have the wrong
view."

"It's Elrod's house."

"Yeah—the back. I only told her as much as I had to. I
didn't want the *house*—it stays the same all the time. I
wanted shots of the *flags* in front of the house—they
changed. Look!"

Stauffer took the picture dated Wednesday and
studied the brilliant miniature of the colors.

"Just like Saturday, there are no more than three
above the crossbar," Harty pointed out. "And that's the
highest thing on the island, the thing easiest seen from a
distance, say, by someone who's hiding out . . ."

"By God, they *were* changed!"

"Wednesday's flags were a white oblong beside a blue fork, on top; the middle one was a blue field with a white square in the center; and the bottom flag was a white one, crossed from the four corners in red. Thursday"—he shifted to a new picture—"the top one was a yellow horizontal stripe, a blue horizontal below that, and another yellow under the blue. The middle flag . . ."

"I can see that for myself," Barney cut in. "But where are we gonna find out what they mean?"

"Where the flags are—at Elrod's."

"Then what 're we waiting for?" The little detective was suddenly in motion. "Not that I'd put any dough on how much good they'll do us. Where'd we get off showing a jury a lotta trick colors? They'd laugh us outa the courtroom."

"Like hell they would. These things are the McCoy. Anyone who is familiar with them can read them just as plain as if it was the alphabet hanging up there at the top of the pole."

"But that stuff's over and done with. Even if it wasn't, it wouldn't help. They never hung the name of the murderer up there. They won't tell you anything."

"But they're going to bring me something!"

"Christmas presents, maybe?" Stauffer said scornfully, and lapsed into silence to mull over Harty's words through the rest of the hike.

The sergeant was doing some quiet, earnest mulling on his own account. He had told Barney something about moving the point of the triangle a little, but it was really more than that. More on the order of making the triangle turn square by adding a fourth corner to it, he thought.

That the buoy was no longer in place and the storm had wrecked Elrod's little dock did not impede the development of his notion. Spiles still stuck up out of the water, like corpse-fingers, to mark the site of the pier; and a detailed government chart of these waters could be brought into court to convince even the most mulish jury of the position the buoy had once held.

Cass Harty blamed himself for having failed to investigate the overobvious. After all, the buoy had been in plain sight from the very beginning; and it was maddening to remember, now, that its hollow booming note had been one of the first things about Sand Head to impress itself upon his senses.

"What I'm after should be right over here," he said, as they reached Elrod's house and strode across the porch. "It's the logical place to keep it." He tossed aside the kapok cushions that made a seat of the broad low flag locker and lifted its lid.

The interior of the chest was bright with colors of the stowed bunting.

"Had enough of them, didn't he?" Stauffer commented.

"Yeah, but this is the important thing." Harty picked up a large thin book whose black cover was stamped in gold:

H. O. No. 87
INTERNATIONAL
CODE OF SIGNALS
(American Edition)
Vol. 1 Visual

Barney began to look more hopeful as the sergeant sat down on the edge of the open locker and attacked the book.

"It turns out we were right when we figured we could disregard those little flags on the side halyards, Barney," he said after a few moments. "They're numeral pennants and not worth a damn to us. But the others are letters and"—he checked Wednesday's picture—"white-oblong-blue fork is 'A'; blue field-white square in center is 'P'; and white field with red x-mark is 'V'."

"APV," Barney repeated. "That 'll get us no place. What kind of talk do you call that?"

"Tell you in a second." Pages spun beneath Harty's fingers. "According to the book, you can signal with from one to four flags. Now, in the three-flag grouping . . ." He progressed through the alphabetically keyed code meanings in the back of the book and found APV halfway down the first column on page fifty-four. "It means 'Again'," he exulted. "Get it? Morgan Elrod was on the loose Tuesday night, and Wednesday the 'Again' signal was flown."

"Do I get it? And on We'nesday night Wade got killed! *Again,* huh? Get after those Thursday signals, Sarge."

"Yellow, blue and yellow stripes horizontal, mean 'D'," Harty translated. "White and red, half and half, vertical, mean 'H'; and this funny-looking one, black, yellow, blue and red quarters, is 'Z'—DHZ." He turned to the rear pages again. "Means, 'Keep clear'."

"The same flags were kept up there on Friday."

"Saturday brought a new signal—the same one that's up now." Harty was studying a photo which duplicated the flags currently snapping at the masthead. Blue and red divided horizontally; yellow and blue, vertically; and a blue, a white, and a blue stripe, horizontal. "EKJ," he announced. "It means 'Danger'."

"H'm! Things were getting tougher Saturday."

"Nowhere near as tough as they are right now." The sergeant thumbed pages to a wanted symbol, then whipped a trio of flags from the locker. The first was blue with a white x-mark; the next had a broad blue stripe for its upper half and an equally wide red one as its lower; and the last was white, divided into four squares by a blue central cross.

"What 're you gonna do with them?"

"Switch signals on whoever's hiding out." Harty went down the porch steps with a single leap.

"What do they say?"

"MEX means 'Rendezvous'." The trio of flags comprising the danger signal came fluttering down and Harty set to work to reeve in his substitute colors. When they were secure, he pulled strongly on the halyard and watched their bright progress toward the peak. There the wind caught them and they swelled away nicely under its pressure, standing out stiff as triple starch.

"A guy—*any* guy could see them a long way on a day like this."

"So, what then?"

"He comes marching in," Harty chuckled. "Since Thursday the signals have kept him away. He's been waiting for this. He'll be in, all right."

Barney wanted all details pinned down. "When 'll that be?"

"I don't know. There was no time set in the Wednesday signal, which would make it look as if he knew what time they'd want him. If I fly extra flags now, to set a time, it might make him suspicious. Maybe it'd even scare him away completely."

"This 'll be Morgan Elrod?"

"I'd bet a year's pay on it. The in-again-out-again stuff matches perfectly with the signals—and don't forget the hot bonds in Wade's office. McNiff sold 'em to a gent named Morgan. Nice?"

"But would the screwball know what the flags mean?"

"Screwball? How long do you think his screwiness will last, once he knows he's all clear in town? I'd say not more than three seconds—unless he has to use it to get himself out from under this business."

"He hid out," Barney recounted thoughtfully. "He bought hot paper off Tootie, he'd naturally know all about that gun, he figures to come into his cousin's dough, and he plays like he don't know how to swim but he usta take cups for it in college. He'll be worth seeing. Where do we wait?"

"I'll wait in the house. It's a gamble that he'll come there, but I think it's a good one. I know he was here Wednesday—Randall admitted it."

"I'd like to gamble so safe in the sweepstakes," Barney said, following the sergeant through the door they had forced on Saturday.

Harty crossed the sunroom and went to a closet in the

hall. He came back with a golf bag slung on his shoulder. Stripping the leather hood back, he turned it down inside and then closed the door. Next, he stood the bag on end, six inches away from the doorknob.

"What are you doing—setting up a Maypole?"

"This is a burglar alarm—Sand Head style." The sergeant twisted the knob and opened the door precisely seven inches. The golf bag toppled over, its steel-shafted contents clanking like a conclave of ancestral Elrodian ghosts. "I don't want anyone to sneak in on me while I'm keeping an eye on things out front."

"I'm here, ain't I?"

"But not for long. I want you to get down there with MacIver. Check on Dunster's speedboat on the way. I promised to give Tootie a break and he's going to have it. The water's getting calmer all the time, and if things break right for me here, I'll cut loose with my gun and you and the boss can go through with your end of the stunt."

"Aw, hell! I wanted to hang around. I'd pay a buck to see that guy's face when he walks in on you."

"A deal's a deal—and I made one with Tootie." The sergeant moved the bag aside for the little detective's exit. "A guy's got to have some honor."

"In a racket like this?" Barney muttered. "I'm damned if I can see why."

3

The sergeant knew he was in a night club—that part of it was all right. Kay was at the table with him and a girl named Arlene, whom he remembered from someplace, was along, too, and they were watching the floor show. It was a good show, except that the tap dancer was Randall Elrod; and that couldn't be right because Randall was dead. Very peculiarly dead.

Even so, the sound of his feet got louder and louder until it was more than any one person could possibly make, and the sergeant's eyes opened and he peeped around the back of his chair and saw figures moving on the porch outside.

"Come on, let's beat it," Laura was saying. "They're not here."

"Are you sure?" her husband asked. "I thought the shades upstairs were drawn."

"Ronnie!" Her sharpness indicated a return to propriety. "Can't you keep your mind . . ."

"I could, but I don't want to. It's no fun."

"Well, I don't think there's any of that stuff going on," Laura decided. "Mr Tenny isn't that kind of a fella. I heard him ask Kay to marry him, last night."

Gresham muttered something both peevish and indistinguishable. Marriage was evidently still a tender topic with him.

"No sense in you two coming to blows over it." Good Ol' Chet attempted the role of peacemaker. "Why don't you run along? I'll wait for them to get back from wherever they are."

It was still daylight outside, but the sun was declining. Harty looked at his wrist watch and cursed his sleepiness. Kay and Tenny should be returning from the san, where they had gone to complete the arrangements for transferring Elrod's body to New York, any time now.

"Go ahead," Chet urged. "I don't mind waiting."

"I guess not." Ronnie sounded slightly and not at all amiably drunk. "You wouldn't be getting set to make a pass at Kay, would you?"

"I'm not—but what would you do if I were?"

"I'd wish you luck," Ronnie said. "And I'd be sore as hell we didn't sign that contract to split our profits fifty-fifty."

Cass Harty heard a sound like a wet pasteboard beer coaster being dropped on a tile floor. He did not need to look to know that Gresham had had his face slapped.

"That was no way to talk in front of a lady," Laura said. "A specially when she's your wife. Come on now.

You, too, Chet."

Three pairs of feet went down the porch steps.

The sergeant slithered to the window and watched them cross the lawn.

Near the concrete base of the flagpole, Thornton stopped. His neck arched back and his face tilted skyward. Apparently he was either studying the weather, or taking in the significance of the altered signal.

If he touches those halyards, Harty thought, he's my man. No one who's on the level would have any reason to tinker with them.

For more than a minute Thornton stood, hands on hips, at the foot of the mast. Then his arms began to move.

The detective's breathing quickened as Chet continued in wide, slow movement. Then, as it concluded, Harty cursed silently.

The man was simply stretching.

The sergeant watched Chet hurry after Ronnie and Laura and could not help wondering if he would be back. As the three figures faded into the horizon, a new idea struck the detective. There was no way of telling when the flag summons would be answered, but it must certainly be after sundown. It would be wise to be prepared.

Leaving his chair, Harty went up the stairway on the jump.

He started in the spacious game room on the top floor and visited, in speedy turn, every chamber in the rambling house. In each room he flicked on whatever lighting equipment was in evidence, from the midget shaving bulbs beside the bathroom mirrors to a cantaloupe-sized two-hundred-watt affair that swung above the ping-pong table.

When the last light of all, located in a bijou wine closet in the basement, had been turned on, he went back to the main floor, stopping long enough, en route, to raid a tool chest and a leather-trimmed case of fishing tackle.

A black metal box was fixed to the wall of the hallway near the kitchen door.

Cass Harty opened the box and yanked the handle of the switch that was inside.

Every light in the house went out.

He said, "Swell!"

There was still enough daylight left for him to work by as he went along the hall and around the corner into the living room, pausing at intervals to twist into the yielding woodwork the small screw eyes he had looted from the tool chest. When the last one was placed to his satisfaction, he returned to the house switch. Fastening one end of the stolen fishing line to the handle, he ran the other through the sequence of tiny metal rings. When it had been drawn through the last one near the living-room window, he cut the line and sacrificed a suspender button to snub the end and keep it from sagging back through the bolts. Efficiency, he thought, was to be preferred to modishness, and he was not a wearer of braces anyway.

Experimenting, he tugged at the button. The line gave springily for an instant. Then it tautened, the switch handle responded, and lights blazed from cellar to roof.

Again the sergeant said, "Swell!" He was confident that the stage was well set as he went to the hall and cut the lights off.

Turning from the switch, his nearness to the kitchen reminded him that he was hungry and his wrist watch confirmed the fact that nearly a dozen hours had passed since breakfast.

He hummed the entire ten lines of the astonishing double limerick about the "Two Young Ladies from Birmingham" as he scouted through the huge but sparsely furnished refrigerator, where the remains of some tinned corned beef looked like the best bet. A chemical analysis might have said otherwise, but it looked better than the dish of venerable pork and beans, or the potato salad that resembled a shuffle of green-moulded potato chips. Gnawing the dry beef savagely, he pried the cap from a bottle of beer and went down the hall to resume his post near the window.

Motion beyond the Dunster house caught his eye before he could sit down. Two figures, male and female, coming from the settlement at a casual pace. He was glad there was still enough light to let him identify them as Kay Franklin and Adrian Tenny.

Tenny, who wants to get married, he thought, and the babe he has his eye on. A weak eye, at that—a pair of weak eyes. Tenny and a girl and a dozen strands of rope. If they go near the flags . . .

With a wave of her hand, Kay disappeared into Dunster's house.

Tenny waved back at her and circled the building, going down toward the cabanas.

They can't be going swimming, Harty told himself. If they were, she'd go down there too. She changed her suit there the other night. Anyway no one's been in the water since the storm started, except me—and that was business.

Nobody had been in the water.

Since Saturday no one would have wanted *to go in the water!*

And LeMoyne Dunster was still missing.

With the care of a master jeweler fitting brilliants into a coronet, Sergeant Cass Harty labored to find the right spot for these two new points in his adjustable mathematical figure which had once been a triangle. He had made considerable progress with it, too, before Tenny came into sight again, walked to the porch steps and, with an air of patient waiting, sat down. He dragged a match across the sole of a shoe and held it to a cigarette, then leaned back, resting an elbow on the step above him. Framing large glasses, his face was turned to the house where the sergeant waited.

"It'd be a damned poor bet that he can even see the mast at that distance," the sergeant said aloud. A moment later, he amended it to, "But he ought to get a look at the flags soon."

Wearing a different and gayer dress, Kay had come out of the house, taken Tenny's arm, and started with him over the sand.

Cass Harty watched them follow the footpath around the curve of the lawn and pass the mast without any observable reaction. If the changed flags meant anything to them—if they had even noticed the change—there was no way to tell.

He ghosted back from the window as they came up on the porch and damned his forgetfulness when a key clicked in the lock of the front door. Of course Tenny would have one!

". . . please! You're not to start that again," Kay said as they entered. "I'm sick of the whole question of marriage."

"I'm mad about you, Kay," Tenny said, "but I can't understand you. Would you like me more if I acted like Gresham—or Wade?"

She laughed thinly. "In that case, I'd . . ." She broke off as a push button of the lamp in the hall clicked beneath her finger without producing light. "What's wrong? This doesn't work!"

"No?" More clicks meant Tenny was satisfying himself about it. "The master switch for the whole house is here. I'll have a look."

Cass Harty made a connoisseur's choice among a guttural Yiddish blasphemy he had learned from Stauffer, a resounding Erse oath which was a heritage of his ancestors, and an intricate and improbable Gallic obscenity he had admiringly heard a professional lady of Aix-le-Bains employ upon her maquereau in the early spring of 1918 and which he had reserved for some superemergency ever since.

It came in handy now. He had hoped the line would remain undiscovered until the flag signal was answered, but . . .

"Kay! Do you know anything about this?" Tenny

asked. "Something damned odd. A cord tied to the switch. It goes that way."

Cass Harty saw his hand would have to be played differently. He stepped into the hall, gun in hand—to let them know there would be no half measures. "O.K.," he said crisply. "I don't know what you had scheduled, but there's got to be a slight delay. Step right in here." He motioned them toward the darkening living room. "And sit down."

"You? Well, I'm damned." Annoyed, Kay flattened her mouth into a burlesque of the sergeant's hard line and pointed a mimicking forfinger from her hip. Quoting the "Handies" of yesteryear, she snapped, "What's *this?*"

"Get moving!" The gun emphasized Harty's order.

"I'll tell you what it is! It's a dumb detective making the mistake of his life. Adrian and I haven't anything to do with what's been going on here. Maybe you feel like a big guy behind that gun, but the whole place is laughing at the way those G-men showed you up. I'll go in and sit down, all right—because I want to see how silly you'll look when whatever you're planning fails to come off."

"You, too, Tenny," Harty told him. "Get in there and park it. And," he added as Kay began to babble a joint protest with her eyeglassed suitor, "there's a third thing for you to do— and I'll enforce it."

"What's that?" Tenny mumbled.

"It's easy." The detective saw them seated and then settled himself into a chair for what could very well be a long wait. "Keep your mouth shut."

MONDAY
(NIGHT)

HOURS PASSED with no sound heard in the pitch-black interior of the living room but Tenny's exasperated puffings-out of breath as he shifted in his chair and Kay's gentle, and very probably spurious, snores.

Prolonged near-silence made the sudden small clack of a key fumbled against a lock seem almost preposterously loud. A careful footstep was heard at the rear of the house. The signal was answered.

Cass Harty was out of his chair and soundlessly across the room, his hand muffling Kay's startled mouth, long before the swinging door of the butler's pantry began to creak. He whispered "Quiet!" in her ear and marveled that Tenny had the good sense to be silent.

The pantry door groaned like rubbed leather as it swung back into place.

A gun was in Harty's left hand, the palm of his right was smeary with lip rouge as he groped for the button on the end of the string. He thought: He's coming this way!

A figure moved darkly, tentatively, in the blackness of the hallway.

As Harty's fingers closed around the line, Tenny cleared his throat noisily.

"Who's that?" The figure stood monument-still.

Cass Harty drew gently on the line, taking up its slack with laboratory care. He felt the first moment would be the most important, and he wanted that to occur in the living room.

"Answer me, goddam it!" The voice was tinged with hysteria. "Is anybody here?" Quick, ragged-nerved paces brought the man well inside the room.

The sergeant yanked on the taut string, then leaped sidewise, cutting off exit.

A flood of sudden illumination staggered Morgan Elrod like a blackjack swipe behind the ear. He shaded his eyes with his hand and spat contemptuously at Adrian Tenny, "So you sold me out? I might have known!"

Change from blackness to glare was even harder on Tenny's pale cods'-eyes. Saying nothing, he blinked back at Elrod.

"So you got this cheap double-crosser to signal me in," Morgan snarled at the sergeant. "First he talks up that stuff about McNiff and gets him reported to Rev Crane; and then he pretends to be helping me and turns me in. Well, how much good do you think it's going to do you?"

Cass Harty said, "I'm not sure." He looked past Elrod to Tenny, convinced that the nearsighted man was astonished by the news of the change in flags even though he had walked directly beneath them. Bad sight, triply bad! he thought. The buoy . . . the queer choice of gun . . . the otherwise inexplicable death of the Messingers.

The interlock was almost perfect.

"It 'll get you nothing," Morgan yelled. "You'll never make that charge against me in town stand up. It won't stick, I tell you! Larsen 'll testify I'm not responsible. Randall will go to bat for me."

He's not faking that last, Harty decided. He doesn't know about his cousin. Two and two always have made four and, by God, they still do. He said, "Randall Elrod is dead!"

Morgan's face showed he did not want to believe it. The man with the heavy eyeglasses leaned forward in his chair. "It's a rotten situation you're in, Morgan," he said solemnly. "I'm afraid you'll have to take your medicine."

"Tenny," the sergeant said curtly, "your sight is bad?"

The man seemed almost pleased to agree. "The best optometrist in Chicago told me it could hardly be worse."

Chicago! Did that have anything to do with what the sergeant had been trying to remember since Saturday? "I'll accept his judgment," he said. "Is that why you didn't notice the flags outside now spell MEX?"

Tenny's face changed—but not greatly. "I doubt I ever really noticed them at any time—I don't know what they mean." He made the change serve as the start of a careless laugh. "Why should I?"

"You're not familiar with the use of marine signal flags?"

"Of course not! I've always lived inland. I've made occasional trips East, but up till last November I'd been in Chicago for ten years as manager of Elrod's office there."

Chicago, huh? Chicago!

Little bits of black wood?

Of course—*Chicago!*

The association of ideas which had been coquetting with Cass Harty's memory came clear at last. A newspaper story, under a Chicago date line, read while he was in Uptown General Hospital recovering from the bullet wounds received on Cardaff campus . . . That held the key.

Let'ssee, now . . . How did it go?

Needy family ... no coal . . . burned some old battery cases . . . acid-soaked wood gave off gas when ignited . . . two dead. Doctors performing autopsy amazed at duplication of symptoms of meningitis in brain of victims.*

The above incident occurred on October 19, 1935. Two members of the family were killed outright, and a third was not expected to recover. It was remarked that the gas, which technicians called fully as lethal as any used in the World War, was offensive to the sense of smell; but the necessity for heat made such unpleasantness endurable, vide: New York Times, Sunday, October 20, 1935.

There was driftwood in the shack the first time I was there, Harty recalled.

Replacing the driftwood with the death-laden battery

cases from the settlement junk pile indicated premeditation and made Randall Elrod's death first-degree murder.

"Tenny knows what the flags mean, all right," Morgan Elrod said. "He kept me informed that way, right along. Told me when the coast was clear for me to come in and when to stay away."

Harty allowed the major riddle to rest in abeyance for a moment. "Why stay away at all?"

"Because you were going to arrest me for that trouble I had. He told me you'd take me back to town with McNiff. That's why I shoved you overboard. I lost my head—I admit it."

"You're a playful sort of a guy! I suppose you crashed that bird over the sconce in the night club because he stood between you and the bar." Harty chuckled. "Why"— he continued—"why did you leave the san Wednesday night and then go right back to it again?"

"The signal had been flying all day. I was coming to answer it, but just as I got to the beach I heard a gun go off. I knew our souvenir piece was missing from the game room upstairs, and I was afraid, after what happened that morning, that you'd blame me. I'm in trouble enough . . ."

"Not any more—the proceedings against you have been dropped. The fix your cousin was working for must have gone through," Harty told him, and thought: I've got it all lined up. Eyesight, gun, flare of furnace, buoy, dinghy, false tips so's suspicion'd fall on Morgan. I've got my man, all right—everything but the motive!

Footsteps crashed across the boards of the porch interrupting the tightly knit chain of reasoning. He nodded at Morgan Elrod and said, "Let them in!"

Stauffer entered alone, his face serious. "They phoned from Keyesport that the newspaper boys have started. If you figure to do anything about Tootie that don't leave us much time."

"How's the setup down there?"

"They'll take McNiff away in the morning. Water's calm enough now, but the cameramen and newsreel boys 'll have to have their whacks at him. Our heroes are getting ready for that stuff now." Barney laughed. "Three of them are shaving and the other's taking a bath."

Cass Harty looked at his wrist watch and said, "We have time enough." Rev would be guarding the jail for another hour.

"I hope so," Barney breathed fervently. He took a familiar-looking sheet of ruled paper from his pocket. "Here's your answer from Albany," he said. "It was phoned over this morning, right after we left."

"It's about time." The sergeant began to read the reply to his inquiry about the corporate structure of Wade Enterprises without much interest. So the firm had paid income tax on earnings of slightly better than a million and a half dollars last year, had it? That was not startling news now.

From behind thick lenses Adrian Tenny watched closely.

Gen Crane's humpbacked scrawl was hard to decipher in places, but Harty read on. Of course it took three people to apply for papers of incorporation, everybody knew *that*. Of course the applicants were not necessarily the moving spirits behind the company being formed, everybody knew that too. But . . .

The sergeant's impatience with the extraneous details of the message vanished as he saw who the three incorporators of Wade Enterprises were.

Why, he wondered, why hadn't he recognized just how widespread the use of names of underlings, in filing such papers, actually was? Hadn't he seen enough of it in the past to know that the stunt of junior clerks, typists, or even office boys, fronting for the real big shots was a corporate commonplace?

So Tenny had been Randall Elrod's right-hand man, eh? And he wanted to marry Kay, who was Wade's girl Friday, did he?

"Who's this guy?" Barney whispered. "The screwball?"

"Yeah—only he's not so screwy."

"Then whatta you gonna do with him?"

"Nothing. It's the other bird I'm interested in."

"My ears are not as weak as my eyes," Tenny said. "I heard that. Just why are you interested in me?"

"Because you were down here last fall. Because you bought some stolen bonds from Tootie McNiff. Because you were so eager to get married. Because you're such a swell marksman. And because five men are dead—one of whom never had a fair chance at living."

No one seemed to notice he said five instead of four.

"Wait a minute, Sarge," Barney objected. "How could he of bought the bonds? Tootie said that fella *didn't* wear glasses—and this guy's never without his."

"Tootie also said that both times he met the buyer, the man was waiting for him at a prearranged time and place—seated at a particular table, And, both times, *he stayed after Tootie left!* He had to stay, because he didn't dare go out in the street without putting his glasses on—and if he did put them on in front of McNiff they would have helped identify him!"

"Talk like that only helps to clear me," Tenny said. "You admit my eyes are bad, and then say something about my ability to shoot straight. Don't make us laugh!"

"I'm trying hard not to," Harty assured him. "As a matter of fact, your weak sight was the first important lead in this case—right at the very start—if I'd been smart enough to catch it. There's always a reason when murder occurs, but there didn't seem to be any in the killing of the Messingers."

"And was there?" Kay asked.

"I'll get to that in a second. The first words I ever heard this guy say were in surprise that Messinger was on the Head and he followed that up by asking if you were safe. Both remarks were obviously sincere. He really was worried over your safety, Kay, especially so because he didn't know what was what after he saw Messinger.

He thought he was drawing a bead on Charley Wade. A bathhouse operator told one of my men that Messinger usually wore a gray suit, but on Tuesday he sported a black-and-white one, just like Wade's; and he had the same heavy build—enough like him to fool a man with bad sight. The boy's death came about either because Tenny was unfamiliar with the size of the pattern his gun would throw, or because of plain callousness. Maybe he didn't care how many people got hurt, just so he reached his objective. But when he actually saw one wrong body, and one unplanned-for body, lying there, he got scared stiff—there was no way to tell how many others might have been hit and he was afraid you might have been among them. Those two unguarded statements, followed by Wade's death the very next night, should have made it plain that Wade and not Messinger was the man our friend was after."

"But why hurt poor Charley? They never had any trouble."

"He never had any trouble with Elrod either," Harty pointed out. "But both Wade and Elrod had to be gotten out of the way if Tenny's plan were to work out."

"What plan?"

"*To get control of Wade Enterprises!*"

"But . . ."

"But, nothing!" Cass Harty slapped the folded paper across his hand. "This message from Albany says that the applicants for papers of incorporation of Wade Enterprises were LeMoyne Dunster, Kathryn R. Franklin, and Adrian Tenny; each holding five hundred shares of capital stock."

"I just dummied in the transaction," Kay offered. "Charley was wrangling through the courts with his wife and he thought her lawyers wouldn't be able to get at the shares if they were listed in my name."

"Of course. And Tenny fronted for Randall Elrod, chiefly, I suppose, because Elrod wasn't eager to have his association with Wade a matter of business record. He told me as much when I talked with him Thursday night, but he was able to deny any shares were listed in his name without telling a flat lie. To him, Mrs Wade's charge of wanting to get control of the business was so absurd that he never even suspected that that was what this heel was up to all the time."

"But even if Randall had been killed when Wade was," Kay objected, "Adrian still wouldn't have control of the business. Only one third of the shares were listed in his name."

Cass Harty grinned at her. "For a babe who was smart enough to think up that gag of mailing 'old newspapers' home to her mother—and to play me along," he said, "you don't seem to be using what's under that shiny black thatch of yours. You never were particularly fond of Tenny, were you?"

The shiny black thatch moved from side to side. "No. I never was." She showed no surprise at hearing that the ruse of the package had been discovered.

Harty decided she had probably phoned her mother to check on its arrival. "You weren't fond of this lug," he said, "but you never took time out to ask yourself why he was always proposing to you?"

"No. Proposals—of marriage, or otherwise—are not exactly a novelty to Mrs Franklin's only daughter."

Evidently her self-interest was not always as enlightened as he had thought. "Don't you see that with Tenny keeping the stock that was rightly Elrod's, if he married you and persuaded you to hang on to Wade's, he'd dominate all policies of the company with a two-thirds voting power. And he'd collect two thirds of the very juicy profits. A million bucks isn't hay!"

"Are you sure about all this?" Kay asked.

"You can't go around the facts. And while you're thinking that over, Toodles, give this a whirl. Just try to figure out how long Tenny would have let you live once you were married and he got you to make a will in his favor."

She was convinced. She turned on Tenny and her arm swung up.

His head bounced back and blood began to leak from a corner of his mouth.

"Dunster could show all this up, even if you didn't," Morgan said. "He knows who really owns the shares."

"Dunster musta had an idea what was in the wind," Stauffer told them. "Gen Crane got it from Rev that it was Dunster brought the G-men in. He called 'em from Keyesport, We'nesday, and asked 'em for God's sake find a federal angle down here. That's why he stayed over on the mainland so long, waiting to call them back and see if they could move in."

"Where was the fed angle in this thing?" Harty asked.

"They used McNiff. He went up to see a girl friend of his in Connecticut, last year, driving a car he borreyed off a pal. The car broke down and Tootie left it there and come back by train. Well, it turns out the pal had swiped the car over in Brooklyn; so Tootie taking it across a state line made it technically a federal offence."

"Don't you see Dunster called in the G-men just to draw attention away from himself?" Tenny said suddenly. "He's the man you want. You'll see when you find him."

"You can't bluff me, Tenny." Harty was himself bluffing a little. Basing the shot on Tenny's otherwise inexplicable visit to the cabanas while Kay was changing her dress, he said: "Dunster has been dead since Saturday. His body is in the cabana—you went down there to see that no one had disturbed it, just before you came over here."

"The cabana ... I never thought . . ."

"Yes, the cabana—and I should have known it last night. You've always been jealous of Kay, but when you met me near the cabana you practically chased me up here to her and guaranteed you'd stay out of the way—anything to keep me from going into the cabana. The joke was on you; I hadn't intended going in there." He turned to the others. "He hid the body in there because he thought nobody'd go near the place till the storm ended. He figured he'd have a chance to get rid of it in the meantime."

"But this guy didn't go on the boat with Elrod and Dunster," Barney said. "How come they're both dead?"

"A good analytical chemist will back up my idea on Elrod," the sergeant told him. "I'm not so sure about the boat end of things, but it must have gone like this: Do you recall why Tenny—who was asked first—said he couldn't go on the sail?"

"No." Barney rubbed the back of his ear. "I kinda forget."

"He *claime*d he couldn't find his glasses, which was the bunk. He knew where they were; a guy with sight like his has to know where his glasses are—but he was stalling and trying to establish his presence on land. He had had the whole of Friday night to set the stage in the shack and he was sure to get results, since the roughening water was a challenge to Elrod to take Jubilee out. Tenny let them start, then intercepted Jubilee on her way toward West Point, a stunt that was easy enough to do since he walked in a straight line on dry land while they were proceeding in a series of tacks. He must have signaled them in, gotten Dunster back to the cabana on some pretext, and taken care of him there. Then he joined Elrod, told him his glasses were found, and made some excuse for Dunster; and they got under way. The rest was easy. *Tenny*, not Elrod, turned the boat over. Elrod's touch of grippe, which he'd been nursing since Thursday, made him an easy victim. Tenny must have started the fire in the shack and told Elrod he'd go for help, or for some dry clothes. Easy?"

Stauffer demanded grimly, "You gonna come clean?"

"I admit nothing." Tenny's myopic gaze was steady on the sergeant's face. "There's no weapon—and even if you had one you'd never make a jury believe I could aim well enough to kill a person at any distance. Expert testimony about my sight will acquit me."

"Go easy with that stuff—your sight is just what will convict you. A person with good eyes could have trusted them to aim a revolver—and he'd have killed no one by mistake. You had to use the punt gun because you couldn't see well enough to aim accurately at a man and hit him with a single shot. But a wide scattering pattern, flung at a figure clearly silhouetted in front of a roaring fire, made your job easier."

Tenny started with surprise at hearing the weapon named, but he said nothing.

"No other person in the case would have needed to use the punt gun," the sergeant said. "You left the party . . ."

"I can see where he had his chance Tuesday night when he was supposed to be up at this house," Barney cut in. "But when Wade was killed you saw him yourself, sitting in the lifeguard's tower."

"*I* saw his monk's cowl robe in a damned vague light," Harty answered. "And when I sent you over there to look around, *you* saw, among other things, one of those conical floats the guards take along when they go out for a rescue in a bad sea. If that thing was stood on end and Tenny's robe thrown over it, he was free to streak for the pier and cast off the dink. Everyone thought he was still in the tower. He managed that part very, very cannily. He was no special pal of young Gresham, but when the kid got soused to the ears and took a brodie off the tower he rushed to his assistance. Other men, older friends of Ronnie, were glad enough to stay near the fire; but Tenny, who knew there was nothing out there to be afraid of, almost sprained an ankle in his hurry to get going. It was a smart way to steal a head start."

"All the time he was pretending to help me he was putting me under suspicion." Morgan foamed into rage. "I ought to kill him."

"The state of New York will take care of that," Harty said. "But let me finish. He got into your cousin's boat and sculled toward the buoy"—Tenny started again—"he looped a rope from the stern of the dink, about a spar of

the buoy; and, since the buoy was offshore from the
fireplace, aiming the gun became simply a matter of
waiting for the tide to swing the dink, bow on, toward
land. When bow, rowlock and gun, all in line, were
pointed at the flame which even Tenny could easily see,
he pulled the lanyard and the thing was done. The gun
was hidden, afterward, in the float—an idea which
probably suggested itself to him last fall when Kay hid
under there and frightened Wade and him."

"By God! Sarge, you've got it," Barney said. "What
about . . . the other?" His head bobbed toward the west
wall.

"We'll need him," Harty agreed. "I'll bring this prize
along. You hop down there and wait for the signal. I'll let
go with it as soon as it's safe. Got keys?"

Stauffer patted a jingling pocket as he went through
the door. "Open anything *I* ever seen."

"You've worked out a very ingenious frame-up,
Sergeant." Tenny made one last try to brazen things out.
"But you fall down in one spot. You can show that the
stock was in my name, that I stayed in Elrod's house and
knew about the punt gun, that I asked Kay to marry me.
But you can't prove the dinghy was ever tied up to the
buoy—you're simply guessing, there—and unless you
prove that, there's no case against me."

"Hell! That's already proved," Harty laughed. "In my
cigarette case are strands from the dink's stern line. They
came out of a joint in the frame of the buoy, and the fact
that they were jammed in there tightly enough to stay in
place during the storm is a damned fine indication of the
amount of strain that was put on the line. When we add
that to McNiff's identification of you as the purchaser of
the bonds that were slipped over on Wade, and then sling
the rest of the stuff at the jury nice and fast—you won't
have a prayer."

"But you haven't got McNiff. The G-men think he's
the murderer," Kay said. "It was even on the radio."

"We'll have McNiff, all right." Cass Harty handcuffed

his prisoner securely and led him outside. "And we'll have him soon." He studied the radium dial of his wrist watch in silence, while several minutes ticked off, giving Stauffer time to reach the jail. "And this," he said, "is the way we'll get him."

Morgan Elrod, Tenny and Kay stared at him in amazement as he drew his automatic and pointed it skyward.

Ten shots volleyed into the night air.

"What on earth did you do that for?" Kay asked.

There was no reason to tell her that the shots would bring the four federal men on a gallop from the hotel, leaving Rev alone at the jail, or that MacIver and Barney would rush up to tell the Sand Head officer that McNiff had escaped and was currently engaging in a gun battle down the ridge. The rest was up to Tootie. If he remembered his instructions he would hide beneath his cot and Crane, looking in at the window, would see an apparently empty hoosegow. He could then be depended upon to hurry away toward the sound of firing, and the inspector and Barney would be free to convoy McNiff to the waiting speedboat.

"I'm just celebrating the Fourth of July," Cass Harty said. "It doesn't come along for another month yet, but what the hell?" He quickly fitted a new clip of cartridges into the gun and nudged Tenny to get moving. "Before I go, Kay," he asked, "what did you do when you failed to wait for me on the ridge Wednesday?"

"I went to the house. I was nervous about some . . . money I had. I wanted to see that it was safe."

"Practical Kay, the boys called her." He quoted his favorite catch line. "*And the boys were right!*" He knew whose money it was, but he doubted that he'd do much about it. There was the question of jurisdiction, for one thing, and, for another, it would be hard to prove. And he had just finished one hard job.

"Faster, you," he told Tenny.

They strode through the darkness toward the bay,

Harty with gun ready. Anyone who would try to take *this* prisoner away was in for a stunning argument.

"Oh, Sergeant." Kay's voice floated mockingly after them. "What about that sail we were going to have?"

From the west came shouts of hurrying men, and, further back, a worried clamor originating with Rev Crane.

"I think we'll let that wait," Harty said as he goaded Tenny to a more speedy pace. "Was that all?"

"Yes," Practical Kay said, "except one thing. How would a girl go about getting hold of that roll of newspaper she was sending to her mother?"

In spite of the oncoming agents, Harty stopped in his tracks, rumbling with laughter. "I can't take that up with you now," he said. "But you'll be going back to town in a day or two. The place where you can get the information you want is listed in the phone book—under the Hs."

THE END

Resurrected Press Books in *The Chief Inspector Pointer Mystery* Series

Resurrected Press Books in H. Ashbook's *Detective Spike Tracy Mystery* Series

The Murder of Cicely Thane (1930)

The Murder of Stephen Kester (1931)

The Murder of Sigurd Sharon (1933)

A Most Immoral Murder (1935)

Murder Makes Murder (1937)

Murder Comes Back (1940)

Murder on Friday (1941)

AVAILABLE FROM RESURRECTED PRESS!

JOURNEYS INTO MYSTERY

A collection of three novels of travel and mystery from some of the best known writers of the Edwardian Age

A man is mysteriously murdered on the night express from Rome to Paris. Which one of the passengers is the murderer. The Countess? The General? The clergyman? The maid who disappeared?

A sapphire necklace stolen from a cab in the London fog. A ship's steward who is either more or less than he appears to be. A jewel thief who criss-crosses the Atlantic in search of victims.

A grand London hotel. A missing German prince. A murdered man whose body disappears from the hotel. These are the challenges facing an American millionaire and his daughter after he buys The Grand Babylon Hotel.

- **The Rome Express – Arthur Griffiths**

- **The Voice in the Fog – Harold MacGrath**

- **The Grand Babylon Hotel – Arnold Bennett**

AVAILABLE FROM RESURRECTED PRESS!

THE EDWARDIAN DETECTIVES
LITERARY SLEUTHS OF THE EDWARDIAN ERA

The exploits of the great Victorian Detectives, Poe's C. Auguste Dupin, Gaboriau's Lecoq, and most famously, Arthur Conan Doyle's Sherlock Holmes, are well known. But what of those fictional detectives that came after, those of the Edwardian Age? The period between the death of Queen Victoria and the First World War had been called the Golden Age of the detective short story, but how familiar is the modern reader with the sleuths of this era? And such an extraordinary group they were, including in their numbers an unassuming English priest, a blind man, a master of disguises, a lecturer in medical jurisprudence, a noble woman working for Scotland Yard, and a savant so brilliant he was known as "The Thinking Machine."

To introduce readers to these detectives, Resurrected Press has assembled a collection of stories featuring these and other remarkable sleuths in The Edwardian Detectives.

- The Case of Laker, Absconded by Arthur Morrison
- The Fenchurch Street Mystery by Baroness Orczy
- The Crime of the French Café by Nick Carter
- The Man with Nailed Shoes by R Austin Freeman
- The Blue Cross by G. K. Chesterton
- The Case of the Pocket Diary Found in the Snow by Augusta Groner
- The Ninescore Mystery by Baroness Orczy
- The Riddle of the Ninth Finger by Thomas W. Hanshew
- The Knight's Cross Signal Problem by Ernest Bramah

- The Problem of Cell 13 by Jacques Futrelle
- The Conundrum of the Golf Links by Percy James Brebner
- The Silkworms of Florence by Clifford Ashdown
- The Gateway of the Monster by William Hope Hodgson
- The Affair at the Semiramis Hotel by A. E. W. Mason
- The Affair of the Avalanche Bicycle & Tyre Co., LTD by Arthur Morrison

RESURRECTED PRESS CLASSIC MYSTERY CATALOGUE

Journeys into Mystery
Travel and Mystery in a More Elegant Time

The Edwardian Detectives
Literary Sleuths of the Edwardian Era

Gems of Mystery
Lost Jewels from a More Elegant Age

E. C. Bentley
Trent's Last Case: The Woman in Black

Ernest Bramah
Max Carrados Resurrected:
The Detective Stories of Max Carrados

Agatha Christie
The Secret Adversary
The Mysterious Affair at Styles

Octavus Roy Cohen
Midnight

Freeman Wills Croft
The Ponson Case
The Pit Prop Syndicate

J. S. Fletcher
The Herapath Property
The Rayner-Slade Amalgamation
The Chestermarke Instinct
The Paradise Mystery
Dead Men's Money

Fergus Hume
The Mystery of a Hansom Cab
The Green Mummy
The Silent House
The Secret Passage

Edgar Jepson
The Loudwater Mystery

A. E. W. Mason
At the Villa Rose

A. A. Milne
The Red House Mystery
Baroness Emma Orczy
The Old Man in the Corner

Edgar Allan Poe
The Detective Stories of Edgar Allan Poe

Arthur J. Rees
The Hampstead Mystery
The Shrieking Pit
The Hand In The Dark
The Moon Rock
The Mystery of the Downs

Mary Roberts Rinehart
Sight Unseen and The Confession

Dorothy L. Sayers
Whose Body?

Sir William Magnay
The Hunt Ball Mystery

Mabel and Paul Thorne
The Sheridan Road Mystery

Louis Tracy
The Strange Case of Mortimer Fenley
The Albert Gate Mystery
The Bartlett Mystery
The Postmaster's Daughter
The House of Peril
The Sandling Case: What Would You Have Done?
Charles Edmonds Walk
The Paternoster Ruby

John R. Watson
The Mystery of the Downs
The Hampstead Mystery

Edgar Wallace
The Daffodil Mystery
The Crimson Circle

Carolyn Wells
Vicky Van
The Man Who Fell Through the Earth
In the Onyx Lobby
Raspberry Jam
The Clue
The Room with the Tassels
The Vanishing of Betty Varian
The Mystery Girl
The White Alley
The Curved Blades
Anybody but Anne
The Bride of a Moment
Faulkner's Folly
The Diamond Pin
The Gold Bag
The Mystery of the Sycamore
The Come Backy

Raoul Whitfield
Death in a Bowl

And much more!
Visit ResurrectedPress.com
for our complete catalogue

About Resurrected Press

A division of Intrepid Ink, LLC, Resurrected Press is dedicated to bringing high quality, vintage books back into publication. See our entire catalogue and find out more at www.ResurrectedPress.com.

For announcements and updates on upcoming publications, LIKE us on Facebook!

www.Facebook.com/ResurrectedPress